I0730303

BEYOND
THE
HORIZON

THREE EPIC TALES

THREE VITAL QUESTS

Beyond The Horizon

Copyright © 2025 by Ray Keipert

All Rights Reserved etc. No part of this book may be reproduced or used in any manner without written permission of the copyright owner except for the use of quotations in a book review.

This book is a work of fiction. Apart from known political and historical figures, names, characters, places and incidents either are products of the author's imagination or are used fictitiously. Otherwise, any resemblance to actual persons, living or dead, events, or locales is entirely coincidental.

Any Scripture quoted is from the New Living Translation (NLT) version.

Book cover design and Interior formatting by 100 Covers.

ISBN E-book: 978-1-7637541-3-3
     Paperback: 978-1-7637541-4-0
     Hardcover: 978-1-7637541- 5- 7.

BEYOND THE HORIZON

RAY KEIPERT

ALSO BY RAY KEIPERT

Life's Winners and a Few Losers

Five in the Quiver

A Hand of Aces

Code 1990

'We can make our plans, but the Lord determines our steps.'
—Proverbs 16: 9 (NLT)

'The only impossible journey is the one you never begin.'
—Tony Robbins

'Life is either an adventure or nothing at all.'
— Helen Keller

For Norm Hawkes

CONTENTS

INTO THIN AIR — 1

SURF BREAK — 83

RETRIBUTION — 177

FOREWORD

Well may you wonder, what was the rationale for these three novellas under the title of 'Beyond The Horizon?' A wish on the author's part to indulge a desire for travel or simply reminisce over past trips abroad? Perhaps both?

In any case, I trust you will enjoy reading the various tales of the book's three separate quests. They involve a school reunion leading to the dogged investigation of a teenager's mysterious disappearance, high-level embezzlement impoverishing a developing country and an international terror plot threatening our very civilisation.

Plenty of challenges and much intrigue abound in the pages of 'Beyond The Horizon' as you, the reader must ask: how can our characters achieve their demanding goals against such overwhelming odds? That's a good question, but as you follow the many twists and turns of 'Into Thin Air', 'Surf Break' and 'Retribution', all is eventually revealed...

Ray Keipert

INTO THIN AIR

CHAPTER ONE

It was a pleasant Easter Tuesday in Perth, the start of the much longed-for school holidays, but poor Alex Deverell wasn't appreciating the 'love' that day. Not when he'd been labouring in his front garden for what seemed like hours (but in reality was only about thirty minutes) to dislodge a large dead tree root. Urged on by his kindly elderly neighbours, the Williams- themselves well past helping physically- he'd alternately used both a mattock and a crowbar to break each separate root one by one. Still, the taproot held on obstinately.

'Come on you so-and-so, break!' Had the Williams not been encouraging him from the other side of the fence, he might well have resorted to more graphic language. After one more mighty heave with the crowbar, the stubborn taproot finally gave way, with Alex almost losing his balance through the effort. 'Got ya!'

'Whacko!' His neighbours were exultant, with Mrs Williams offering to bring out a cup of tea to celebrate. Alex wiped his brow and considered the kind offer before replying- once he'd caught his breath - 'Thanks anyway, but I think Sonya's about ready to bring me one, with morning tea as well if I'm lucky. She left me alone to do this job because she had student maths papers to mark, and needed a bit of quiet time.'

His hope was then rewarded, as Sonya appeared as predicted, carrying a tray of much-needed refreshment. With the excitement over, his neighbours returned to their own, more gentle, gardening routine.

'Just in time, love. Thanks!' After hauling the dead root over to his trailer for removal to his local rubbish tip's vegetation section, along with other results of a long weekend's gardening session, Alex gratefully collapsed onto a porch chair to partake of his wife's tea and cakes. He had barely sat down when Sonya spoke.

'So, what's next on the job list?' He groaned. Sonya, a meticulous organiser, loved lists.

'I think bill paying. I've had enough gardening, it's time to have a session on the chequebook.'

He didn't know that Sonya had already set the bills out carefully on his study desk, along with the household budget she had thoughtfully prepared.

With the tea and snack finished, Alex was psyching himself up for the long chequebook session ahead when they both heard a small motorbike approaching, to the accompanying tune of the neighbourhood dogs barking.

'Ah, the postie. I wonder what mail he'll bring today.' Any thought to distract Alex from the task of bill paying was welcome.

The motorbike pulled up at the letterbox, and as the cheery postie gave them a wave and moved on to his next delivery, Alex strolled down and extracted three letters.

'Not another bill!' Alex gingerly opened the first envelope and noted that their electricity account would be an addition to the coming payment session. The next letter was more neutral; a regular circular from a local real estate agent firm, Hutton and Marchant, inviting homes for listing. The Deverells home suburb of Craigie in Perth's attractive northern belt always had "buyers waiting", as the monthly epistles from Hutton and Marchant declared. This letter was for recycling; the Deverells were staying put.

'What's the other one, Alex?' It looked rather intriguing, with a postmark from Guildford, Surrey, in the United Kingdon. 'Isn't that where you taught once, darl?' Sonya had a good memory.

'You're right. I wonder what it is.' There was no point in speculating further, so Alex tore open the envelope. Then he whistled.

'It's an invitation to a Twenty-Five Year Reunion – Class of 1970.' Hey, that was certainly out of left field. Alex read on. It was from the high school in Guildford in the UK, where he'd spent a happy year teaching back in 1969 and 1970. Australian teachers were especially sought after in Britain in the 1960s, and, as a twenty-eight-year-old with seven years' experience teaching English and history in Western Australia, his application was eagerly processed. Crestwood County Secondary School was an excellent posting. Guildford in Surrey allowed easy access up to London for weekend and holiday sightseeing. Then, when the school year was over at the start of summer, a European tour was on the itinerary before a return to Perth and the resumption of teaching. All in all, it had been a great experience.

'So, when is the reunion?' Sonya could sense a UK holiday coming up.

'Saturday, July 22nd. In the school common room. Staff and former students. Partners welcome.'

'Oh, dammit!' His wife was clearly upset.

'What, love?' Her reaction was a bit puzzling.

'Don't you remember? I've promised to look after Charlotte's 'terrors' all that month and into August, while we're both taking our long-service leave. She's got a block of work lined up, her first stint back in the workforce since the twins were born. If it goes well, it'll be part-time employment for her from then on. I can't let her down.'

Oh, yes, now he recalled. Their elder daughter had married young and presented her husband with twin boys on their first wedding anniversary. With them now being eighteen months old and quite a handful, Charlotte was venturing back into a secretarial career, albeit somewhat tentatively. They couldn't disappoint her; a promise was a promise. Then Sonya brightened.

'Well, you could go by yourself for two weeks or so and take a bite out of your leave. I'm sure there'll still be enough time to finish repainting the house after you come home.'

Alex definitely recalled that arrangement! A bit of a 'busman's holiday', although he didn't mind house painting. But it was not a bad suggestion – a solo trip for the reunion and some sightseeing afterwards. Memory lane beckoned. He appreciated Sonya's encouragement.

Putting aside the chequebook for a few minutes, he dashed off his acceptance, ready for posting the next day. The invitation had stirred his long-ago recollections of England and teaching, as well as his brief courting of Sonya. It had been with a pang of guilt at leaving her and a sudden last-minute reluctance to go that Alex had left in the first place, and only after Sonya assured him she'd wait for him to return. She had been teaching mathematics at the same high school in Albany, and had summed up Alex well. He was a man worth waiting for.

So she did. On Alex's return in October 1970, Sonya was there, and the two immediately rekindled their romance. Alex did casual teaching for the rest of the Western Australian school year, then secured a permanent secondary appointment in 1971.From there, his career didn't look back. Marrying at the end of that year, the couple settled in Craigie, into a home that was a constant "renovator's delight".

Fortunately, this hadn't been a burden for Alex and Sonya, Once their day jobs were done, they found plenty of time to indulge their desire for decorating. The two of them spent many a weekend scouring galleries for works to display throughout the house, and became something approaching connoisseurs. Alternatively, they'd haunt antique stores looking for knick-knacks, delighting in general bric-a-brac. Parenthood was very important to them, and they were devoted to their two daughters, Charlotte and Elizabeth, both healthy, happy girls.

Fast forward to 1995, and Alex was fifty-four and a very satisfied head teacher, as was fifty-two-year-old Sonya. With their many achievements behind them, they both felt they had so much more to look forward to.

Now the prospect of a trip back to the UK had turned up, visiting Alex's old haunts and catching up with his former colleagues. It was very exciting. How had the intervening twenty-five years treated them? And what had life held in store for his former students? He did recall one unresolved issue concerning one of them, a very sad case. He'd followed the situation after returning to Australia, but then forgotten it. Was there any news since?

As Alex made arrangements for the trip in the next few weeks, one thing was for sure.

He'd soon find out.

CHAPTER TWO

The Qantas 747 dipped its wings as it descended towards Heathrow Airport after the long flight from Australia, broken only by a brief stopover in Bombay. Seated in his economy class seat in the midsection, Alex couldn't suppress a yawn. It was certainly a long haul, the longest flight he'd made since returning from Europe in 1970. Sure, he and Sonya had enjoyed more than one holiday in scenic New Zealand, Fiji and Norfolk Island with the kids. But a holiday in Phuket was as far afield as either of them had ventured until now. It was true; travelling to the UK certainly emphasised the tyranny of distance. But once you arrived, it was all worth it.

Following a smooth landing and the usual exit procedure from the 747, he endured the wait for luggage. There were the usual delays getting through Customs in the non-EU gate, but no real problems. Before long, Alex found himself at the pre-arranged desk for Bargain Car Rentals. Waiting his turn, he fervently hoped everything would fall into place. Finally, he reached the front of the queue.

'Hello. Alexander Deverell from Perth, Australia. I've booked a Ford or similar vehicle for a maximum of three weeks, but will probably only need two. Unlimited kilometres.' He had his passport and International Driver's Licence for verification.

'Certainly, Mr Deverell, all the paperwork is in order. Do you want to take out full insurance?' He decided he did, and signed the form. As a left-hander, Alex was used to people watching him as he signed in that slightly ungainly way he needed to adopt. Why was it so 'interesting'? Ignoring the unwanted attention from the man at the desk, he finalised the remaining arrangements, and picked up the key to his Ford Fiesta. The clerk directed him to the nearby parking area, easy enough to find. As promised, the car had a full tank of petrol and was freshly cleaned. Alex did a final inspection, walking around the vehicle to check for any unlisted bumps. He found none; the car was in perfect condition.

Armed with a map showing the best route to his first destination in Surrey, Alex was soon on his way, carefully negotiating the exit from the surrounds of Heathrow. Thank goodness they drove on the left! An unfamiliar change to the other side of the road, as in Europe, would have been a real shock to the system. He followed the signs out of the endless roundabouts. Yep, there was the start of the A3, just the road he needed.

As he drove, he reflected on the last time he'd driven this road. After he'd received his appointment to the Guildford school in 1969, he had taken a flat in nearby Godalming. It was only about six kilometres away from the school, but gave him some privacy after hours. Situated in Butts Lane, just off the High Street, it was both convenient and ideal, affording an easy walk down to cafés and shops. Once he was settled, Alex had bought a Volkswagen camper, so he was set up for weekend trips whenever he wanted – except in winter. That season's weather was a bit too brisk for the outdoors!

Life then had been close to blissful, although working as an English and history teacher, as for any discipline, had its inevitable ups and downs.

The turnoff to Godalming approached. Goodbye, A3 trunk road. Alex steered the Ford onto the exit and was soon crossing the River Wey and driving into the town's High Street. Obviously the shops had changed in twenty-five years, but the street was definitely still recognisable. With great anticipation, he headed along the familiar route to Butts Lane.

This was the first disappointment. The old block of flats had vanished, redeveloped in recent years for a more grandiose establishment, much taller and a lot more modern. Still, every trip down memory lane had its downsides, there were bound to be surprises. Alex parked the Ford and got out to have a good look around. He felt the need to stretch his legs after the long plane trip, and a walk would do him good.

He headed back towards the High Street. There was little left from 1970 that looked familiar. What had been the name of his favourite café? Alex couldn't remember. But he recalled exactly where it was and found it right away. Now called the 'Traveller's Rest', he walked in and ordered a coffee and a snack before finding a table. There were a few other customers, but none took any notice of him. The barista showed interest in his accent.

'You're Australian?'

Alex nodded, guessing it was still a slight oddity. 'Yes, I'm here for a workplace reunion. I was last here twenty-five years ago.'

'Well, welcome back to the UK. I guess it's changed, eh, cobber?'

Alex winced privately but smiled, helping the man enjoy his little joke. He hoped the coffee was better than the old-fashioned slang, good natured as it was.

Following his refreshment, Alex strolled along the High Street looking for recognisable places and was gratified to find some. Then it was back to the car and his real destination, Guildford, where he'd booked a room at the Black Horse. He checked the map, but remembered the way: take the A3100 for six kilometres. As he motored along, he relished the delightful balmy July weather, as warm as you would want. He recrossed the River Wey and drove down Guildford's High Street. This was the heart of the shopping district, a real hub with its shops, boutiques and department stores.

He drove past the Friary Centre. It had still been under development in 1970, but now it had become a major shopping precinct. *Wow*, thought Alex. *Stunning*! Following his map, he turned off and drove down the two streets to the Black Horse. With a parking spot for the Ford readily available, he went in to register.

On completing the check-in formalities, Alex took his luggage up to his room, fortunately a quiet room at the back. He unpacked and made himself at home. Next, he plugged in his brand new Nokia 2110 mobile phone, checked in with the local UK network, and set it up for global roaming. This would make communicating with home easier, and he tested it immediately with a phone call home to Sonya. She was grateful to hear he had arrived safely, but he kept the call short. Time was money! Then, resisting the urge to stretch out on the bed to have a snooze, he forced himself to go back to the car. There was one important venue that required a visit- the real purpose of his trip.

The Crestwood County Secondary School!

CHAPTER THREE

The school was just past Guildford Cathedral, whose imposing structure and modern architecture dominated the town's skyline. Alex recalled the cathedral was completed in 1961, just a few years before he began teaching there.

Crestwood County Secondary School had accommodated about six hundred students in Forms One to Six, with Alex teaching both English and history in the first five forms. At the time, he had been the only overseas teacher, but he recalled a woman from France who had assisted the French language teacher. What was her name- Monique Arnaud? Coincidentally, there was an Yvonne Arnaud Theatre in the town, named after an actress with the same name. Alex had always wondered if they were related.

And who was the languages teacher? Ah, yes, Genevieve Townley. She also taught religious education- for what that was worth. He and Sonya were nominal Anglicans, only going to church occasionally, more to admire the setting and architecture than anything deeper. They had nothing against religion, of course, but didn't take it too seriously. But he'd respected Genevieve for her beliefs.

Outwardly, the school didn't look any different, although on closer inspection there were a couple of extra classrooms. It was Thursday, and the reunion wasn't for two days. School for the year had just concluded, so there were no students present. With only a few tradesmen on the premises and the grounds apparently open to all, Alex took the opportunity to stroll around. The oval was exactly as he recalled, so, too the main building. As Alex wandered through the grounds, a persistent memory shadowed the edge of his mind. Slowly, as the details flooded back, the traumatic event came back into focus.

It was a week after school had finished, around the middle of July, 1970. He'd said his goodbyes on his last day of teaching and been given a wonderful farewell present, a magnificent beer stein. He was at the start of his three months' European travel, and was somewhere in the south of France when he'd seen a British newspaper with the startling headline: *Boy vanishes. Huge mystery*. Intrigued, Alex had read on. He couldn't believe what he was reading. It was one of his students, Bobby Russell!

Fourteen-year-old Bobby had vanished from a shopping trip in Guildford, where he lived with his parents and two elder sisters. He'd just completely disappeared, which was quite unlike him. Police were following up significant lines of enquiry and were questioning at least two suspects. However, despite the "promising leads", Bobby was never found and nobody could be pinned for the crime. Once back home in Perth, Alex had kept in touch with a couple of former colleagues, but the trail just went cold. It was a real mystery.

But most people don't like unsolved mysteries, especially if they leave behind bereaved families.

And the poor Russell family had been grieving for a long time.

The next day, a Friday, Alex did some more sightseeing. Close to the Black Horse was Guildford Castle, a prominent landmark overlooking the town that dated back to the eleventh century. Alex was intrigued. He had been there back in 1969, but revisiting it now reminded him of the town's rich history and heritage. He took some photos on the new Canon digital camera he'd brought with him. Sonya would be interested to see them when he got home.

Then, putting the Ford Fiesta to good use, he took a jaunt over to Reigate, down to Crawley and Horsham, then Billingshurst, Haslemere and back via Godalming to Guildford, ending with a much-needed rest in his room at the Black Horse. Although he already missed Sonya and his family, being a carefree tourist had its consolations.

Tomorrow would bring the reunion. The big question would be: had the Bobby Russell mystery ever been solved?

CHAPTER FOUR

Right on midday, Alex left the rental car in the school's parking area, noting the streamers and bunting at the entrance to the building that housed the staff common room. He joined others making the same way to the venue, thoughtfully signposted for those who may have forgotten the way. Students who were now married were able to bring their partner, although it was likely few would. This was a personal reunion for those who'd been at the school.

Welcome signs were on display, along with the names of all the 1969/70 students and teachers. More streamers and balloons complemented the décor. Drinks and refreshments were poured. As Alex entered, there were cheery cries of 'Mr Deverell! Welcome back!' as former students and colleagues rushed to shake his hand. 'All the way from Australia – fancy that!' Some he recognised, others he did not. Alex reflected how we all age at different rates; some people seemed barely to have changed while others were almost unrecognisable. He was certainly gratified, judging by their easy recognition of him, to be in the former category. Name tags, thoughtfully provided by the Reunion Committee, were of great assistance.

The MC was a former colleague, Scott Geddes, who had taught economics and geography. At a few minutes past twelve he called everybody to order. 'Quiet please. Let's make an official start. Remember, anybody not paying attention will be sent to the headmaster's office!' They all laughed, although back then it would have been no laughing matter for any student.

The festivities unfolded according to the schedule. Firstly, a roll call of those former staff and students who were present, with a record of any career achievements since leaving the school. Secondly, a sad list of those who had passed away, including the 1970s headmaster. The MC made special mention of Bobby Russell, which answered Alex's as yet unasked question. The mystery had never been solved. Some people dabbed at their eyes. The memory was very moving.

Finally, before mingling for private catchups, there was an exceptional shout-out for one teacher from 1970 still at the school, dear Genevieve Townley. Now sixty-five and a widow, she intended never to retire, if possible. To the cheers of all present, Scott presented her with a special award. Genevieve beamed, greatly honoured. Teaching was her life's work.

To recognise career achievements, ex-students and former teachers were allowed to bring something related to their present occupation. One student had become a significant author and displayed their published books; another was a film producer who always seemed to gravitate back to Guildford, for some reason. Others publicised their building or plumbing companies, handing around their business cards.

One former teacher who had become an environmentalist really got into the act, displaying photos on the wall. Another was Cressida O'Neill, an art teacher who had retired at forty after receiving a large inheritance and was now a famous artist. She had brought along a magnificent oil painting to the reunion, a self-portrait, and donated it to the school. It was quickly hung on a prominent wall to be fussed over, along with a catalogue of her other works. Alex remembered she had given a painting to the school before, when she taught there. It was still on the common room wall. He strolled past the various displays, had a good look at the two paintings, the author's books, the photos, the extensive film material and business cards. Moving on, he shook his head. It was too much like a trade show for his liking!

An hour of "memory lane" followed. This was more like Alex wanted. Being a bit of a novelty himself, there was much backslapping for the popular teacher from former students and colleagues alike. Some posed the inevitable question: 'Do you know so-and-so who migrated to Australia?' and he smiled inwardly each time. *No, mate, it's a big place!* If he only had a dollar for each occasion he was asked!

Needing a break from the adulation, as wonderful as it was, he strolled over to the catering section. There, he noticed a woman aged in her forties, crying quietly in a corner. Instinctively, he went to comfort her.

'I'm sorry to intrude, but can I help?' She looked up at him through her tears.

'Oh, you're Mr Deverell, aren't you? Bobby's teacher? I'm...' She paused as her emotions got the better of her.

'You're Bobby's older sister?'

She nodded. 'Harriet Russell.'

'I guess the mention of his name just now was upsetting. Do you want to talk?' Again she nodded. They went into the kitchen and pulled up a spare couple of stools. As Alex waited for her to begin, her thoughts came out like a flood.

'I nearly didn't take on this catering job, but in a way I wanted to. I run the firm, Excelsior Catering,' Harriet explained. 'I was eighteen the day he disappeared. My sister, Natalie and I never forgave ourselves for not being right there with him. But he was only in the café opposite, you know!'

'Harriet, why don't you tell me the story from beginning to end. I wasn't in the UK when it happened, so only got it in bits and pieces.'

'It was Saturday, July 25th, 1970- a date I'll never forget. It was a week into the school holidays, which meant something to Natalie and Bobby, but I'd already left school and was working in the hospitality industry. I still am! Bobby had got a voucher from New Age Nails here in Guildford, a two-for-one offer. It was only valid for that day, and only at a certain time. He was quite a sweet brother and wanted Natalie and me to get our nails done- the works- for half price. He came with us. We had had two technicians working on us at the same time, side by side.'

'So how did he disappear?'

'Well, he started off waiting on a spare seat but soon got bored, even though he mentioned something vague about being interested in the process. The technicians really gave us a great treatment and it took quite a while. So I told him to go across the way to a café and get himself a cold drink and a snack, then wait there. I offered to pay and he got the money from my purse and left us. We never saw him again!'

'Goodness. What a shock!'

'Absolutely. Once we were done we went over to the café, which was very crowded. Bobby definitely wasn't there, we checked every table. One of the waitresses sort of remembered him getting a drink and a snack but had no idea what happened to him. So we left and scoured the shopping centre for an hour. There was no sign of him. We found a public phone and called our parents, who rushed here and spoke to the mall's security. We all searched again, but no luck. Finally, security phoned the police. We made a statement and were then so upset our worried parents took us home, hoping he'd turn up by himself.'

'So it then became a police matter?'

'It sure did. They followed up their suspicions, but to no avail. Bobby was never seen again. Now you know why I'm still so upset!'

'Harriet, I completely understand. If there's anything I can do...' Alex felt helpless. What could a visitor from Australia do, especially when he was only here for a couple of weeks?

'Mr Deverell, I remember Bobby liked you as a teacher. Maybe you've got some fresh ideas...?'

'Please call me Alex. Harriet, I'm not sure what, but I'll see what I can do. Why not give me your contact details and I'll stay in touch.'

'Thanks so much. If anyone can do it, you can, Alex!' She scribbled her number on a piece of paper.

'I'll certainly try. Bye for now.' He embraced her, took the paper and went back to the celebration. As of that moment he hadn't the foggiest idea what he could do that hadn't already been done before.

Not the foggiest.

Alex rejoined the group, thinking perhaps inspiration might strike. There were still plenty of former staff and students to re-connect with, and it was a pleasant experience, long anticipated. The present headmaster, Arthur Northcott, was enjoying it as well, relishing the occasion. Genevieve Townley was a focal point. Everybody knew her. Alex left her for now, given she had a crowd of eager well-wishers around her. There'd no doubt be an opportunity later to have a chat.

He gave Scott Geddes a vigorous handshake. He'd always liked Scott. Now a head teacher of economics and geography at Willowbrook Academy, an exclusive private school on the northern fringe of town, his position was set. Scott confirmed he'd be there until retirement. Hearing about Alex's career back in Western Australia, Scott showed interest in a trip there.

'You'll be welcome anytime, Scott. We've always got a spare room in Craigie!' They shook on it.

'Mr Deverell, fantastic to see you!' Two of his former senior students, Mark Delandro and Ann Telfer, approached him. Alex learned that Mark ran a well-known building business in Guildford, while Ann was an experienced film producer in London. Oh, that was her. He'd seen all the promotional material. It was a bit curious she kept returning to the Guildford area.

Alex moved on to meet Gordon Reynolds, another former student, now a Conservative Party politician representing a constituency in the West Country. As expected, Gordon was very urbane and definitely had the gift of the gab. In a nice way, though. One surprise was Keryn Hume. Alex remembered she was of a practical bent; he'd got that right; she now ran a prosperous local plumbing firm. In fact, she often did jobs for Mark Delandro. Why not, they'd known each other for ages.

After this Alex met up with some of his former colleagues. Their conversations followed a predictable pattern. There were several commiserations over those who had passed away or been uncontactable for the reunion. One of the staff he wasn't especially keen to connect with was Hector "Boyo" Wharton. Boyo had taught physical education, had a surly attitude and wasn't very fond of the students- or his fellow staff members. It was said he later developed a drug problem. Was he dealing? He was never convicted, but the rumour persisted. Whispers ran around the room. Either way, he was there with his partner and glad-handing those prepared to speak to him. Alex didn't bother, other than a brief greeting before moving on.

Much more engaging was Fred Yeo, formerly of the art department, also now retired. Fred wore a garish coat and looked the epitome of an art teacher. He told Alex he'd only ceased teaching two years previously and was enjoying retirement. 'Lots more time to paint, I love it!' Fred was standing with Cressida O'Neill, who was decked-out in an eye-catching dress. Alex would have loved to speak to her, but she was distracted by a former student, whom she was praising enthusiastically. Fred took Alex aside.

'Alex, you should talk to Cressida when she's free.'

'Sure- any special reason? I was just about to see her. I always liked Cressida, she has a great personality.'

'She's left me for dead, career-wise. I mean, I do some dabbling in my workshop over at Dorking but she's really hit the art scene. The major buyers line up to get her works. You may want one of her paintings as a souvenir of your trip. I'm sure she'd help you out.'

'Really? It's fantastic when teachers do well. Good on her!' After some more catching up, Alex moved on. Fred had his own former students to talk to. Arthur Northcott called the Australian over, wanting to ask about teaching arrangements in his state.

'My antipodean friend, is there any way we could set up a permanent exchange teaching program with your state? I'd love to start one before I retire. Of course, we have individual exchanges as you'd know, but a permanent program, also applying to non-government schools and properly organised, would be terrific.'

'Arthur, I suggest you correspond with our Minister for Education. Here's the name and details.' Alex took out his pocket notebook and pen and jotted them down. Arthur went away, satisfied. Yes, it would be an exciting initiative.

The discussion with Harriet Russell preyed on Alex's mind. Scott and Genevieve were now available, and he went over.

'If you're both free for a bit, can I have a word?'

'Sure,' they replied, almost in unison.

'It's about poor Bobby Russell. A few moments ago I comforted his grieving sister Harriet, who's doing the catering today. She was crying in the kitchen. I think we all realise it's so very long since he disappeared, but of course it's the not knowing that gets to Harriet and her family. Rather rashly, I promised to do what I could to solve it.' They raised their eyebrows and looked at each other knowingly.

'I know, pretty daring, not to mention unrealistic. I'm only in the UK for about two weeks so it's a big ask. No doubt the word 'impossible' just flashed through your minds.' Their nods confirmed that last bit. Genevieve spoke first.

'Alex, you must be psychic. You may not remember from back in 1970, but I don't just teach religious education, I believe strongly in the Christian message. Just this last Sunday in church I prayed for that very thing, and here you are, wanting to do something. So yes, I'm on board!'

Scott looked at Alex and raised his eyebrows. With a nod, Alex agreed with his unspoken thought. *Spare us the religious fervour!* Nevertheless, from a humanitarian point of view, there was a clear need.

'Count me in, too!' said Scott. 'Let's do what we can. What's your plan, Alex?'

Sadly, Alex didn't have one and his stomach churned at the thought of how and where to start.

'Give me a little while and I'll come up with one. Look, we want to enjoy the reunion for now. How about we meet back here at, say, ten am tomorrow and I'll go through it with you. Genevieve, as you're still on staff here, you'd have a key and permission for after-hours access?'

She nodded.

'OK, ten o'clock it is. Put on your thinking caps and we'll get cracking then.' They shook on it.

Turning away to see another of her students, Genevieve reflected on the unexpected answer to her prayer. She'd have to attend St Jude's early service tomorrow to be back here by ten, but that was a minor matter. So no Sunday sleep-in!

But that was a small sacrifice.

CHAPTER FIVE

Punctually at ten the next morning, Alex and Scott arrived at the entrance to the building to find a spritely Genevieve ready to let them in. The two men, meanwhile, were suffering somewhat from too much imbibing and a raucous dinner with several of the former staff and students at the nearby Frog and Toad Hotel. It had gone on till rather too late. Nevertheless, Alex was as ready as he'd ever be to outline his way forward.

Thanks to Excelsior Catering's well-established cleanup procedure, the common room was now stripped of the celebrations finery and back to its normal state. Nothing more was scheduled there until school was due to resume in early September, following the long summer vacation. They had the place to themselves, thanks to headmaster Arthur Northcott's blessing. He was quite happy to hand the key over to Genevieve; he and his wife were off to the Dordogne for their annual French holiday. So now, ready for the project, she asked the inevitable question.

'Well, Alex, what's the plan?'

'Right, it's this. Firstly, do a research and background check. We need to gather information from newspaper archives, police reports and whatever we can find online about Bobby's disappearance. Interview Harriet and, if possible, other family members, including Natalie. Also friends and acquaintances. Get a timeline of events.'

'Got you.'

'Secondly, visit the scene- the café he went into before he vanished. I realise it could well have changed, but it will give us a feel for the case. Maybe the surroundings will give us a clue, say, an alleyway next to it, for example. Take a photo that we can study at our leisure. Not that this case will give us much leisure!'

Genevieve smiled. She thought not.

'Thirdly, interview witnesses and look at persons of interest. I'm no sure how we can get these. We can at least ask for a copy of the police report, and- if they give it to us- see who they investigated. Then check on any leads before contacting the cops. In other words, do their legwork for them. They can claim the credit later, no doubt they will. What do you reckon?'

Scott spoke first. 'All that sounds good to me. What do you think, Genevieve?'

'I agree. Look, the school library has a complete file, all hard copy. Nothing's been put on computer yet so we can troll through it for our research, as your first point, Alex. I suggest we do that now for a start. If you're happy, follow me.' They did.

Minutes later, Genevieve had assembled the full file on Bobby Russell. Accessing the library computer, Alex began typing a document based on the miscellaneous material they unearthed, listing the following facts with accompanying details, all set out:

- The Russell children's visit to the nail salon
- The two sisters' vain search for Bobby in the café opposite and the shopping centre
- A similar search by the mall security staff and police

- The police investigation and the interview of the two main suspects, before termination as a 'cold case.'

The trio discussed the two main suspects, fleshing out the newspaper reports. There were originally three until Surrey police found their number one suspect was still in jail for a similar kidnapping offence. Scratch him. Suspect number two then featured as their main person of interest. He had form for abducting children. Initially disbelieving his claimed alibi, the police grilled him extensively until an analysis of the facts showed he couldn't possibly have been in Guildford on that date and was telling the truth. It turned out Newcastle police stopped him for a traffic offence just after lunch that same Saturday. So Surrey police released him without charge.

Suspect number three had an absolutely ironclad alibi; he was being treated in hospital all that weekend for chronic cirrhosis of the liver. The doctors gave him three months to live. That was an optimistic assessment; he died two days after his release. The police had reached a veritable dead end as there were no other clues. It was all a bit depressing. Still, Alex felt he had to take the lead.

'Well, there was nothing to go on there. Whoever did it was an unknown offender, so it's quite a mystery. We'd better move on to visiting the scene. How about it?' Scott volunteered the transport.

'I'll drive, I've got my car right outside.'

Minutes later, after piling into his Vauxhall Corsa, they were on their way to the High Street and the mall. The question was, would they find a nail salon where it had been in 1970? And the café?

The answer was yes, although both had been renamed. The nail salon was now called Lovely Hands, and the café renamed as The Jolly Sandwich. Starting with the nail salon, Alex explained to the manager that they were unofficially following up a cold case matter. She showed interest when Alex started asking a series of questions.

'So how long have you worked here?' he asked her. 'Can you tell us if the layout has changed in twenty-five years? Would a customer have been able to see who came and went into the café opposite?'

'I'm pretty sure it's always been the same, I've been here for years,' said the manager. 'I used to come for manicures as a teenager and then I did work experience before getting a full-time job. I remember clearly how it was back then. We get the customers facing away from the window for privacy, so they're not obvious to anyone looking in. So they'd never notice the café, nor would the technicians, because they'd be too busy.'

That verified Harriet's story. After taking a photo, they then moved over to The Jolly Sandwich. The school library report had conveniently included a sketch map of the only helpful piece of information from the café waitress; where exactly Bobby had been sitting, just to the left of the main door. Once again, a couple of questions directed to the current manager confirmed there had been no significant change to the décor. The very same seat was still there. The library report showed Bobby had finished his strawberry milkshake and left part of a sandwich on his plate. Maybe he wasn't hungry or did something - or someone - cause his sudden departure? Who knew? Next door there was an alleyway that led to the car park. It was an ideal location for a sudden getaway, but you'd need a willing victim. How would a fourteen-year-old boy be willing?

They took another photo and walked back to the car in silence, thinking about what to do next. Alex spoke first.

'Look, I think we need to interview Harriet Russell again and check Bobby's effects at home. It's likely the family still have them. Next, maybe go over our library file again. Finally, let's talk to someone from Surrey police in Guildford; maybe they'll show us their file and notes.'

'Good thinking, Alex. Why don't you go to Harriet and we'll do the cops. After that, meet back in the common room.' Scott was right onto it.

'Agreed. Just give me a lift back to my car in the school car park and then I'll get going. I'll phone you when I'm back at the school.' Having a mobile phone connected to the local network was proving to be a big advantage. Both Genevieve and Scott owned mobile phones, Genevieve with a similar Nokia, and Scott with an Ericsson.

Alex met Harriet at the Russell family home, which was about a kilometre away from the school. She and her husband lived three doors along in the same street, Oakdene Road.

Mr and Mrs Russell, a couple in their early seventies, were at home. The stress of having a missing child had evidently weighed heavily on them; they looked older than their years. Despite this, they were polite to Alex and grateful for his visit.

'Do come in, Mr Deverell. It's an honour to have one of Bobby's old teachers visit us. Harriet tells us you're following up our dear son's disappearance.'

'That's correct, Mr and Mrs Russell. With your permission, I'm hoping Harriet will show me his effects.'

'Certainly. His old room is upstairs, we've never changed it. We live in hope that he'll return- though that's now a vain hope. Realistically, we expect he's buried somewhere out in the woods, but we'd just love to know where...' Mrs Russell reached for a handkerchief, as she'd no doubt done many times over the years.

'Of course.' Alex was embarrassed and needed to change the subject slightly.' I'm aware you have another daughter, Natalie. Is she still living around here?'

The diversion worked. 'Oh, she emigrated to Australia in the late 1970s, wanting a fresh start. She chose Brisbane in Queensland. Being Australian, you'd know it of course.'

'Indeed I do. All right, I'll just stick to Harriet's version then. Harriet, can you please show me Bobby's room?'

Bobby's room was immediately on the left at the top of the stairs. Most prominent was a neatly-made bed, gathering dust, possibly never used in all the time since his disappearance. Perhaps nobody would dare. In his mind, Alex ticked off what he saw. Sporting pennants on the wall, a painting. A small chair with some of the boy's books on it. He evidently liked Enid Blyton and W.E. Johns: *The Famous Five* and *Biggles* featured noticeably. Next to the wardrobe stood a cricket bat, ball and hockey stick.

'OK if I look inside?' Alex gestured at the wardrobe, keen to continue his mental catalogue.

'Of course. Check anything you like.'

A set of shelves held Bobby's underclothes, summer shorts, hairbrush, comb, nail clippers and pullovers, along with a few other personal effects. Hanging up were his school uniform, shirts and trousers and a couple of winter coats. At the bottom of the wardrobe lay a thick folder. Alex took it out. Inside were a number of paintings. He looked carefully at each one, and was very impressed.

'Very good, I like his style.'

'Yes, the wall painting is his, too.' Harriet was happy to show it off.

'I think that's about all. Do you have anything else relating to him?'

She bit her lower lip. 'Only his last school report, plus the one from the year before, as well as that damned brochure that led us to the nail salon. The brochure wasn't of much interest to the police, though I did show it to them. They just noted it then let me keep it. It felt like my last connection to my dear brother, in a sense. I don't think the school reports will tell you much, but you're welcome to borrow them, and the brochure.'

'Thanks, I will. The reports just round out my knowledge of Bobby. As I taught him, my own comment for English will be on the last one, but it will be good to look at the rest of it. I would have written in my assessment of his progress and passed it on. However, only the form master would have seen the final version with all the teachers' observations. So this will be a first for me. And the brochure is worth a look at, too.'

'No problem, I put them in the wardrobe in his underwear drawer. Please give them back once you're finished with them.'

'For sure. Well, I think that's all for now. I'll be back in touch. Bye, Harriet.'

'Bye, Alex.' With a further farewell to her parents, he was soon back in the Ford and motoring to the school. Once there, Alex made a mobile phone call to the others, telling them he was ready for their return. For one thing, the brochure was interesting in its own way, and the school reports threw up an anomaly. But had he made any progress? Maybe yes, maybe no. It was too early to tell.

It was all definitely food for thought.

CHAPTER SIX

Scott and Genevieve confirmed exactly what the newspaper reports had claimed about the police investigation of Bobby's disappearance. Inspector Hamish Mackenzie had been the senior constable called to the shopping mall on the day of Bobby's presumed kidnapping. Mackenzie, along with his colleague, had immediately assessed the situation and gathered whatever evidence was available. As it happened, he was still at the same police station, having risen through the ranks. He was happy to answer questions from the two teachers, starting with his memories of that day.

'Yes, Mr Geddes and Mrs Townley. A constable and I interviewed the one waitress on duty in the café that afternoon. The poor girl was run off her feet, what with the Saturday afternoon crowds. She recalled the boy, the milkshake and sandwich provided. However, there was a foul up with someone's order- a rather bossy matron as I understand- and the woman unloaded on the waitress quite unfairly. In short, a young teenager who'd paid for his meal, and was sitting quietly in the corner close to the entrance, went completely unnoticed. Once his seat was vacant, it was quickly filled by another customer. So that's it!'

'No doubt. Well, at the start of the investigation, you concentrated on three major suspects.' Genevieve put the newspaper report in front of Inspector Mackenzie, who nodded.

'Yes, it's all in the paper. Reported unusually correctly in this case, would you believe. We were sure- almost 100% - that it was down to one of them. They all had form, you know. I must say, with hindsight, this meant we let the trail elsewhere go cold and once we realised all three were innocent, well, it was too late to find the real culprit, try as we did. We're convinced it was a new offender, one unknown to us, who did it. However, we had no other leads and eventually designated it a cold case. What is curious is, there have been no similar crimes since.'

Scott wouldn't let that point rest. 'You mean this is a one-off? Surely there have been plenty of abductions since?'

'Sadly, yes, but we've always been able to make an arrest. And we've tried to tie the Bobby Russell case to later crimes but were never successful. So I stand by the assertion that it was a unique event by an unknown offender. Quite unusual.'

'Thank you, Inspector. We'll take that on board. We appreciate your time.' They shook his hand and left.

Back in the school car park, Alex had an opportunity to study both the school reports and the salon brochure before the others arrived. Just as they pulled up, he called out, 'Hey, I've just thought of something. Go on up to the common room and I'll be back soon.' Puzzled, they nodded.

Slamming the driver's door shut, Alex took off back to the mall, parked the car and ran to Lovely Hands as fast as his legs could carry him. Would he be in time before it closed? He was in luck; the manager was just packing up for the day. Out of breath, he stammered his request.

'Sorry, I won't keep you long. Can you please have a look at this brochure. I realise it's many years old but is this the sort of leaflet that this business would have given out in 1970? What I'm saying is, you were a teenage customer then. Did you see it?' She had a close look.

'Certainly not. I vaguely recall we got home leaflet deliveries along with our mail through our front door, but they were properly printed. In any case, there was never such a "two-for-one" offer. We'd lose too much money. Frankly, we've never been short of customers, not with the type of people who live in Surrey.'

'Just what I was thinking. This brochure is an amateur job. It looks as though it was an office production, not a quality printer, maybe the type you'd find in...' He stopped himself in time as the penny dropped.

'Well, if you've got what you need, do you mind if I close up now? My husband is waiting to give me a lift home.' She nodded in the direction of a man outside, impatiently checking his watch.

'No, of course not- but is it OK if I come back another time if I need to?'

'Oh, sure. Bye for now.'

'Goodbye, and thanks.' He rushed out, muttering a mumbled 'sorry' in the direction of the husband, who scowled in reply.

Alex had no intention of spoiling their domestic felicity.

Back in the common room, Alex suggested they meet in the library from now on. All the records were there and, after all, they had the school premises to themselves. They agreed, but not before having some refreshment, which Genevieve insisted on preparing. While she was in the kitchen, Scott reviewed his notes and Alex filled in the time with a brief stroll around. He noticed something curious. 'Hmm, that's a bit odd!' He made a mental note to follow it up, then Genevieve returned with a tray bearing cups of tea and some cream buns. A welcome respite. Once they had finished their tea, she spoke.

'Look, we agree we're searching for a new offender and probably someone Bobby knew well enough to go off with. It may have been a local person or even someone who was at the reunion. I've been having some thoughts, so let's concentrate on those who were at the school in 1970 and could have been in the area on the day of the abduction- for that's what it surely was. I've made a list. Alex, we can eliminate you, of course. You were clearly in the south of France!'

Alex was relieved. 'Sure, if anyone asked, I could show my passport stamps, the date of leaving the UK and my eventual return there at the end of September. Yes, please cross me off the list!'

'Me, too!' Scott piped up. 'We were away on holiday on the second day of the summer vacation- a trip to Iceland as I recall. I've got my old passport as evidence. And you're definitely not a suspect, Genevieve.' She smiled, hoping she was well and truly above suspicion.

'Right, so here are the others, in priority order.' She gave them each a copy of her list.

Familiar names. Students Mark Delandro, a Rupert Jones and a Will Sorensen, plus five others. Scott had the best and most recent knowledge.

'I feel we can eliminate Mark Delandro. Sure, he was friendly with Bobby but we never witnessed anything untoward. Nor has he been involved in anything since. He's an honest builder around Guildford with a good reputation. Squeaky clean.' Genevieve nodded.

'However, Rupert Jones has been a bit dodgy. Admittedly, nothing to do with young boys or the like. I think he wrote some dud cheques, then his boss asked him to leave his firm for other dishonest practices. Now he's a real estate agent, which may make you smile, and doing well. I feel there's nothing to go on there.' They crossed off Rupert Jones.

'On the other hand, Will Sorensen has been nothing but trouble in the area. He has form for punch-ups in nightclubs, aggressive driving and road rage. The man's an antisocial pest.'

'I get that, but would such behaviour make him likely to abduct a teenage boy?' asked Alex. 'I mean, it would hardly make Will likeable enough to entice a boy away, would it?' They agreed and Will was now off the list for now. On they went and, other than a couple of question marks against a pair of 'maybes', the rest of the student list was eliminated. Then it was the staff's turn. Almost all of the male staff members were automatic suspects, and the three discussed them in turn.

Genevieve, who had remained at home for that 1970 summer vacation, had already put a line through those teachers who were definitely away overseas, or far from Surrey, at that time. Of course, that left a large number who could be suspects. These included the headmaster, who was just a bit too close to some of the students, although there were never any adverse official reports. So they concentrated on priority targets, two who were prominent.

'Well, our number one suspect is a man I never liked when I was at the school, but I'm trying not to let it colour my judgement,' said Alex. 'He called me either a convict or a colonial. His little joke, I suppose. On his better days, he'd boast about English cricket victories and I'd retaliate when the Aussies won. It could have been good natured, but in his case it wasn't. However, I didn't like the way as a physical education teacher he related to the students. Definitely too suss for my liking. Also, since he retired to his rural setting, there've been rumours, as I just heard at the reunion.' Scott and Genevieve nodded in agreement. Those were their thoughts, too.

'Fine, but let's also look at man number two.' Scott wanted to be even-handed.

'This one's a much nicer character- and I'm wondering if he's a bit too nice. Exactly the sort of person who could have inveigled his way into Bobby's confidence. I see in Bobby's 1969 school report he wrote wonderful comments about the boy's progress in his subject. That was not confirmed by a later teacher in 1970, I may add. It could have been the very thing to worm his way into the poor kid's good books. However, we'll need to find evidence – that's only a supposition.'

At this point somebody yawned. Alex looked at his watch and realised the hour. They needed to call it a day, even though it was not yet dusk outside, thanks to English summer time. He had a thought.

'We need evidence. How about I follow up our number one man tomorrow. All I need is his address and I'll keep him under surveillance- and do whatever else is necessary.'

Alex looked at his friends. 'You two chase up our second prospect. Keep your phones on and we'll rendezvous back here in the library with the details before deciding on our action.'

They were enthusiastic. 'Yep, let's sleep on it and get cracking tomorrow. Alex, this is where he lives.' Genevieve handed over a piece of paper. 'You've got a local road map, of course?' He had.

'Alright, sweet dreams, both of you!' It had been a long day but Alex bounded down the library stairs like a younger version of himself.

Tomorrow he was going to well and truly bowl it up to Hector "Boyo" Wharton.

CHAPTER SEVEN

Early the next morning, Alex gunned the Ford Fiesta from Guildford to Godalming, then on to Witley, Chiddingfold and finally down to Haslemere. Here, just south of the last landmark, he turned off onto a narrow laneway that would lead him the short distance to Boyo's rural property. He'd equipped himself with a pair of binoculars and a small but powerful torch from a sporting goods shop not far from the Black Horse. Fortunately, the shop proprietor was an early riser. Also, the obliging hotel chef had packed him a picnic lunch along with a full water bottle, so he was properly provided for. Just as well, this could be a long day.

A small copse of flowering hawthorn trees just beyond the rural estate boundary offered an excellent vantage point to observe the house as well as shelter the Ford from any prying eyes. From here, Alex could easily see who came and went, which- if the reunion rumours were in any way justified- would be a series of intermittent visitors. However, tying any activity to Bobby's sad disappearance so long after the event was quite another matter. Well, all he could do was undertake surveillance and see what turned up.

For the first hour nothing happened. Then a car appeared, a real old banger, driving along the lane before stopping right outside the house. A pair of scruffy teenagers emerged. Boyo came out of the house and greeted them roughly. Alex could barely hear the words, relying on some skill as a lip reader to get the gist of the conversation.

'The usual deal?'

'Yep.'

'Dough first, don't forget.' The first scruff handed over some notes and received a bag of some substance in return. Both teenagers then jumped back into their old vehicle, turned around and sped back down the lane.

OK, he was into narcotics dealing. So what would that have meant for Bobby, assuming Boyo had kidnapped him? Murdered him to shut him up after a drug deal went wrong? Was there any evidence young Bobby took that stuff? Not really. Yet this was all pretty unsavoury, so Boyo was a definite maybe. It could be a promising line of enquiry. He'd have to keep his eyes peeled for the rest of his watch, hoping to learn more.

Two more cars arrived in the course of the day, with the same outcome. Alex observed a bag of drugs exchanged for cash, each time with Boyo's flippant and dismissive attitude. Clearly, these addicts were just a means to an end for him. What a nice little earner! Alex wondered where he got the drugs. He wouldn't have a lab in that separate barn building, would he?

The chance to answer that question came just on dusk. Boyo emerged from the house, went over to the barn and opened the large main door. Inside was a large van, which he started up and drove out before stopping and carefully closing, then locking, the door. He then drove the vehicle along the lane and out of his property. In the distance, Alex heard it revving its way along the link road in the direction of either Guildford or possibly even London.

So, the man was a possible drug cook and most likely a wholesaler. The daytime customers were only the small fry, the major trade would be either in town, or maybe the capital. This warranted further investigation.

Alex waited till night fell to make sure the place was unoccupied. He carefully made his way down to the barn, wearing a small backpack containing his phone and camera. With no chance of jemmying open the main door- which would also "tip his hand" - he went around to the back, finding a small window with a blind pulled down to stop prying eyes. He'd checked his car boot earlier and found a tool for prising off the hubcaps in the event of a tyre change. It would serve as a jemmy. Thanks, Ford Motor Company! He levered the window up, and heard the catch snap. Bingo! Pushing it fully open, he leaned in, knocking aside the blind as he tumbled down onto the barn floor. He was in.

Well, look at that! What do you know! He flicked on his torch. Before him stood a fully-equipped drug laboratory. It wasn't operating, but the appliances were still warm. Boyo had clearly done a decent "cook up" and was now away in delivery mode. It was time to record the evidence. Alex quickly took the camera out of his backpack and started snapping away, the discreet flash hardly noticeable in the large barn.

Then he heard it.

The sound of a key in the lock in the smaller front door, next to the main door. The handle turned, and the door opened. In came a woman he recognised as Boyo's partner from the reunion. He hadn't actually been introduced but recalled someone mentioning her name. *Deirdre*, he thought. Panic-stricken, he ducked silently under a large table, his heart racing, and lay motionless, praying she wouldn't notice the jemmied back window. She didn't. She began tidying up the paraphernalia Boyo hadn't put away, muttering as she did so. This was hardly a dream job and judging by her attitude, something her partner should have attended to. 'Swanning off as usual...' Alex heard her complain. All the while, he lay there as quiet as a mouse, wondering what to do if discovered.

Fortunately, after what appeared to be aeons of time, she finished the job and vanished through the front door. Alex only emerged once he heard the lock click. Even then, he waited a full minute before resuming his photographic evidence. After a last look around to check, he retreated the same way he'd come in, ensuring the broken lock was hidden on the floor under a nearby bench, the blind put back in place and the window properly closed. It was as neat as it could be and would hopefully pass a casual inspection. Bad luck if it didn't.

Then it was back to the Ford for the return drive to Haslemere, where Alex had found accommodation at the King's Arms, a three-star hotel. Sure, he could have gone straight to Surrey police over Boyo's drug lab but he hoped to get some inspiration, or better still evidence, to prove involvement in Bobby's disappearance. Maybe the poor boy was buried somewhere on the rural property? Alex's mind was working overtime. It was certainly plausible that Bobby Russell had been murdered because he was too honest to go along with Boyo's drug empire and had to be silenced. Who knew?

The next day, provisioned again with a picnic lunch and a supply of water, Alex returned to the same hawthorn trees for more surveillance. He was rewarded by seeing the van that had left yesterday return before being reparked in the barn. Judging by the easy way it moved, it was empty. Empty for the next delivery, once Boyo had cooked up another batch. Again, three lots of customers came to buy a supply of their favourite narcotics. It could be any drugs; it was impossible to tell from a distance. Speed, LSD, MDMA, heroin, cocaine… plenty of possibilities.

It was late in the afternoon, and Alex had picked up his binoculars to verify the day's final drug sale. He took a step away from the car to get a clearer view. It proved a disastrous move.

Away from the protection of the trees, the late summer sun glinted off his binoculars...

Bang!

What the heck!

With an almighty crash, a rifle bullet splintered his car windscreen, showering him with shards of glass and leaving his face bloodied. Then two more rounds hit the Ford, completely shattering the windscreen. Shocked, Alex dropped the binoculars, jumped into the driver's seat, started the motor and roared away. Skidding through a U-turn, he took off in a panic as more bullets whizzed past or drilled into the vehicle. He zigzagged furiously until he was out of range, hearing only one more round ricocheting off the bodywork. Glancing into the rear view mirror as he raced down the lane, he could see the dust of a vehicle in hot pursuit. He swerved onto the main road. Haslemere was his destination and salvation- if only he could get there in one piece.

Whatever the speed limit was, Alex exceeded it. It was only when he sped through the town limits that his pursuer gave up the chase, doing a quick turn-around and retreating. For now, Alex was safe. Unaware if there was a police station anywhere, he sought refuge back in the King's Arms. He left the shattered Ford out the front and staggered up to the reception desk. Young Prudence Croker was on duty and she jumped up, shocked at his blood-peppered face.

'Sir, are you OK? Please, have a seat while I call an ambulance.'

Alex held up his hand. 'No, please phone the police first. It's urgent!'

Wherever they came from, Surrey police were highly efficient, arriving just as the helpful Prudence had patched him up using the hotel's first-aid kit. Alex quickly explained what he'd seen.

'Five kilometres south, a property just off the main road, left along Shepherd's Lane. Hurry! It's owned by a Hector Wharton. He has a drug lab in his barn and I've observed him doing drug sales and a probable drug delivery. Uses a large van. You can get him and his female partner, Deirdre, if you're quick. But please come back here when you're finished- there could be more to this story!'

The police rushed out, telling Alex to wait there. Smarting from Prudence's liberal application of antiseptic, he was in no mood to do otherwise- especially when she insisted on getting a medicinal brandy for him from the bar. Then another.

Over an hour later, the two police officers returned to report back. 'Sir... Mr Deverell, is it?' Alex nodded. 'We found the property vacated. The Whartons have fled, but we've put out an all-points bulletin to locate them. However, you were right. There was clear evidence of a sophisticated drug laboratory, no doubt with a distribution network as you claim. We thank you for your initiative in uncovering it. Don't worry, we'll ensure they're brought to justice.'

'That's great. I'm sure you'll catch them sooner or later. Hopefully sooner.'

'Indeed. Now what was the other matter you wanted to discuss?'

Definitely grateful for his second brandy, Alex related the tale of Bobby, their quest for a solution and deep suspicion of Boyo's involvement. The sergeant raised his eyebrows.

'So you feel the poor lad's body could be buried on the Wharton property?'

'It's a definite possibility. That's the theory I'm pursuing, anyway. In 1970, Wharton's drug involvement would have been in its infancy, and I feel Bobby may have got wind of it. His family assure me he never liked or touched drugs. So, to cover his tracks Wharton could have done away with the lad. There's no doubting the man's murderous intent.' Alex patted his injured face for emphasis. The sergeant got the point.

'Look, we'll do a search, even use cadaver dogs if necessary, although after a quarter of a century that would be a bit of a stretch. Rest assured, we'll go over the place with a fine-tooth comb.'

'Thanks, most appreciated. Look, here are my contact details. I can't do any more here so I'll head back to Guildford in the morning, if I can get the Ford windscreen fixed up. You can contact me there.'

'Wonderful, Mr Deverell. I'll do that. Goodbye for now.'

'Goodbye, Sergeant – and thanks.' He got a cheery wave in reply.

Young Prudence Croker was an asset to the King's Arms. 'Mr Deverell, I'll ensure your car gets temporary patches for the bodywork, along with a new windscreen if you can wait till midday tomorrow. My uncle runs Speedy Smash Repairs in the street behind us and he'll do a rush job. I just phoned him.'

'Prudence, you're a bottler!' She reddened with pride, though puzzled at the expression. *These Aussies were a funny bunch*, she thought, *but they have plenty of guts.*

'It was my pleasure to help!' Then the young receptionist returned to her desk duty as Alex, more tired than he imagined, dragged himself up the stairs to his room to collapse on the bed. He'd buy Prudence a big box of chocolates before he left. Just before he dozed off, his last consoling thought was about the Ford. *How good was it that I took out full vehicle insurance with the car rental company!*

Still, explaining away a number of bullet holes in the bodywork would be a trifle unusual.

CHAPTER EIGHT

Meanwhile, Genevieve and Scott's journey over to a country area south of Dorking was relatively uneventful. They found Fred Yeo's rural holding quite easily, even though neither had ever been there. While he wasn't the major suspect in the case, he could be seen as just 'a bit too nice', and that in itself might be grounds for suspicion. Sometimes criminals- confidence tricksters and the like- adopt just such a veneer. Genevieve checked her profiles. Fred was in Guildford on the day of Bobby's disappearance, though he had gone abroad soon after. This could also be seen as suspicious.

A converted oasthouse on three hectares of land served as both Fred's home and a base for his post-school career; he was a popular and well known artist in the area. He lived there with his wife, Hannah, also a former art teacher. Their two adult children had left home years ago to establish themselves in their own professions- nothing to do with art. Perhaps having grown up in a home overrun by artwork meant they'd had their fill. Whatever the case, the oasthouse was now for Fred and Hannah alone.

The two amateur sleuths' first port of call was the local community arts and crafts centre to collect any information relating to Fred Yeo. They found copies of two brochures, which they took and studied over in a quiet corner.

The first brochure advertised regular art classes held at the centre, once a week throughout the summer. Students needed their own supplies and were to be given instruction in the different mediums, especially watercolours and oils. Gouache was also available as an extra. The rates charged were quite reasonable, certainly a fair price. The maximum number set for the class was realistic in view of the space available.

The second brochure was for private classes at the oasthouse. Some were for one-on-one classes, at other times in a small group of two or three, never more than five. The names Fred and Hannah Yeo were featured, implying both would be present. So despite Fred's own comments about his "modest career", it seemed he certainly enjoyed a good local reputation. Was he simply being self-effacing, or was he here hiding something devious?'

Genevieve enquired at the counter.

'We're interested in these classes by Fred Yeo. What can you tell us about him? I assume you know him well?'

'Oh, yes. He and Hannah have lived around here for years, they are both retired teachers. He was at a secondary school over at Guildford, I think. People like his classes, and the ones he and Hannah give at home are very popular.'

'We realise some people have a bit of an artistic temperament and art classes can sometimes have their frictions, if you like. Does that ever happen with Fred and Hannah, or in their classes?' Genevieve was fishing, and getting a bit desperate. Scott wondered where this was going.

The woman frowned. This all seemed somewhat unusual.

'I suppose occasionally. There may have been one or two who were asked to leave. Come to think of it, there was one woman who wanted to exhibit her own paintings and had a bit of an argument. I think she was an ex-school student of Fred's, now that you mention it. She'd looked him up for some help but it ended badly. Fred reacted and we saw another side of him. No longer Mr Nice Guy!'

'Thank you. You've been very helpful. We'll think it over. Bye for now.'

Embarrassed that she may have been indiscreet, the woman was pleased to see them go. She'd keep quiet in future. The walls have ears in a place like this. Intrigued, she wondered what those two were about. Did they want to enrol in a class and were sussing things out? Oh well, Fred and Hannah had plenty of students, even if that woman and her male companion went somewhere else.

Back in the Vauxhall, the two had a quick conference. Was there a case for highlighting Fred Yeo as a possibility? They agreed, yes. He was in the area on the day, had written up Bobby Russell as a boy of great potential, seemed to have given him special attention in class, and he wasn't quite as nice as he seemed, especially if there was some frustration or ruckus involved. Perhaps he had some nasty plan in mind and got frustrated with Bobby, and reacted by killing him. It would be interesting to see if there was a body buried on the Dorking property...

Oh, the perils of building castles in the air. They were just about to discuss their likely next step when Genevieve rubbed her sore eyes, then cleaned her dirty spectacles. She really needed to get her eyes checked by an optometrist, her regular examination was rather overdue. That done, she took a final look at the dates she'd listed for the 1970 summer holiday Fred and Hannah had taken, verified by a police interview. She froze. They'd left for a three-week painting holiday in Italy on July 20th, not August. She'd misread the month. Fred was out of the UK on the day Bobby vanished, and not in Guildford at all!

She checked herself before saying something she'd regret. 'Oh, no!' was all she could utter as her vain castle suddenly collapsed around her. Whatever you might say about Fred, he was off the list. Completely innocent.

'Sorry, Scott I've mucked up big time. Fred's not our man. Let's go back to Guildford right away.'

It was a sad and frustrating trip home.

'Alex, what on earth…?' Genevieve was clearly shocked by the sight of Alex's face, pock-marked by the effects of the exploding car windscreen; the normally shatter-proof glass had been unable to resist the force of three rifle bullets fired in quick succession.

'A bit of a story.' They were all ears as he went through the drama of Boyo Wharton.

Scott whistled. 'Yep, I never especially liked him, either. So, have the cops had any luck tracking down him and Deirdre?'

'Not so far, but they'll keep us posted.'

After the disappointment of scratching Fred Yeo off the suspects' list, Genevieve brightened visibly. This one really looked promising.

'Right, so let's list the points in favour of wrapping up this case with Boyo being charged over Bobby's murder.' She went over to the library whiteboard, board writer in hand. Out they came, a sense of optimism filling the room.

Guilty of drug manufacture and supply- beyond doubt. An attempt on Alex's life- he was lucky to survive. Drug trafficking with teenagers- clearly observed. No alibi for Bobby's disappearance, he was simply "at home" on the day. An extensive rural property that was ideal for burying a body. A background in dealing with teenagers and every chance to "silence" a problem child if something went wrong, maybe one who disapproved and wanted to blow the lid on the whole setup...

'Yes, it's all circumstantial but compelling. All we need is for him to be caught and confess. Or for the cops to find evidence of a buried body on his land. Either way, we've got him, once he and his wife are located.' Rubbing his sore face, Alex could see the end in sight.

Scott smiled. 'I think we're all agreed.' The other two nodded, satisfied. 'Let's leave it for now and go home. We'll reconvene once you've heard back from the cops.'

'Exactly. We can wait till then.' Genevieve was of the same mind, too. On that note, they all left.

Stretched out on his bed at the Black Horse for some much-needed relaxation, Alex contemplated a nice hotel meal and a drink. He was keen to phone Sonya at home and let her know all about what he'd been doing, but decided to wait until the case finally broke. Once Boyo was in custody, it would be a done deal. Tough as nails that man might be, but police interrogators would be tougher.

It would be case closed. And finality for the long-suffering Russells, once poor Bobby's body was located.

He could hardly wait.

CHAPTER NINE

'Hector Wharton interview beginning at nine ten am. Detective Sergeant Edstein and Senior Constable Fogarty of Surrey Police present. You are represented by your solicitor and have been duly cautioned. Video recording has started.'

Hector and Deirdre had been captured at Dover as they were about to travel to the Continent in a desperate bid to escape justice.

The smarmy look on Boyo's face soon vanished under the vigorous questioning. He might well have been an original "bovver boy" from the mean streets of London's East End, but the softer life in rural Surrey had well and truly removed the grit that justified such swagger. The evidence against him was overwhelming. It was a long list. Following the execution of a search warrant, police officers confirmed a well-established drug laboratory on his property. Traces of narcotics were in his delivery van, and there were photo-recognition shots of him passing more than one checkpoint in London. No denying it, he was the delivery driver. Confessions from a number of teenage customers were now available, naming him as their supplier. His fingerprints were also on the high-powered rifle that had fired at Alex Deverell.

Wharton gulped. He'd be going down for a long time, and his property would be forfeited under proceeds of crime legislation- not that he was likely to ever get out of jail to again enjoy his rural ambiance. But it wasn't over yet.

'Now, Hector Wharton, we're moving to a further charge, one even more serious. This is your opportunity to confess all to us.' Boyo and his solicitor raised their eyebrows, the latter with his pen poised. Edstein continued.

'I refer to the 1970 summer school holidays disappearance and presumed murder of one Bobby Russell on the twenty-fifth of July of that year. You were his physical education teacher at that time and, from our reliable enquiries, just beginning your drug supply network. Is that correct?'

'Yes, I agree with your last point.' The crestfallen Wharton felt further resistance was useless. He'd employ a fallback tactic in the hope of beating a more serious charge. His solicitor put a restraining hand on Wharton's right arm. The interrogator continued.

'Good. We allege you encountered Bobby Russell as a potential client for your nefarious trade, tried to get him on side but failed. It's likely you saw the boy as a representative for his year group, hoping to get a string of similar victims. We allege he reacted against your proposition and indicated he'd report you either to his parents or the police. You enticed him from the Guildford café to your rural holding, where you murdered him and disposed of his body. At this moment, we're continuing the search of your property under the terms of the warrant mentioned above.'

'No, never, I absolutely deny it! You'll find no body- there isn't one!' His solicitor nodded vigorously in support before offering his legal advice.

'I state for the video record that my client definitely denies the charge you have levelled. He maintains his innocence. We believe this is simply a fishing exercise on your part to clear up a cold case. It's a travesty of justice! Where is your evidence?'

The interrogator back-pedalled somewhat, perhaps he'd overplayed his hand.

'Well, we'll see. All in good time. As stated, we're conducting a full property search and the truth will come out. Our best cadaver dogs will find any body that might be buried there, so this is your last opportunity to make a clean breast of it. One point we could have added, you have no alibi for the date Bobby Russell disappeared. According to our 1970 records'- he indicated a folder on the table- 'you were simply at home on the day. Is that correct?'

Wharton sighed. 'Actually, that's wrong. I admit I lied when asked back in August 1970 at the time the police were trawling through school staff members. I wasn't at home that day, far from it.'

'That's interesting, so you're an admitted liar. Well, where were you and how can you prove it?'

Wharton's swagger wasn't entirely gone as he rose to the occasion. 'Look, I was keeping up my appearance as a tough geezer, a habit I had when I was a bovver boy up in the East End. You know, maintain my reputation as invulnerable, even down here in Surrey. Be invincible if you like...'

'Go on.'

'The week the kid vanished, I was in hospital up in London. Went into Richmond Private Hospital on the twenty-first and stayed over a week. Didn't move from the ward or the rehab unit all that time. It was a double hernia operation. I'd been pumping iron too vigorously for too long to impress everyone and did some damage to myself. Believe me, tough East End characters don't go in for hernia operations, it's a sign of weakness. They just hide the damage. Only wimps can't put up with it. I guess I was a wimp.'

'We'll need verification.' Energised, Wharton's solicitor rose to the fray.

'I suggest you both go and look for it. The hospital will have records. Until then, withdraw your accusation. We have nothing more to add.'

Somewhat crestfallen, Edstein and Fogarty terminated the interview. It was a disappointing end to a likely slam dunk. Wharton seemed sure of himself and they'd immediately check his latest declaration. If true, he was exonerated on the kidnap and murder charge and a search for a buried body on his land would be fruitless, even though they had all the other matters on him. And they were enough to keep him banged up for years.

Sadly, though, it meant the cold case of Bobby Russell was still open.

Later that day, Alex Deverell took the devastating phone call. Yes, incontrovertible evidence faxed down from Richmond showed Wharton had indeed been an in-patient on the dates declared. There was proof of his extensive double operation, details of his rehabilitation and discharge, far from fit, more than a week later. Orders to recuperate at home for at least a month, light lifting only.

Bad as he was, Hector Boyo Wharton wasn't their man. The grounds search was called off and the dedicated cadaver dogs returned to base.

Gloomy and frustrated, the three sleuths were back to square one. There were absolutely no firm suspects. However, they decided to sleep on it and meet back at the library the next morning. Perhaps to wind up their efforts, give the case away and go about their business. Alex envisaged a quick trip to the Lake Country in the north of England – it would be fantastic to revisit it. Before that, he would phone Sonya. After all that frustration, how he missed her. He'd play tourist for a few more days then fly home. He'd certainly done his best; all three of them had. It looked like this cold case would stay cold.

Genevieve Townley was equally disappointed. As a longstanding member of the school community, she suffered profound loss over the injustice of the unsolved case. A woman of faith, she couldn't imagine enduring the pain of that loss for the rest of her life, and had sought prayer and counselling over the years. It was still so much to bear. She could only imagine what it must be like for Bobby's family. Even finding the poor boy's body would have been progress. It just seemed so unfair.

Bereft of inspiration, there seemed only one thing to do. After tossing and turning during a restless night and already running late for the ten am meeting, she nevertheless took a sharp detour.

Simon Carstairs, Rector of St Jude's Anglican Church in Guildford, had just completed a draft of his coming Sunday sermon when he was alerted by a frantic knocking on his study door. He opened it and a frustrated but determined Genevieve Townley burst in.

'Sorry to intrude, Simon but I need help!' Noting she was in a right state, Simon calmly told her to sit down and explain.

Out tumbled all the frustration of the Russell case. It wasn't the first time she had sought his counsel, but this time it seemed more urgent. Once she'd paused for breath, Simon offered an observation.

'Genevieve, I'll certainly pray again for a solution. I agree, we need divine guidance.' It was then Genevieve glanced down and saw Simon's sermon lying on his desk. The title jumped out at her: *You will know the truth and the truth will set you free.*

Immediately her face brightened. 'Of course! The Gospel of John, chapter eight, verse 32. Simon, that's the answer! I could kiss you!'

Taken aback, the rector knew that would be highly unethical and wondered what to do. Fortunately, he didn't have to wonder long. With a simple 'Bless you!' Genevieve turned around and bounded towards the door and flew down the flight of steps rather faster than a woman of her age might consider safe. 'Say a prayer after me, I've got to rush off. Toodle pip!' As a dedicated man of God, Simon Carstairs was used to answered prayers.

Just not at such warp speed.

Energised after the revelation, it was Genevieve's turn to motivate the other two. Alex and Scott were on the verge of giving up. After all, how could three amateur sleuths, mere high school teachers, succeed in cracking such an old case when the considerable efforts of the UK's police forces had failed? It was definitely time for a conference and a brainstorming session. They needed to summarise known facts and assumptions, and revisit questions. Genevieve began.

'Let's agree in the search for the truth and its freeing effect- that's my inspiration for today!- we have learned it was an unknown offender and apparently a one-off. Can we assume the offender was at the reunion? It's at least possible, as Bobby would have only gone off with someone he knew and trusted. If it had been a forced abduction, he would have yelled out and resisted. He was fourteen, after all.'

The two men nodded. They were all unified on that point.

'The next thing is to go over the profiles again, there may be something we've missed. We need to check for an unusual item in someone's background, a possible clue.'

They went through the list again, keen to find an anomaly somewhere. For the brainstorming session, Genevieve suggested they simply call out any apparent discrepancy or fact from the list and she'd write it up on the whiteboard. Then they could put in the name it matched.

'Off you go, you can start with the two cleared suspects if you like.'

'OK, a convenient hernia operation and an alleged drug dealer.'

'Next one, a trip to Italy. Also convenient – perhaps too much so.

'A film producer who noses around Guildford.'

'A builder who seems too good to be true.'

'A large inheritance and early retirement.'

'A female plumber with a large clientele.'

'A headmaster too close to his students.'

'Then there's the old 1970 nail salon brochure – there's something funny about it.'

On it went. Some people had more than one entry. In school reports, one teacher had praised Bobby for his talent, while another had simply said he was a "middling student". The "too close" headmaster had now died, so that avenue was closed off.

The teacher who retired early had become quite famous but that could simply mean secondary school teaching had been the pathway to a better career. Matching the comments to the person didn't get them any further, so they reached another dead end.

'Can anyone see a pattern? Anyone stand out?' Like the others, Alex felt this was getting them nowhere. 'Come on, a line of enquiry?' They shook their heads. Genevieve suddenly felt the truth she was so eagerly pursuing must be a mirage. But in her mind, she kept repeating the same Bible verse. Over and over the words *truth* and *free* kept coming back. Divine intervention?

'Alex, I share your frustration. As does Scott, I'm sure.' The latter nodded vigorously. 'So what is your gut telling you, my Australian friend?'

Suddenly, inspiration struck- from where, Alex had no idea. It had something to do with the nail salon. 'The nail salon. That's where I think we can break the case. I reckon it revolves around the old 1970 brochure, so I'm going back there right now!'

'Go, man, go!' The other two cheered him on. 'Then come back and we'll get cracking!'

With a cheery wave, Alex was quickly out the door.

CHAPTER TEN

Hardly had Genevieve Townley vacated Reverend Simon Carstairs' study than there was another similarly urgent knock at his door. Curious, he opened it. There stood one of his more recent parishioners, Roxanne Jessup.

'Roxanne, please come in. What brings you here today? Whatever it is, please have a seat.'

Rather out of breath from her rush from his church's small carpark, she was pleased to do so.

'Simon, I've just got to get something off my chest. Look, you've been preaching lately about the importance of honesty and there's something I was very dishonest about in my past. For some reason it's come to the surface and I want to get it sorted. However it works out.'

'Wonderful. Is it private between you and God, or do you feel the need to talk about it?'

'The last one. I feel I need to tell you in confidence and then make it right somehow.'

'Alright...'

'Years ago, when I was a business manager, I took a one hundred pound bribe to perform a favour. It was nothing extraordinary, and it seemed harmless at the time. However, something terrible happened soon after that might have been- could have been- a consequence of what I did. I didn't immediately see the connection, and I certainly had no idea back then of what I might be getting involved in, but the fact I'd taken a bribe preyed on my mind. It wasn't honest to take it, was it?'

'No, of course not, but we're all human and make such mistakes. If you confess it to God…'

'I have already, just last Sunday, quietly in church. He gave me the message that He forgave me but I needed to make restitution somehow.'

'What do you suggest?'

'Go to where the business is now and make an ex-gratia payment to it. Heaven knows where the person is who offered me the bribe. But the business is still there, under a different name. I'll feel better if I do that. I've calculated how much time has elapsed since taking the bribe and what the money is worth, plus interest. I'm determined to make a clean breast of it and tell the present manager all the details.'

'Roxanne, I approve. I'm sure you'll feel better when you do that.'

Relieved, she rose to leave, even as Simon was ready to offer a consoling prayer. Like Genevieve, she too caught a glimpse of the coming sermon's title. Perking up, she offered a farewell thought, gesturing as she did towards his draft document.

'Simon, I feel I've found the truth and I'm free indeed. Bye for now.' Seconds later, his brief visitor was gone. His silent prayer of blessing went after her.

Imagine that- two women so impressed by his sermon, all from a glance at the title. And he hadn't even given it yet!

It was going to be one heck of a message on Sunday.

Braking rather too hard and inflicting a little more damage on his now battered Ford Fiesta, Alex pulled up in the car park closest to the nail salon and fairly sprinted through the mall, desperate to see the manager again. He was confident this time he'd find out the truth. Fortunately, the same woman was on duty and the only client present was finalising payment, ready to leave. Resisting the urge to interrupt, he waited until she was out the door. He had Harriet's old brochure ready in his hand.

'Hello again, forgive me for troubling you once more. I'm still following up that cold case I mentioned.' The manager didn't mind. She was alone and business was slow that day. Still, she could see she might not be closing up anytime soon.

'This old 1970 brochure puzzles me,' explained Alex, showing it to her. 'Do you think they put out many like it back in 1970? You told me you've been working here for years and were familiar with the process then.'

'You're right, I've never seen anything like it. It's pretty amateurish, looks like it was run off on one of those old spirit duplicators that were popular back in the 1970s. They were kept by places that just wanted a few copies for the staff or whoever. We're much more professional now.'

'Thanks. Anything more you can tell me?'

She glanced at the door. There was nobody else coming for their treatment. Time to unburden herself. 'In fact there is. Would you like a cup of coffee?' Alex readily agreed.

Minutes later, she placed two steaming cups of coffee on a convenient table.

'Today's been a funny day. Less than an hour ago I was visited by a previous manager, a woman called Roxanne. She wanted to admit to something wrong she'd done years back. She'd taken a bribe from someone to offer two particular teenage girls a special treatment, as a one-off. They would bring along a brochure confirming a two-for-one offer, and Roxanne was given a hundred pounds for going along with it. The person bribing her was actually going to pay full price for the second treatment, anyway. So it was money for jam. Strange, but true!'

Alex whistled. He was onto something here.

'Anyway, she's now got religion or something and had a guilty conscience. She insisted on paying me three hundred pounds as compensation, so that she'd feel relieved. She called it an ex-gratia payment. I tell you, I can't afford to look a gift horse in the mouth, so I wrote it up as a donation to our salon. I don't want to feel guilty in the future so I recorded it properly. Maybe the owner will give me a bonus in gratitude- if I'm lucky!'

'Sure, I hope they do. Did you find out why that person offered Roxanne the bribe?'

'Not exactly. But the reason why the old manager felt so guilty wasn't only the money. According to her, the teenage girls' brother came with them, mentioning some story about a special interest in remembering the various steps in applying varnish, but he got bored and went across the mall to a café. Then vanished! It's been a cold case since, a quarter of a century would you believe. I assume that's the one you're following up? So Roxanne held herself responsible morally. As she said, 'If I hadn't agreed to the bribe, that poor boy might still be alive. It was all my fault.'

'Would you believe it indeed! However, I hope Roxanne doesn't beat herself up too much. Now, do you know where I could find her? I need to follow this up.'

'I do. She gives beauty treatments from a home studio here in Guildford, and gave me her business card in case I felt she owed me more money. Perhaps she now sees herself as a Good Samaritan! She's not far away, a house up in Empire Lane.

Why don't you take her card, I won't need it any more. She's at Number 10.'

'Thank you, you've been very helpful. Bye.' Taking the card, Alex ran off so fast he left half a cup of coffee untouched.

Number 10 Empire Lane, here I come!

Alex pulled up and parked right in front of the house; fortuitously, a client had departed just seconds before he arrived.

His ring on the doorbell was answered promptly, for which he was very grateful, unwilling to waste any time unnecessarily.

'Hello, my name's Alex Deverell and I've been given your details by the manager of the nail salon down in the mall. I'm following up on an important matter that I understand you're aware of, and feel you may be able to help me. May I come in and explain?'

Roxanne Jessup was getting the feeling the process of divine forgiveness for her past transgression was taking a strange course, but was open to it. Anything for complete absolution!

'Yes, Mr Deverell. Please come in. I'm happy to help you however I can.'

Over yet another cup of coffee- he could hardly refuse- Alex outlined his quest, details of his colleagues, and the urgency of the situation, especially as he would be returning to Australia within days, solution or no solution.

A tearful Roxanne dabbed at her eyes as she again confessed her regret at taking that bribe. Without it, she believed that Bobby Russell would still be alive today. Sympathetic as he was, Alex wondered why the police hadn't worked this out that very day.

'Don't you see, Mr Deverell? I could hardly confess to taking a bribe. I'd have lost my job, or even worse, the police might have seen me as somehow complicit in the boy's disappearance. Sure, the teenage girls showed them the brochure and the police remarked that it didn't look too professional. I simply lied and told them we had only a small budget for publicity and would do a better job next time. The police seemed happy with that explanation and gave the girls the brochure back. It didn't seem relevant.'

'Logical enough. So no doubt you never mentioned the person who bribed you?'

'No, of course not, absolutely no way, even though the whole arrangement seemed dodgy. That never hit me. That is, until I heard messages in church and my guilt really surfaced. I think you know the rest.'

'Yes. Roxanne- may I call you that? Just one more thing. Who exactly bribed you?'

'Of course you want to know. It may well relate to the case, now that I think of it. Let me write the name down on a piece of paper.' She did.

As she handed it over, Alex raised his eyebrows but said nothing. Of course, that definitely made sense. It brought a lot of loose strands together. He rose to go.

'Thank you! You've been more helpful than you know. We may now be able to solve a very cold case.'

Roxanne rose to see him to the door. Again, he left a hardly-touched cup of coffee. Time was of the essence and Alex had to race back to the school so they could start solving the mystery once and for all.

As his Ford Fiesta departed with a squeal of tyres, Roxanne Jessup felt in her very soul she'd obtained absolution. Somehow, without really knowing it, she'd revealed the truth and was now free.

Free indeed.

CHAPTER ELEVEN

'Right, we're definitely onto something here. This could be the breakthrough we need.' Alex suddenly had a real spring in his step, having returned to the school library at a speed that was lucky not to have attracted police attention.

'How so?' Scott was incredulous. Alex enlightened the other two, then showed them the paper with the particular name.

'OK, let's check it against our brainstorming points.' Scott wanted to be sure. So they did, very carefully.

'There's a definite clue when you go through them again. I wonder how we missed it the first time?' Genevieve was on board with the theory, Scott too.

'Well, it's time for action! Don't forget, we've lost years and years already and I've got to return to Australia soon. We have the address from our notes, haven't we, and the three of us can surely sort this out. If you're ready, let's go! I daresay the old Ford will be up for another run.' A minute later, Genevieve, clutching her file of material including the all-important address of their quarry, was locking up the school before they rushed to Alex's vehicle.

Alex drove, with Scott as navigator in the front passenger seat, his road map spread out on his lap. Genevieve stretched out comfortably in the back.

'Don't worry, we won't need the map yet. I was on this same road before, you know.' Alex certainly was. They sped through now-familiar towns, barely slowing for the populated area speed limit signs. Witley was a blur, then for the second time in recent days the Ford entered Haslemere, then left it.

'Direct me from now on, will you. New territory.'

'Sure. I know where we're going. The next place is Petworth. But please slow down, we don't want to get booked.'

'Whatever you say.' Minutes later a sign flashed by. 'Petworth coming up, not far. Now, time to go over a plan of action. Let's hope our target is at home.' They all were of the same mind: Alex would do the talking, although all three would play a vital part. It all depended on timing and distraction. If it came off, they'd be in with a chance.

With Petworth behind them, they drove quickly through the open countryside. The last major settlement before the turnoff to the south was Chichester. Reaching the town in good time, Scott did a visual check. This was a location even the travelled teacher was unfamiliar with and he had to carefully examine the map. Fortunately, a signpost cleared up any doubt, and the Ford began relentlessly eating up the kilometres towards its final destination on the West Sussex coast- the Selsey Peninsula. During his year living in Britain, Alex had motored through the area, but didn't recall the exact location they were headed for.

'So what can you tell me about where we're going? This Selsey Peninsula?' The helpful Genevieve was keen to enlighten him.

'Oh, it's the southwestern tip of West Sussex and a pretty isolated place. No doubt that's why it was chosen- its remoteness, far away from prying eyes. Surrounded by the English Channel on three sides, it really feels secluded, as I remember it, though I haven't actually been anywhere near here for donkey's years.'

'Sounds right to me. So what else does it offer, Genevieve?'

'Long stretches of beach, salt marshes and low-lying countryside. The only people who usually come here are nature enthusiasts who want to observe the wildlife. There aren't many neighbours for the few home owners who do live around here. I tell you both, our theory is sounding better by the minute. Somebody really wanted to be alone. Well, let's do what we can to prick that bubble.'

'Or lance the boil, more like it.' They all felt the built-up frustration of a quarter century's unsolved major crime. 'Well, not too long now. Let's hope there'll be someone at home.'

Minutes later, Scott had good news. 'We're almost at the tip of the peninsula and straight ahead I see a homeowner's sign for the very place we're looking for- Selsey Bill Cottage. Slow down, Alex, or we'll go over a cliff into the Channel. Now turn in to your left. Good gravy, this place is remote. Yep, here it comes.'

Their progress up a very long driveway towards an imposing rural house seemed like a date with destiny.

CHAPTER TWELVE

'It's now or never!' Alex was adamant. The other two nodded. Genevieve offered a silent prayer. He parked the Ford at the edge of the driveway and they walked up to what appeared to be a mansion. They knocked on the home's front door. Then knocked again.

After a third knocking, the door opened to reveal a squat man in his sixties, quite bald, his face unshaven. His clothes, hardly stylish, had seen better days. He squinted at the uninvited visitors.

'Yes?'

Alex spoke. 'Hello. I'm Alex Deverell, a teacher from Australia. These are my colleagues Genevieve Townley and Scott Geddes, teachers from a secondary school in Guildford. We used to work with Cressida and just the other day reconnected with her at a school reunion. I'm about to return to Australia and am interested in her art work. We gather she now has an excellent reputation in the art scene. There may be a market for her in Perth, my home city. May we see her?'

'Mr- er- Deverell, I'm afraid this is most irregular. We don't conduct business from here, this is where Ms O'Neill plans and completes her superb paintings. She needs solitude, as you may imagine. Surely she told you she has an agent in London and all business is transacted through him? And for that matter, how did you get this address? Cressida never gives it out.'

'Forgive us, sir. We didn't get the full story at the reunion and someone got your details from old school records. But as we've come a long way and I'm about to leave the UK, may we please see her?'

'Oh, alright. I'll call her and see if she's free. I'm her business partner, Winthrop Lewis, by the way.'

'Thanks, Mr Lewis. May we wait in the hallway?'

'Yes, I suppose so. Come in.'

As he left, they gave each other knowing looks. Quickly sizing up the house, it looked like an artist's paradise; old, with many nooks and crannies. The walls of the high-ceilinged hall displayed several dazzling paintings bearing Cressida O'Neill's trademark signature "Cressida O'N". The closest, a still life entitled *A Jug of Cannas* would be worth many thousands on the open market, given her fame since she retired from teaching.

Winthrop Lewis returned with a far from pleased Cressida O'Neill in tow. Gone was the effervescent, free-spirited, artistic sexagenarian from the school reunion, in her colourful clothes and the zaniest glasses in the room. In her place was a rather irritated looking woman with bedraggled hair, wearing baggy jeans with frayed cuffs and a well-worn, paint-smeared artist's smock.

'I gather, Mr Deverell, you're interested in my art? Well, here's my business card so please contact my agent re any purchases. He'll have a full catalogue, I assure you. I definitely don't transact business here. If you were that keen, you could have spoken with me at the reunion.'

'Yes, I agree I should have,' explained Alex. 'I realise that's normally the case, but you seemed very occupied with our former colleagues. However, as I just told Mr Lewis here, I'm about to leave for Australia. I was so impressed by your artwork in the staff common room at Crestwood that I talked my friends into coming straight down here to sound out a deal. A last-minute thing before I jump on a plane home. So may we please have a few minutes of your time? That's all it will take. May I request we go through to a room where there's more natural light?'

Impatiently, Cressida looked at her watch. Then snorted. 'Alright, five minutes then. Come this way, outline your deal and make it snappy!' She and Lewis guided them in the direction of another room. As they moved along the hallway, the three stopped twice to make appreciative comments about the paintings on display. Once they reached the sunroom, which was bathed in natural light, Alex continued his spiel.

'Thank you. As I said, I loved the still life you donated to the school in the late 1960s and often studied it. Then the self-portrait you showed at our reunion the other day- it was magnificent. An absolute likeness. You must have used real skill to capture that when you painted yourself in a mirror.' Cressida glowed with the praise, her ill-temper now dissipating.

'Well, I've had decades of practice, as you know. You would recall my work from the time we taught together all those years ago.'

'Of course. Well, as we came in through the hallway, I couldn't help but notice the still life, *Roses in Bloom*. That one is the sort of painting I was hoping to find. With your permission, may I photograph it? I'd like to show an art dealer acquaintance in Perth, who would be just the person to establish a market for you in Australia. I take it you haven't expanded there yet?'

'No, not yet, but I like the prospect. So far I'm well-known throughout the UK, Europe and North America. Come to think of it, the antipodes would be a new market. Yes, of course, take the photo and write up a description. This could be useful.'

'Fantastic. Perhaps Genevieve could help Winthrop get the painting down and bring it here. I'll have my camera ready.' Cressida was prompt to agree.

'Thank you. Winthrop, bring in the painting, will you.' Winthrop and Genevieve left to do so, returning with it a minute later. At Cressida's urging, Winthrop carried it in and placed it on a chair, carefully checking it was in the best light. Alex and Scott busied themselves with slight adjustments, here and there, a bit more one way than the other, then the reverse. Oh, dear! At last they got it just right, taking one photo after the other. Nobody noticed Genevieve in the doorway, slowly backing away.

Alex did, of course, right on cue. Once he and Scott finished fussing over the painting, extolling its virtues, he had a whole spiel on art prepared, relevant to any artistic work he could see in the room. How grateful he was for all those long-ago weekends he had spent with Sonya trolling through galleries to find paintings to decorate their family home. The experience had given him a certain expertise. After having milked *Roses in Bloom* for all it was worth, the two of them found more "masterpieces" to photograph, praising the artistic virtues of each. Alex went on to deftly insert comments about acrylics, the different aspects of watercolours and oils, and even detoured into a spirited discussion on sketching. It was a class act.

To top off the performance, aided by Scott, he conducted a personal interview of both Cressida and Winthrop, took their photos together, noted down their history as artists and connoisseurs, getting ample material for a long blurb for his "coming story". He assured the pair all this was to be passed onto Western Australia's favourite and most influential art dealer, along with a detailed account glorifying all Cressida's paintings.

Five minutes of her time? The flattered artist would willingly give up a full hour or even longer.

Alex, the master interviewer, laid it on thick and fast. He could go all day without stopping if he needed to.

In the meantime, Genevieve didn't waste a second of the opportunity she had, and slipped through the first door she found leading away from the hallway. It led into a lounge room full of antiques and the oldest settee she'd seen for a long time. How grateful she was for the season; at any other time of year the gloomy house would need all its lights on. As it was, the mid-summer sun streamed through a gap in the slightly-opened old-fashioned curtains and she was able to find her way about without having to turn on a light.

At the end of the lounge room there were more rooms- quite a lot more. Quickly Genevieve checked each one. They were all empty. Finally, there were just two more doors to check. Which one? She thought she heard a slight movement coming from the other end of the hallway, and offered a silent, desperate prayer for divine help. A calm feeling took over her, and she felt guided by an unseen hand. It directed her to try the one on the right.

Quiet as a mouse, Genevieve carefully opened the door and stepped inside. Her heart stopped. A man sat at a desk, his back to her, contemplating something he was writing. He appeared unkempt, but not dangerous. Emboldened, she approached him. He looked up at her, questioning. It was a face she recognised. Finally, it was time to ask the simple question; one she had been wanting to ask for twenty-five years.

'Are you Bobby?'

'Yes. Who are you?' Then he looked at Genevieve closely. 'Mrs Townley?'

With tears in her eyes she replied. 'Yes, Bobby, I am. And I'm here to take you home. Your family desperately wants you back. So please, leave that and come with me, quickly.'

'I've tried to escape before but they always catch me and bring me back. Can you really help me leave this time?'

'Believe me, I will. Just come now, before it's too late!'

Looking relieved but a little frightened, Bobby got straight up and followed her without a sound. The two quickly but quietly found their way back to the hallway. Genevieve held a finger to her mouth, signalling Bobby to stay silent. In the adjacent room, she could hear Alex, with supportive and interested comments from Scott, holding forth on matters of art. He was in top gear now, waxing lyrical on the debate between oils and watercolours. It was a topic he just couldn't leave alone. Then he moved to the technique of gouache, praising Cressida's undoubted skill across the board...

The final hurdle was the front door, which Genevieve opened and then closed behind them with only the slightest 'click.' Thank heavens someone- Winthrop?- had lubricated the hinges. There was not even a squeak.

Her heart beating fast, Genevieve guided Bobby down to the Ford, opened the back door and motioned him to get inside. He did, feeling safe at last. She had one final task. Turning on her mobile phone she texted both Alex and Scott, to be sure at least one would react.

'Got Bobby, he's safe in the car. Wrap it up now and let's go.' Inside, both men's mobiles pinged. Glancing casually at the screens, it was clear something had grabbed their attention.

With Alex's spiel rudely interrupted, Cressida looked around her. Where was that woman, Genevieve?

Alex had a ready answer. 'She just texted. She's diabetic and started having a turn. Had to go back to the car for a snack. You can't wait too long or it affects you. She's sorry about that.'

'A bit rude not to say goodbye to us. Oh, well, is there anything more you have to say? I think you must have got all my details for your art dealer. Is that it for now?' Even Cressida had a limit to the flattery she could absorb.

'Yes, thank you both for your time. We've got everything we need, believe me. We'll go now but I promise you, somebody will be in contact.' Both Alex and Scott shook hands with the pair, then left down the hallway.

As they turned to leave through the opened front door, Alex couldn't resist a final farewell.

'Somebody will definitely be in touch- and soon. You can bank on it!'

Driving as if he'd been transported to Brand's Hatch, Alex revved the poor Ford Fiesta away from its parking spot but slowed down once Scott cautioned him. They didn't want to raise attention and such an exit was far too suspicious. However, once down to the end of the driveway and with a right turn onto the access road away from Selsey Bill, his speed picked up again. By then all four of them were ecstatic- Bobby Russell in particular.

Out poured a jumble of questions. What happened? What did they do to you? Couldn't you get away? And from Bobby: Why are you all here? How come? Mr Deverell, didn't you go to Australia? How did you find me? On it went. But they still had a plan to complete, so they needed to focus. Alex took charge.

'Next stop, Chichester police station. We need to wrap up the case!' Yes, they did need to, and bring about justice for Bobby's many lost years. As the Ford entered the town, they found their immediate goal in the main street. Alex parked right outside and all four rushed inside with newfound energy. The bored desk constable asked their business, wrongly assuming a routine matter. Once they told him, suddenly inspired, he sprang into action.

'There are three constables on duty right now but I'll call in every senior officer I can. Please come this way. Amazing- the boy freed after twenty-five years' captivity!' At the urging of the three teachers, the police formed a squad, ready to race down to Selsey Bill Cottage. Justice was imminent. With Genevieve present as his supporter, Bobby Russell made a full statement. The local inspector issued an arrest warrant, at the same time insisting on a police escort for Bobby, Alex, Scott and Genevieve back to Guildford.

With the paperwork done and the police car leading the way, lights flashing, Alex smiled with satisfaction. Forget Brand's Hatch. With official protection, he could now indulge his urge to do some Formula One driving- and it would all be legitimate.

Jackie Stewart, eat your heart out!

EPILOGUE

Alex drove the battered Ford Fiesta to Heathrow Airport with Genevieve by his side. She wanted to be there in the departure area to farewell him. After that, being on holidays with a sudden amount of leisure time at her disposal, she was more than happy to catch an airport bus back to London and do some shopping and sightseeing in the capital before taking the train home to Guildford. Scott, along with many former Crestwood students and colleagues, had all given their heartfelt goodbyes. The last few days had been tumultuous; a whirlwind of emotions.

As Alex turned the Ford into the airport carpark, he glanced at his passenger. Genevieve smiled at him. They were still glowing from recent events. Surrey police had informed them that Cressida and Winthrop had indicated they would plead guilty to kidnapping and false imprisonment of Bobby, meaning they would be serving a long term of incarceration themselves. Bobby's family exulted over having him back home again and couldn't wait to make up for his lost years, and would most likely be compensated by the seizure of Cressida's famous art works.

'Well, Alex- what are you going to say to the car rental chaps?' The departing tourist had been thinking the same thought himself. With the much-the-worse car at least now safely parked, he jingled the keys in his hand and grimaced as they approached his final hurdle- Bargain Car Rentals.

Within minutes Alex was at the head of the queue. Sighing nervously, he handed over a comprehensive police report, accounting for the state of the Ford Fiesta, to the incredulous customer representative. It was almost possible to read his thoughts as he read through it. Police operation? Car chase? Bullet holes riddling the bodywork? A smashed windscreen with an emergency replacement? The poor car would be a complete write-off. A total loss! The clerk shook his head. Twice. He would need to check all this with his supervisor. With a curt 'Wait here!' he left the desk to talk to his superior behind the screen. Alex and Genevieve could hear every word.

'These cursed Australians- who do they think they are?' The clerk didn't hold back, much to the amusement of Alex and Genevieve. 'Thrashing our cars like it was a damned Dakar rally! Don't they have their own outback races like "Back to Bourke Bashes" or whatever? This is the United Kingdom, for goodness' sake! They need to go on the black list!'

'Remember the Bobby Russell case, just solved?' A second, much calmer female voice intervened.

'Of course.'

'Well, it was down to this gentleman and his colleagues. Didn't you see the TV news? We've never seen the like of it.'

The supervisor came out to talk to Alex and Genevieve in person.

'Mr Deverell, on behalf of a grateful British public and Bargain Car Rentals in particular, thank you for what you and your colleagues achieved with the Bobby Russell matter.' She shook Alex's hand warmly. 'And this is Mrs Townley with you, I assume? It was our pleasure to provide you with a vehicle and we'll accept all expenses. We'll return your full deposit and it'll be in your bank account directly. There's nothing further for you to do.'

'Thank you, that's wonderful. I really appreciate it.' Alex and Genevieve couldn't believe their ears.

'Goodbye, Mr Deverell and safe travels. Best wishes to you, too, Mrs Townley.' No sooner had they left, astonished, than the supervisor turned to the clerk. 'Get the Fiesta and get your camera ready. Just think of the advertising campaign we can run with this one. Bargain Car Rentals help crack cold case!'

In the few minutes until check-in, Genevieve was curious and still had questions. 'Alex, how did you suspect Bobby was still alive and doing all those paintings?'

'I guess it all just fell into place. Cressida had donated a painting to the staff common room in the late 1960s when she was teaching at the school, I remember it from when I was there in 1969 and 1970. It's still there, and featured during the reunion. She had signed it normally, as she did, "Cressida O'N". However, the second painting she brought to the reunion the other day, the self-portrait, had the same signature but this time it was signed by a left-hander. Not only that, but the style was far superior to the earlier one.'

'You're left-handed aren't you?'

'Yep, that's why I noticed it. And I remembered Bobby was left-handed, too, from teaching him. I was very sympathetic to him because of that. When Cressida gave out catalogues of "her" paintings at the reunion, I looked carefully at them and reckoned they were all signed by a left-hander. Of course, I didn't have any more to go on but that at the time.'

'So that's how you started to work it out?'

'Oh, we all helped with parts of the puzzle, you know that. Scott was a terrific support, you were a great encourager and your infiltration of the Selsey house was inspired!'

'I can see it all now,' said Genevieve sadly. 'Poor Bobby lost a quarter century of his life under enforced house arrest. Chilling stuff, really. Cressida set up that nail salon appointment to trap him! She would have handed him the brochure after school and told him to pass it on to his sisters as a 'secret surprise' and told him not to mention her name. So much for the special "art assignment" on nail varnish technique she gave him as a cover, to ensure he'd go too. I daresay she bribed him with the offer of a treat in the café opposite if he went along with it, and kept their little secret.'

Genevieve was angry all over again on poor Bobby's behalf.

'Exactly.' Alex went on to elaborate. 'Knowing the time limit of the special nail deal, Cressida was able to lie in wait in the crowded café opposite, ready to hear his report and reward him with a treat- something extra to the milkshake and sandwich he'd already bought. Once he'd had it, she sweet-talked him into going outside and down an alleyway to the nearest parking area, probably for a further "surprise". Her accomplice, Winthrop, was waiting in their car. After a quick trip down to Selsey, the two of them kept the poor boy there to paint on demand. Cressida made him sign each painting as herself, and subsequently racked up an absolute fortune from Bobby's genius-level paintings.'

'So how do you reckon she put her plot together?' Genevieve was curious.

'From teaching Bobby, she knew he was a child prodigy. Remember, Fred Yeo had correctly recognised Bobby's budding genius, as mentioned in his 1969 school report. As a distraction, Cressida talked down Bobby's ability while she hatched her plot, only giving him a mediocre mark the following year. It threw everybody off the scent!'

Genevieve continued as the penny dropped. 'The catalyst must have been when she came into her large inheritance at the end of 1969, as we both remember from her excited news in the common room that day. Cressida inherited her late parents' house, Selsey Bill Cottage, with a fortune to go with it and was able to retire from teaching at only forty.'

'Yes, her scheme was to piggy-back on a child prodigy and disguise her own merely mediocre talent. They either locked poor Bobby inside or on the rear courtyard all the time he was kept there. As we found out when the cops raided the home, the section where they normally confined the boy was entirely secured so he couldn't escape.'

'Unbelievable, that they'd go to those lengths to claim fame from his paintings and make money!'

'I know, it's shocking! By chance on the day we arrived, they must have been about to put him back in his lockup area when we interrupted them. So they left him sitting in that chair doing an "assignment" to prepare yet another masterpiece painting. Then you found him- that was so inspired, Genevieve! The whole arrangement came out in a secret diary Bobby kept, found by the cops, detailing how he lived, including some unsuccessful escape attempts. It appears they let him outside occasionally for supervised walks around the property, tethered to one of them. As the place was so remote there was no chance of a nosy neighbour upsetting their apple-cart.'

'Yes, and as he unloaded to us in the car once he'd got away, they were also very adept at using psychological pressure to keep him there. Lots of 'we're your family now' statements, which helped to paralyse his will to resist. Constant bribery with his favourite sweets and treats. Wow, we'll all be eternally grateful to you for being the catalyst to solve that enduring mystery. Let's be happy Bobby and his family now have their lives back. And Cressida and Winthrop have got their just desserts!'

'I agree. Well, it's just about time to go, and I need to phone Sonya at home- a very overdue call, might I say. Thanks for all you and Scott did. There'll always be a spare room for you at our house if you want to visit us in Western Australia. I promise you, the trip won't be as dramatic as this one!'

'Thanks, Alex. It was great to reconnect, despite all the drama. Look, can I leave you with some reading matter on the plane trip home? I feel I was inspired from above to see this through to the end. What I'm saying is, you may like some spiritual uplift as well. In short, a booklet from St Jude.'

'For you, Genevieve, I'll take it. I like to be open-minded. It's certainly been a dramatic journey over the last few days. You may have something there, so I'll have a good read of it!'

'Please do. Well, for now, farewell, dear friend!' She gave him the biggest hug she'd given to anyone in years. He returned it with a similar one and a huge kiss on the cheek.

Then before he'd even reached for his mobile phone, Genevieve was gone. He'd sure miss her.

Fortunately, the time difference was compatible with Perth's. They were on the same day at least. Alex dialled and Sonya picked up right away.

'Hello, stranger. I believe you've been up to something! What's this about being on the television news where you are? The Williams came over to say they just caught the tail end of a story here. I've been so busy looking after Charlotte's two terrors I've hardly had time to scratch myself, let alone watch TV. Do tell!'

'Let me answer that with a question. When you were a schoolgirl, were you ever put on detention? I seem to recall some incident you mentioned once.'

'That's a funny one. Yes, in fact. It was for persistent talking in class when I was fourteen. I was kept in for a whole hour by that Miss Murgatroyd. Can you imagine, all that time? I missed my school bus home and had to walk all the way. That's an hour of my life I'll never get back, what a waste. But why do you ask?'

'Dear Sonya. As a fourteen-year-old you lost a whole hour you'll never get back. Imagine that!'

'Yes, so?'

'Well, love, have I got a story for you!'

SURF BREAK

CHAPTER ONE

As he inserted the key into his office door lock that Monday morning, Gary Bishop had two immediate regrets. The first was that today was the second anniversary of the tragic death of his beloved wife, Lesley. The other- and certainly more minor by comparison- was the realisation he'd have to work all day instead of checking out one of his favourite surf breaks, Snapper Rocks or Duranbah Beach.

Yeah, how's that for bad luck! The weekend had been frustrating; stormy and totally unsuitable for surfing, his one great passion. He'd given it his best, trying the breaks until he'd been forced to give up- even Greenmount Beach, which was somewhat more sheltered. No dice. Even his well-designed JS Industries high-performance surfboard was no match for the choppy, unpleasant conditions. Then, on Sunday night, the storm had blown over, giving birth to the working week's ideal surf forecast. Oh, the irony.

'I reckon the surfing god, Huey must be a jerk,' Gary thought. *He's sure been playing around with us. Perhaps he'll be more benevolent next weekend.* Well, he could only hope.

Gary had determined to be in his office early to distract himself from the pressing memory of Lesley by immersing himself in his tasks. So far it wasn't working. With his efficient personal assistant, Jilly Mortensen, not due to arrive for another hour, his grief inevitably intruded. Lesley had died so young, still in her late thirties. An aggressive breast cancer had proven impossible to defeat. They'd fought it together like a couple possessed; sadly, to no avail. After the funeral, Gary had been bereft. Sure, his family, and Lesley's, along with a coterie of friends, had been very supportive, but as a man who was raised to 'suck it up', he felt it was now up to him. He and Lesley hadn't had children, so he was a free agent now, with no responsibilities. But was that a blessing or a curse?

At forty years of age, based in Brisbane as a qualified forensic scientist with the Queensland Police Forensic and Scientific Services facility, Gary had relished his career. Working in state-of-the-art laboratories and known as an expert in conducting scientific analyses, Gary concentrated on DNA testing, fingerprint detective work and toxicology. Later, he took the opportunity of a change to specialising in document examination. As a side interest, he completed a course in Advanced Negotiation Skills- Gary Bishop was a man who liked to be prepared for everything. Each day as he arrived for work, he mentally saluted Queensland Police's motto, "With Honour We Serve." It was his personal maxim, too.

He remembered vividly his reaction to Lesley's final, dreaded diagnosis. He cashed in all his annual leave to devote himself to Lesley's needs. The FSS was very supportive and the couple had managed, especially after Gary extended his long service leave to twice the time on half pay. They got by.

'Gary, I know you don't understand why, but God has his reasons.' The kindly minister at Lesley's funeral meant well, but failed to convince the bereft young widower. As unimaginable grief welled up and filled his soul, he just wanted to scream. *Yeah, right, if God cared so much, why didn't he cure my wife?*' It was an unanswerable question.

His return to FSS felt like an anticlimax, and he passed an uninteresting eighteen months there, constantly wondering where life might take him. Throwing himself into his work wasn't the solution.

Until that phone call came, out of the blue.

'Gary, it's Adam Singh here. Not sure if you remember...' Gary certainly did. Adam had been in his forensic science cohort at the University of Queensland.

'Look, I've just heard your sad news through the grapevine of your wife's death, it took a while to filter through to me. I'm sorry, Gary. Please accept my belated but sincere condolences. Had I heard earlier, I would have come to her funeral, or at least contacted you sooner.'

'That's OK Adam, we haven't been in touch in years. I wouldn't have expected you to.'

'Possibly not. But I'm still very sorry.' *Come on, man get to the point.* Adam did.

'Look, I don't know if you're looking for a new direction in life, but I have a proposal for you. For some time now I've been running a private investigation business in Tweed Heads, just over the border. It's been doing well, but I've just been offered a position in forensic science with New South Wales police in Sydney and it's too good to refuse. Would you be interested in taking over my business as a PI on a walk-in-walk-out basis? In other words, it's yours to run from when you arrive. It comes with an established bank of clients, plenty of work and an efficient PA, Jilly.'

Gary was amazed. Was there a god in heaven after all? Nup, it was too soon to call on that one. His first question to Adam seemed obvious.

'OK, but wouldn't I need a licence?'

Adam had anticipated his query. 'Yes, but I don't see a problem. Just like when I got into the game, you'll find your Queensland forensic science experience will put you in the box seat when it comes to eligibility and experience as 'a fit and proper person'. There'll be an online training course you'll be able to complete quickly, and character references will be a breeze. And there's a fee to pay to the licensing and regulation division of the NSW police force- tax-deductible of course. That's about it.'

'Sounds straight forward, then.'

'It is, in your case. You'll find there's a big crossover between PI work and our profession of forensic science, so you'll be applying your well-honed skills constantly.' Adam was certainly convincing. After further talking to fine tune the details, Gary drove down to Tweed Heads, met up with Adam and checked things out. The office had a beautiful base in Wharf Street, the town's main thoroughfare. Nearby were magnificent beaches where he could indulge his passion in surfing. The location sure offered a great lifestyle combination. Gary could even take over the lease on Adam's flat; the landlord was more than happy. They'd shaken on it to agree.

Weeks later, Adam had left for Sydney and Gary was ensconced in Border Private Investigations' modern, well-appointed office with his freshly-framed new PI licence displayed on the office wall. The delightful Jilly Mortensen was briefing Gary on current client enquiries. The caseload was nothing dramatic, but there were a few ongoing matters which would bring in a regular income.

Things were starting to look up.

CHAPTER TWO

'Gary, there's a Mrs Kayla Westford here to see you. She's a new client who's just heard of us. I'm sorry to say she's a bit upset over something.' Jilly Mortensen's interruption to his reminiscing seemed urgent. In any case it was time to get down to business, so he banished any further reverie for now.

'Sure, please send her in.' Jilly did so, having thoughtfully provided poor Mrs Westford with some tissues, always kept discreetly handy. The visitor, an attractive blonde-haired woman of medium height, entered Gary's office, dabbing her tears.

'Mrs Westford, please have a seat. I gather there's a problem. I'll do my best to help.'

'Thank you. It's a bit of a story.' Mrs Westford was mid-thirties at most, possibly younger. Gary noticed she wore a wedding ring. Was it a husband problem?

'Please, just tell me what's happened in your own words. Are you OK if I take notes?'

'Yes, of course. Look, I've been knocked for six. My husband, Dion, has left me and taken all our spare cash. He's probably overseas now. He's completely cleaned out our bank account and investments. There was $300,000 all up, which we were going to use for a house deposit. We were planning to raise a mortgage for the rest. Now I'm almost penniless with two young children.'

On further questioning, Gary learned Kayla Westford was a teacher at Little Jewels Preschool. She rented a house at Sunrise Point, a short distance south of Tweed Heads. She was thirty-five and had two young daughters, five-year-old Elise and three-year-old Sky.

'Please tell me about Dion.'

'He's three years older than me. A mad-keen surfer. A merchant banker at Zenith Bankers in Sydney, he works remotely from a home office. He's an expert in high finance, works around the clock on international deals. Then he surfs! I know he has a big portfolio of shares and property. I've been at him to cash some of it in and buy us a home but he kept delaying. But I did get him to transfer some to our own account- which he's now cleaned out!'

'I'm so sorry, Kayla- may I use your first name?' She nodded tearfully. 'So what makes you think he's overseas?'

'He always used to go on surfing trips to Bali, coming back with tales of the fantastic waves at Medewi, Canggu and Padang Padang.' Yeah, Gary thought, I've been to those places. The long tube rides at Padang were out of this world... he snapped back to reality as Kayla continued.

'Look, I've heard whispers that on those trips he got involved in the drug trade in Bali. Sometimes he had surfing mates over and there was a bit of wink-wink and nudge-nudge whenever the subject of drugs came up. I'd always give him dirty looks and he wouldn't discuss any of that with me. I'm dead against illegal drugs, don't smoke and rarely have a wine. But I reckon I wouldn't put it past him!'

So that's what he's like, Gary thought. He was into a healthy lifestyle himself, having seen enough of the effects of drugs in his forensic science work to ever touch them. 'So you reckon he could be in Bali?'

'That's my best guess for now. Can you please take my case? I'm desperate to at least get our money- mine now- so I can support my two daughters. Fortunately, I can ask Little Jewels for more shifts if I have to, I'm only part-time at the moment. The only problem is, how do I pay you?'

'The priority now is to solve this problem,' said Gary. 'Leave the money for now, it can be sorted out later.' Gary Bishop knew there were more important things than money. Suffering a personal tragedy set you right on that point.

'Thank you, Mr Bishop. I'll be eternally grateful if you can help.'

'That's OK, Kayla, I promise I'll do my best. But please call me Gary. We're pretty informal around here.'

Might as well start out that way. This problem seemed a real doozy, and Gary felt in his bones they'd be in it for the long haul.

CHAPTER THREE

Gary Bishop's life began in a happy family home in Mermaid Beach on Queensland's Gold Coast. Being an only child, his doting parents could easily afford to encourage any hobby he chose to follow, along with the pursuit of academic excellence. Leisure activities weren't complicated; there was really only one sport he engaged in with a passion: surfing. What else? After all, the family lived in Surfcrest Avenue. Gary quickly progressed from a beginners surfboard to an intermediate board, before specialising in boards from JS Industries, updating and replacing them when required.

There were plenty of local beaches for the teenager, who grew to above-average height, to develop his expertise, as well as his muscles. In addition to Mermaid Beach, there was Broadbeach, Nobby's and Burleigh Heads, and more further afield. The Gold Coast was a paradise for a young surfer who was eager to master the challenging waves, whatever the weather and conditions. With meticulous practice Gary soon became expert in all the moves- he loved perfecting the art of the cutback, then the tube ride, the barrel. Christmas holidays were the best, it seemed like an endless summer, out there beyond the breakers with his best mates.

But of course life wasn't just about the sun, sand and surf.

While the Bishops could have afforded to send him to a prestigious private school, to their credit they encouraged him to progress from the nearby primary school to the closest government high school, Miami State High School, a short distance away. 'We'd rather you mix with everyday kids to learn about life,' was their maxim. Reinforcing the wisdom of that theory, young Gary had excelled there, and after his final exams qualified for entry to a number of university courses in Brisbane.

He chose forensic science, and that discipline soon became a passion for him, equal to his love of surfing. Queensland University of Technology offered the most suitable course in this field, a Bachelor of Science degree in Applied Science (Forensic Science). He enrolled eagerly, finding student digs in Brisbane and applying himself to the rigours of academic study.

In his second year, Gary met a delightful and equally academic fellow student, Lesley Jacobs, who was just as keen as he was on forensic science. A Brisbane girl, she quickly fell for the handsome young surfer from the Gold Coast. Gary in turn was entranced by the lovely Lesley. As soon as they both graduated, they married, setting up home in a flat in suburban Kangaroo Point. Gary was successful in obtaining a position with Queensland Police, while Lesley continued her study for a Master of Forensic Science degree. Securing a tertiary appointment was her ambition.

The clever Lesley Bishop progressed to a Doctor of Philosophy degree, working as a temporary lecturer with the University of Queensland. With a permanent position confirmed back at her alma mater, the loving couple felt life was magnificent. Their dreams had come true. That was until Lesley felt a suspicious lump in her right breast. She was barely out of her twenties.

The onward march of cancer was relentless, and Lesley's thirties were spent enduring one round of treatment after another. They did everything their medical team had suggested:

a double mastectomy, rounds of chemo, radiation, wellness clinics, meditation therapy – the lot. The doctors had even put Lesley on a trial of a breakthrough drug, but in the end, the titanic battle was lost. Gary booked his beloved wife into a hospice in suburban Kelvin Grove for the best palliative care that the dedicated staff could provide. In those final sad days, Gary moved into the hospice with his wife. He spent Lesley's last night stroking her face and comforting her as she lapsed in and out of consciousness, and the hospice chaplain recited prayers and words from the Bible. The brave Lesley looked serene as her shallow breathing began to fade. At dawn, she was gone.

It was her 37th birthday.

Following the funeral, Gary's parents insisted on supporting their grieving son for a long as it took. They'd loved Lesley as their own daughter. For the next two years, he would drive down to the family home in Mermaid Beach every weekend for his own surfing marathon, paddling far out to sea to ride the breakers in. Sometimes, when his grief could not be assuaged by the rigours of the surf, Gary felt it would be a relief if he paddled out to the horizon, never to return. Once he was actually on the point of doing so when a freak rainstorm came out of nowhere, drenching him and hiding the tears streaming down his cheeks.

'Send it down, Huey!' he screamed to the god of the surf, the only one Gary acknowledged. He felt relieved and strangely invigorated by the downpour. He turned away from the horizon and caught a wave back to shore.

Surfboard stacked on top of his car, he was just about to drive back to his parents' home when a nagging doubt assailed him again. 'Where am I going? What's my future? Is this all there is?' It all began to turn dark again. That's when his mobile rang. It was a number he didn't recognise.

'Hello?'

That unexpected phone call from Adam Singh had set him in a life-changing new direction.

CHAPTER FOUR

Gary had plenty of homework to do on the new Dion Westford case. Fortunately, Kayla had the foresight to bring with her a summary of information on her husband, which included a copy of his résumé. On paper, Dion was very impressive, starting with a degree in finance from the University of New South Wales followed by a further qualification in computing and extensive experience in banking with various Sydney institutions, merchant banks in particular. He had an extensive portfolio of investment clients. So what was this wife deserter's mindset?

'What do you reckon? He's left his poor wife in the lurch and abandoned his kids. How do you think he would he treat his clients?' Gary had put in a call to Nick Vassallo, his state police contact in the fraud squad.

'Gary, good to hear from you. I'd heard you'd left the Queensland cops and are now a PI in Tweed. How do you like it?'

'Fine, Nick. I'm onto an intriguing case now.' Gary filled Nick in.

'It's funny you should mention Zenith Bankers. There's nothing definite as yet, but the word around the traps is there could be some clients with missing funds. Maybe that's down to our friend Dion? I've been busy with more urgent enquiries so I haven't followed this one up, but I'll get onto it when I can and if I find anything, I'll get back to you. Stay in touch!'

'That I will. Bye for now.'

Gary went through again everything Kayla had told him. He didn't want to miss anything. The talk of Bali reminded him of his own surfing experiences on the tropical island. Since Lesley's death he'd gone on several surfing trips with mates, and one or two by himself, all in a bid to try and get through his grief. His mates had been very supportive, and it had helped for a time. On one trip, he'd met a local surfer who was a police officer there. They had struck up a friendship. Did he still have him as a contact? People like that were especially important now that he was running a PI business. He scrolled down and found Jimmy Perduwan's details, then called the number.

'Jimmy, long time no see! How are the breaks on Keramas?' He'd remembered the Indonesian's favourite spot. After the pleasantries, during which he was delighted that Jimmy still considered him a friend, Gary got down to the business of Dion Westford. Was he known to the local police?

He was. Jimmy was quite forthcoming. Dion was a leading light on the local party scene and had tried to get a foot into the drug trade there. Pot, MDMA, heroin, speed- whatever was the 'flavour of the month'. Then it stopped.

'So why was that?'

'Westford encountered some heavies who took exception to him muscling in on their territory. Him being an Aussie and all. They made Bali too hot for him and basically ran him out of town. He was out of his league. I don't know what he did as a banker, but I don't think he had a future as a drug supplier. Certainly not in Bali, at least. Actually, he was a bit lucky. If he'd kept at it, we'd have had enough evidence to arrest him and he'd have ended up in Kerobokan. Not the first Aussie to do so, of course.' How true, Gary thought.

'Any idea where he might be?'

'Well, if he's fled overseas as you say, he could be anywhere. Why don't I make some enquiries and get back to you?'

'That'd be terrific, my friend. When all this is over, I look forward to a trip to Bali and riding some waves together!'

'I'll hold you to it, mate! Bye for now.'

As he returned the farewell greeting, Gary knew this was a promise he'd try to keep. Friends were indeed precious.

Three days later the reliable Jimmy returned the call. 'Hey, guess where Dion Westford has turned up?'

'You'd better tell me.'

'Dili, in Timor-Leste..'

'So, he seems to like your part of the world. Just jumped over the border, as it were. Any idea what he's doing? It must be some racket.'

'No doubt some lurk, but who knows what. It could be drugs again but probably not. I think he's had his fingers burned on that score. And given the poverty of East Timor, it's unlikely to be fleecing bank clients. I'll have to leave it to you to chase up from now on.'

'My friend, thanks a million – you're a brick!'

'I assume that's a compliment?'

'Jimmy, you'd better believe it.'

CHAPTER FIVE

Previously known as East Timor, Timor-Leste is a young nation with a tumultuous history. After being under colonial Portuguese rule for centuries, it was decolonised in 1974. In the vacuum left by Portugal's departure, East Timor declared its independence in November 1975, but was immediately invaded by its much larger and more powerful neighbour, Indonesia. Why not? They shared the same island, so it would have been a tempting target for annexation.

A brutal occupation followed, largely ignored by the international community. There were widespread human rights abuses, mass killings and forced relocations. Through all this the East Timorese people resisted bravely. Guerrilla warfare, co-ordinated by the main resistance group, the revolutionary front called FRETILIN, gave the hard-pressed population hope despite the loss of life of hundreds of thousands of civilians.

Eventually, international diplomatic pressure forced Indonesia in 1999 to agree to a UN-sponsored referendum giving the beleaguered populace the option of independence. The people of East Timor embraced it with overwhelming enthusiasm. UN peacekeepers, many from neighbouring Australia, ensured a valid vote. East Timor finally gained independence in 2002, taking the official name of the Democratic Republic of Timor-Leste. Now, in 2017, it was just fifteen years old, and as Gary planned his first trip to the young nation, he reflected on some of huge challenges it had had to face: building a stable government, establishing political and economic institutions, and dealing with huge social and developmental issues. *Well, I reckon I'll have enough of my own challenges over there. Sorting out Mr Dion Westford, for a start.*

'I'd better get my skates on,' he said to Jilly. 'I'll need a visa, I could get one on arrival but to be sure, let's apply before I leave. Let's hope they're quick with it.' In went his application to the embassy in Canberra, located in Beale Crescent, Deakin. A follow-up phone call indicated there should be no problems. Gary certainly hoped not.

Ten days later Gary had his generous sixty-day tourist visa and booked a Qantas flight from Brisbane to Darwin. After a wait of only three hours, he would be on another Qantas flight to Dili, Timor-Leste's capital. Not bad. Checking the internet, he considered himself lucky. Often you had to fly a longer route via Bali, then change planes for the final leg of the journey.

Beginner's luck. Would it hold? Next hurdle: how to locate his quarry once he was on the ground. When Adam Singh had briefed him on his new role of PI, he'd emphasised that it was a 'high contact role'. In other words, you depended on a network of people to pass you information, each being an expert in their own area. Adam supplied his own list, which Gary would add to. One highly recommended name was Eric Dunshea of the Department of Foreign Affairs and Trade.

'He's worth his weight in gold,' Adam told him. 'The man knows everything that's going on. Very discreet, and only passes on what he knows is correct, and then only to approved people. You'll be one of them, of course once I let him know you're taking over BPI. Eric supposedly only connects with police sources, but he knows this is a grey area. Certainly contact him if you need to.'

Gary made a quick phone call to Eric, finding the latter immediately helpful. He soon had the address of Australia's embassy in Dili, in Rua Matires da Patria, along with a useful lead. Dion's location would only be a matter of time.

'East Timor, here I come.'

As he flew to Darwin, Gary began to formulate his strategy. Suss out the target, assess the rogue's likely plot and take counter-measures. He reckoned Jimmy Perduwan was right. Dion was no longer onto a drugs racket, he'd probably have fallen back on something more in his line of expertise. Money, money, money no doubt. But how?

His wait in Darwin airport gave him further time to think over his plan. He'd brought his surfboard, both with the aim of testing the surf there for the first time (would it be better or worse than Bali?) and hopefully making a connection with his quarry. A love of surfing was the only thing they'd have in common. It was also a great cover, prominently listed as the reason for his trip on the visa application form.

The onward flight to Dili was smooth, save for some minor turbulence, and otherwise uneventful. Before Gary knew it, the vast expanse of the Timor Sea suddenly gave way to land. As the aircraft surged downwards to his island destination, he saw below him the Presidente Nicolau Lobato International Airport, just a short distance from the capital. Not long now.

'Ladies and gentlemen, please fasten your seatbelts and prepare for landing.'

A slightly bumpy touchdown followed, but he'd had worse. As the engines revved they slowed, taxied to the terminal, then stopped. Dili awaited.

Impatient as he was to be up and cracking, Gary restrained himself to tolerate the inevitable wait to be free of both the plane's confines and then the airport itself. His luggage collection and passage through customs was smooth, probably because of his surfboard. Australians were evidently still popular in the country, thanks to our nation's involvement in their independence struggle.

'Welcome to Timor-Leste- and happy surfing!' was the customs clerk's cheerful salutation as he stamped Gary's passport. He apparently liked the look of Gary's JS Industries model board.

'Obrigadu -thank you.' Gary always thought it was a nice touch for the tourist to learn a few words of Tetum, the nation's language. Finally Gary was through the barrier and on the lookout for a taxi into Dili. Not all that far according to his research, about six kilometres. He noted the good selection of hire cars at the rank, with plenty of choice. The first driver approached him.

'Taxi to Dili? Ah, surfboard!' Like the clerk, evidently an admirer. 'What type?'

' JS Industries, high performance. Have you heard of Jason Stevenson?'

'No, but it's a very nice surfboard! Now, you want ride to town?' Gary noticed he had a roof rack.

'Sure.' The obliging driver carefully placed the surfboard on the rack, secured it, then lifted Gary's other luggage into the boot. Within a minute, they were on their way into the city.

'You been to Dili before?'

'No, this is my first trip. I want to check out the surfing scene.' Well, that was partly true.

'Great beaches here. Where you stay?'

'Beach Garden Hotel. Convenient surfing there.'

'Yes. But better surf beaches elsewhere. I guess you check later.'

'Right. But that beach will be fine for now.' Gary had other reasons for staying in town. Well, one main one.

That seemed to have exhausted the driver's supply of conversation for a while and Gary was left to his thoughts, mentally running through the tourist landmarks he expected to find in the nation's capital. The Palacio do Governo, the president's official residence. Yes, they were now driving right by it, very impressive. Pointing to it, the driver, alert again, gave the local term.

'Palacio das Cinzas.' Gary nodded in appreciation, wondering why the building had both names.

'Much to see here. Maybe go around in our colourful buses, they take you anywhere. Make sure you notice Cristo Rei up on the headland.' The iconic twenty-seven metre high statue of Christ, placed atop a globe at Cape Fatucama, was not dissimilar to the one above Rio de Janeiro. 'You must visit Resistance Museum. Many killed for independence.'

'I remember all about it. A sad time for you.'

'Right, but better now.' Without further ado, the driver pulled up outside Gary's booked accommodation, just back from the long main Dili beach. He untied the surfboard, lifted out Gary's case from the boot and carefully placed both items on the kerb. The Australian peeled off a large greenback from the wad in his wallet. US dollars were the local currency since independence. A generous tip which was evidently appreciated.

'Thank you, sir! Enjoy your time in Timor-Leste!' Then he was off to scout for another fare.

An alert hotel porter carried Gary's items to the Beach Garden's reception desk, then hovered around while he checked in. Room 205. The lift was temporarily out of action- this was a developing country after all- but the willing porter conveyed everything up to the room, let him in, then handed over the key. Gary dispensed another greenback tip, well-earned.

Making a cup of coffee from the room's housekeeping items, Gary considered his options. Where was the elusive Dion? A phone call to a fresh contact in the Australian embassy might provide the answer. Carmelita Soares picked up right away. Gary introduced himself, quoting Eric Dunshea and emphasising the urgent need to trace Dion Westford.

'Ah, Mr Dunshea, I know him. Of course. Dion Westford? Yes. I'm happy to help you, Mr Bishop. It should take only a few minutes.'

'Please call me Gary. Thank you. Should I phone back?'

'No, I'll phone you. I've got your number now.'

She was as good as her word. Ten minutes later, Carmelita was on the line.

'Gary, Dion Westford is staying at the Hotel Esplanada, not far from you. It's even closer to the beach than where you are. You could walk there in minutes. Very convenient!'

'Thanks so much, Carmelita. So we can assume he'll surf right at the town beach?'

'Yes, if he's happy with average waves. If he fancies something more of a challenge, he'll likely travel further afield, east to Manatuto or even Bacau. But he'll possibly surf where he is for a start. If you want to link up, I'd try exactly where you are. One more thing. He has a much longer visa for Timor-Leste than you. In fact, an indefinite one, which is a bit curious. It's legal, but not many people get them.'

Well, linking up just now wasn't what he had in mind, that was one thing. An indefinite visa? That was assuredly another. Gary was grateful to learn this so early in the piece. It looked like Dion would be around here for a while. What was the so-and-so up to?

'Many thanks, Carmelita. You've been very helpful.'

'No worries, Gary! Hoo-roo for now!' So she was a dab hand at Aussie slang, eh? He liked her style.

After unpacking, he felt the call to check the beach, only a stone's throw away. What do committed surfers say? If in doubt, go for a surf. Gary rubbed his JS Industries surfboard affectionately, keen to try the local spot right then and there.

Time to hit the waves.

CHAPTER SIX

At home in Sunrise Point, Kayla Westford was having a bad day. In fact she'd had a series of them. Her caring mum, Helen, couldn't stay any longer as she had her own needs to attend to back in Sydney. Kayla's father was booked in for a prostate operation and needed some support of his own. The situation was beyond awful. She kept thinking over and over about Dion betraying her by cleaning out their joint bank account and decamping for overseas, the marriage clearly finished.

Gone was her inheritance from her loving late grandparents, specifically bequeathed so the young couple could have a deposit on their own home. Gone, too were the savings from her position as a preschool teacher. Meagre as the salary was, Kayla, through careful budgeting, had been able to squirrel away a significant amount. True, some of the total of $300,000 was from Dion himself, although, given his propensity to spend on his own surfing and travel needs, it was a minor contribution.

'Come on Elise and Sky, time to get ready!' She had to summon every ounce of strength just to get through the day. She needed to organise Elise for the walk to the local Sunrise Point Primary School, then get herself and Sky ready for a full day at Little Jewels. At least the kindly preschool owner, sympathetic to Kayla's plight as a deserted wife, had increased the shifts available. Her salary provided just enough income to pay the rent on their modest home in Clifftop Crescent. Not much of a house, but the view was magnificent.

Yes, she mused, if you have to be miserable, at least have pleasant surroundings. Otherwise, there was not much hope for a future unless that PI, Gary Bishop, could do something. Someone had recommended him and he looked OK.

'I guess we'll see.' Kayla sighed. For now, time was marching on. The girls needed their lunch made and they were all a bit late. There were extra kids arriving for her class today who'd need some orientation, and they were a staff member down because a colleague was sick. After work, she needed to go over her budget to check how to cope with some unexpected bills. Perhaps plead for a loan from her credit union? A definite possibility.

A fresh day, and fresh challenges.

Dion woke up that day in a better frame of mind than his abandoned wife back home. He yawned, slowly got out of bed and walked over to the window of his top floor room in the Hotel Esplanada, which offered a wonderful vista of Dili harbour.

'Great day for a surf, I reckon. Look at those waves. Yeah, when the tide turns it'll be ideal. First, time for a leisurely breakfast.' Talking aloud to himself, he buzzed for room service. His breakfast arrived promptly, carried in by an attractive young waitress. Dion had a moment's lascivious thought, then dismissed it with some effort. Willpower was hardly Dion's forte. The big plan demanded keeping faith with his new girlfriend, Lucia, and if word got out about him trying it on with a waitress, well...

So as much as he would have liked to indulge his urges in that direction, his scheme involved some personal restraint.

This was still a conservative society in many ways, thanks to its Portuguese Catholic heritage, and his outward behaviour had to appear above board, no matter how difficult the personal effort. People talk, after all.

Dion finished his cereal and fruit and checked his watch, calculating the surf would soon be right. 'OK, DHD, let's see how you perform today.' He favoured a brand used by Aussie pro-surfers, a Darren Handley design. It had never let him down and he was certain it never would.

He gathered his beach bag and his beloved DHD and went down in the lift to the foyer, deciding to leave his room key for security with the desk concierge. You can never be too careful. He made the short walk over to the town beach just the other side of the long Avenue de Portugal, and left his bag with an attendant there. He knew the man would take good care of it- for a small tip. This completed, Dion was soon in the surf and paddling out.

'Hey, Dion!' Yes, there she was, as arranged. Exotic, slim, dark-haired Lucia Ximenes, his new girlfriend. She was already out past the first set of breakers and waving in greeting. Excited, he paddled over and they embraced so keenly that she fell off her surfboard. As she surfaced, they kissed, laughing. Then it was time to test the swell.

This beach was hardly the best surf spot in East Timor but it was a convenient meeting location for the two. Dili was where Lucia both lived and worked. Today the waves were above-average, but they were both experienced surfers. They restricted themselves to a few cutbacks, redirecting their boards towards the breaking wave, allowing them to maintain speed and continue along its face each time.

'You beauty!' Dion was enjoying himself. Lucia, too. She impressed him with a "snap" as she completed a quick, powerful turn at the top of one large breaker, spraying him with water as he applauded.

'Nice one!' Then, repeating the same moves a dozen times, they considered their mastery of the ocean complete, with no more likely challenges to their repertoire today. It was time to give the surf away for now and relax over a coffee or two at the Café Encanto, at the top of the beach.

As they emerged from the foam, laughing and joking over their prowess, Gary Bishop – who had been enjoying the same experience and similar manoeuvres a short distance away- observed them closely. So, this was Dion's new love interest. Certainly attractive, probably mid-twenties at most, a few years younger than Dion. Gary bet that this woman was an integral part of whatever scheme Dion was hatching. Doubtless about money; the ruthless former merchant banker worshipped it. Just what exactly he was up to, Gary would do his level best to find out. Then he would set in play a strategy of his own, already starting to formulate in his mind.

Retrieving his own beach bag from Pedro, the dutiful attendant, Gary asked if he knew the dark-haired girl, motioning in her direction as the laughing pair made their way over the sand to the café.

'I know her by sight, senor. She comes here often when that tourist is here and always joins him up at the café after they surf.'

'Thanks, Pedro.' Gary doubled his tip, much to Pedro's delight. Then he carried his surfboard back to the Beach Garden and took a longer than usual shower as he figured his next step.

Phone Phyllis Cameron.

Gary's late wife, Lesley, as devoted to the cause of science as he was, had an abiding side interest in the world of acting, writing and performing plays in a number of amateur productions in Brisbane. It was as a member of a theatre troupe that Lesley had encountered the formidable but nevertheless charming Phyllis Cameron, a Scottish lady of generous proportions, who was just as entranced as Lesley was by the world of acting. Through his encouragement of Lesley's activity, and deriving much enjoyment from her thespian performances, Gary had become equally friendly with Phyllis. The Bishops enjoyed the hilarity of Phyllis's company at many a post-performance party.

Moreover, Phyllis was a tower of strength through Lesley's final battle with breast cancer, helping out with visits to the hospice, frequent hot meals delivered to Gary at home, and even insisting on paying all funeral costs. It appeared she'd been an heiress. She certainly had an affluent lifestyle, but she determined to use her large fortune to benefit society, supporting many needy charities. As Phyllis often declared, 'You can't take it with you when you go!' A childless widow, her fortune was at the disposition of various worthy causes.

Somehow Gary had heard that a distant relative of Phyllis's in Adelaide needed some support and, not long after Lesley's death the Scottish humanitarian moved to the City of Churches. She still stayed in touch- Gary never lacked a birthday present or a kind card on the anniversary of Lesley's death. He, in turn, kept in close contact with Phyllis.

'I may live further away, Gary, but you're still in my heart. If you need anything, just call!'

So he did.

'East Timor is it? A turnup for the books, laddie! But nothing will shock Phyllis!' For sure, nothing would. Gary outlined his plan. With a precocious lilt in her voice, Phyllis agreed instantly. 'You get me a visa and I'll be on my way.' He assured her he would, and he'd be in touch as soon as it came through.

'Bye for now, laddie!'

'Good bye, Phyllis.'

His next phone call was to Eric Dunshea in Canberra, requesting an urgent tourist visa for Phyllis. Could he organise one through their embassy in Deakin? He could, with one proviso.

'Don't forget my birthday, Gary!' Gary promised he wouldn't.

It was done that same day and emailed to Phyllis, instructing a stamped confirmation to go into her passport once she arrived in Dili. She would arrive in three days. Gary had arranged her accommodation on the floor above his at the Beach Garden, in an expansive room where the two of them could talk tactics.

It was time to lay the trap!

CHAPTER SEVEN

While he waited for Phyllis to arrive, Gary was busy plotting and planning. He only had time for one further surf, but even that was calculated. He had 'accidentally' crossed the path of Dion as they both exited the water together, exchanging a casual greeting. 'G'day, mate! 'Great surf, eh?'

Contact established.

But the major activity was back in his hotel room. First, he had put in a call to Pete, a specialist whose name had been given to him by Adam. Pete was a master of his art. Yep, if he dropped his other work he could certainly do the job in three days. That done, Gary turned his hand to downloading financial documents, preparing a prospectus and a variety of background material. He was grateful for his university training, and in particular his forensic science experience with Queensland Police, where his expertise as a document examiner in the fraud squad helped expose dodgy financial deals. This time, he was going to create a fraud of his own.

All in a good cause, of course.

The Café Encanto had a few patrons that morning, but fortunately not too many. An ideal number in fact. From his earlier observations, Gary had noted where Dion and Lucia's favourite table was and arranged with the waiter to be positioned quite close by. He and Phyllis contrived to be seated and ready just as the pair were approaching. Their papers were on the table, pens poised, coffees delivered, and a friendly but businesslike air adopted.

If this were a film set, the director would have called: 'Lights, camera, action!'

Out came their scripted lines, rehearsed in Phyllis's hotel room. It was just like one of Lesley's plays. In order to concentrate, Gary deliberately repressed any memory of his dear departed in this 'play', everything had to go to plan. The pair affected an air of businesslike insouciance- or at least, something approaching it. They focused on the task at hand, without even a sideways glance at the two lovebirds, now ordering their own refreshment. Gary and Phyllis knew they were there, certainly. Peripheral vision worked wonders.

Act one, scene one.

'Right, then, Penelope. Is the prospectus clear? I can run through it again if you like.'

'Pretty clear, George. I'm impressed by the returns to those of us in the private investment syndicate. Getting in on the ground floor in Timor-Leste before any more time elapses. The advantage of a developing country, eh?'

'A golden opportunity, I'd say. Only room now for one or two more investors. How's the Darwin office going?'

'It'll be ready to roll soon as soon as we check out the Mitchell Street premises. Fortunately, the air connection with Dili is much better now and we can get over here anytime we have to- which will be often enough once the syndicate's operation gets going.'

'And exact leads on the source of the, er- wealth?'

'Good clues, I'm confident we can find it, thanks to those maps we now have. General Harbianto's holding can't be far away. It'll no longer be Indonesian, it'll be the property of the state here- with the appropriate compensation to us.'

'Treble our money in no time?'

'More like quadruple, I reckon!'

'Are you serious? A return four times over!'

'Sorry!' Gary, that is 'George' looked around with an air of affected embarrassment while Phyllis-Penelope seemed mortified, apologising to anyone in earshot, especially Dion and Lucia.

'I'm so sorry for my friend. He's getting carried away.' Too late. Their interest was piqued.

'Oh, we couldn't help hearing some of your conversation. What's it all about?'

'A private investment syndicate, Darwin-based, set up to locate something of value here in East Timor. There'll be some stellar returns once we find what we're after. It's a bit hush-hush of course, I'd rather not mention it in public. We were getting hyped-up in our enthusiasm and apologise for disturbing you.'

'Any room for extra investors?' Dion had his own reasons for being a bit desperate.

'Well, yes, but only one or two. The others in the consortium are locked in. Is it something that could interest you?'

Dion suddenly thought he might be a bit too eager. 'Oh, possibly. Could we talk about it?'

'Sure. Where are you staying?'

'I'm in the Esplanada, close by. My girlfriend lives here in Dili. Could you come to my hotel room?'

'Of course, if you think you could be interested. When would suit you?'

'How about in an hour's time? Give us time to have a shower, wash the salt and sand out of our hair and freshen up. Here's the address and room number.' Dion scribbled it on a piece of paper.

Standing up to take their leave, 'George' and 'Penelope' offered the couple their business card, waved them goodbye and left, returning to the Beach Garden café for a more relaxing cup of coffee following their successful performance.

Act one, scene two coming up.

As good luck or divine intervention would have it, Gary and Phyllis's timing couldn't have been better. Dion's grand scheme had hit a snag. While Lucia's placement in her government office was close to ideal, she didn't have full carriage of the situation. It all depended on head clerk Rodriguo Fuentes taking appropriate action. While he had initially agreed to do so, he now demanded a 'down payment' of one million dollars in Australian currency first. In effect, a bribe. He was always going to get a share of the proceeds but wanted to hedge his bets by getting some of it up front.

Dion had the money but it was tied up in his confidential Australian account with the Commonwealth Bank of Australia, the CBA. And therein lay another snag. When laying the groundwork to leave Kayla and start a relationship with Lucia, Dion had opened an account with a local Dili bank, the BNCTL (Banco Nacional de Timor-Leste). But now, thanks to Roberta Koning- according to a frustrated Dion- there were unexpected problems in transferring large parcels of money from Australia.

Roberta Koning was head of the CBA's Foreign Transfers Division. She prided herself on her impeccable honesty and unswerving attention to ethics and procedure. Right from the start, she had her own suspicions about the source of funds in Dion Westford's account. Thanks to her senior position in the industry, she was all-too aware that Zenith clients had missing funds, and equally aware that her client, Dion Westford, a former Zenith employee, was under suspicion. For this reason, she raised every fiscal objection she could find when his requests came in to transfer his large holding to BNCTL. Effectively, by her order, his funds were frozen – but only internationally. Her jurisdiction didn't run to transfers within Australia.

In other words, while Dion had plenty to come and go on, he was actually short of dough for his grand plan.

Despite this temporary setback, Dion Westford congratulated himself on how well things were working out. But then, they always had. As he prepared the room for the arrival of his new contacts, he reflected on his childhood. Growing up in a sumptuous home in an exclusive part of Sydney's Eastern Suburbs, he regarded himself as having been born with the proverbial silver spoon in his mouth. The fact that most people seemed to find the over-indulged boy more than passably good-looking with a precocious gift-of-the gab didn't hurt, either.

Dion's social-climbing parents had enrolled their 'prodigy' in an expensive local private school, Commercia College, where his every academic achievement was lauded. When he graduated, the principal had exhorted the Year 12 students to adhere to the school's 'old boys' network to guarantee continuing success in business.

He could still hear the principal's words, 'Remember, it's not what you know, it's who you know!'

Taking this maxim to heart, Dion had followed it assiduously. He'd used every useful contact he could find, resulting in several promotions within his chosen industry- the banking sector. Merchant banks were his forte. Yes, he'd fattened his own account as he went and the clients at Zenith would hardly miss the funds he'd skimmed. They were wealthy enough. If any thought of morality, ethics or religion intruded into his dealings, Dion dismissed them with his personal motto. *God helps those who help themselves*. He certainly had helped himself- in spades.

The hotel room was ready, refreshments poured from the mini-bar. There was a knock at the door. Here they were, right on time. Dion opened the door eagerly.

'Penelope and George, come in. Please, have a seat.'

'Thanks, Dion. Hello again, Lucia.'

'Hello again to you, too. Please make yourselves at home and help yourselves to drinks. Now, what exactly is your business? Your card says 'Auric Investments'. Intriguing!'

Gary-George began. 'As you will have noted from our business card, we- George Barham and Penelope Christopher – are the principals of a consortium tasked with finding something that has been lost for two decades or more in East Timor. General Harbianto's gold.'

Lucia was quick to interrupt. 'But that's an urban myth, surely? We know it existed once but it could be anywhere. The Timor-Leste government has already searched everywhere.'

At the mention of gold, Dion had perked up. 'What's this about, then?' Lucia filled him in.

'During the struggle for independence, the Indonesian military was under the control of a repressive soldier, one General Harbianto, who specialised in terrorising the population. We hated him. Firstly, he ransacked the country's limited gold reserves, confiscating them. Next, he'd arrest anyone with wealth, interrogating them for being part of the resistance, extorting any gold they might have. If they gave up their property, he'd release them. If not, they'd face a firing squad. Over the years he accumulated quite a lot of gold.'

'What happened next?'

'When the UN troops intervened, he was killed in a firefight with the Australian forces – God bless them. But the stolen gold was never recovered. Other Indonesians could have taken it back over the border to West Timor, or elsewhere. Java, probably. We don't know.'

Phyllis-Penelope spoke. 'You're right, Lucia. At least that's what we've believed until now. But recent evidence that our consortium has uncovered indicates it's still here. We've got maps.'

Dion seemed partly convinced, but Lucia was dubious. It was time for Act Two.

Leaning forward conspiratorially and deliberately looking around furtively, Gary-George took the floor.

'Well, whether we find the gold or not, that's not really what Auric is about!' He had their attention. 'We're more interested in money laundering. International crime gangs want to use East Timor to 'wash' their ill-gotten gains. We'll initially use Auric to commence genuinely searching for the gold, and then contact the overseas crime gangs to begin their operation. We'll siphon funds from abroad through Auric, taking a fee off the top for ourselves. It will be a substantial one, I might add.'

'Not a bad lurk, I'd say!'

'You got that right, Dion! If you're interested in joining us, here's our initial prospectus. It's tentative until the official one concentrating solely on gold search is registered in Australia with ASIC - the Australian Securities and Investments Commission. That will happen soon.'

'So if we want to go ahead, what do we do?'

'Come to a meeting in our Darwin office in two weeks. At that time we'll ask for your $500,000 contribution to be an Auric partner. Then it'll be all-systems go. We expect a quick payoff and can practically guarantee your investment will be returned several times over, given the international crime gang money that will wash through it. And who knows, we might actually find the gold!'

Dion and Lucia exchanged knowing glances. He couldn't transfer his money easily from the CBA to his East Timor bank. But it could go to Darwin! Then, with the profit coming from Auric, he and Lucia could implement their own scheme.

'So we'd just need to transfer the half mill. to your Darwin account.'

'Sure, that's exactly right. It'll all be done from the Australian end.'

'And once Lucia and I are partners, could we – er – use that account to release some needed funds of our own?'

'Absolutely – no problem. It'll be a working account for all partners.'

Dion smiled. This was one way to get around that damned Roberta Koning. She couldn't stop a transfer within Australia. Paying that robber Rodriguo would be straight forward. And then, on with their own scheme.

'George, we're in. Give us the details for Darwin.'

Clever Dion Westford. He was a winner again.

CHAPTER EIGHT

The next two weeks were very busy indeed. Gary and Phyllis took the first available flight to Darwin and booked separate rooms at the Excelsior. Then, having checked vacant business rentals, took a lease on an attractive shopfront in Mitchell Street. Thanks to Phyllis's magnificent budget and supreme generosity, it wasn't long before the hired fixtures, fittings and office equipment were in place.

At the same time she'd put in a call back home to Adelaide to her beloved Torrens Troupers, asking if they could all be in Darwin on a certain date. She explained the props and costumes they'd need- mainly business attire – and sent them all air tickets. What a philanthropist! Unfortunately Phyllis had a dodgy heart. Not knowing how long she had, she wanted to ensure she left the world a better place. This might just be her crowning glory.

In the meantime, Dion and Lucia had carefully checked Auric Investments' website. They were instantly impressed; it was very professional looking. The photos of the two principals, George Barham and Penelope Christopher, certainly did them justice, and the news stories detailing Auric's previous business activities appeared authentic.

Gary agreed. Pete, his IT specialist, had come good. *Not bad for a three-day rush job*, thought Gary. It was a first-rate website.

On the date of the meeting, all was in place. The actors, expertly rehearsed by Phyllis, all knew their lines. The office equipment was installed and working and the boardroom set up for a business meeting, Gary was at Darwin airport in plenty of time to collect Dion and Lucia in a rented late-model Lexus, specially cleaned and shiny.

As Phyllis saw the Lexus with the two passengers approach, she called the troupe to order. 'Ladies and gentlemen, let the performance begin!'

'George' escorted Dion and Lucia into an office that was a hubbub of activity. Sleekly-attired businessmen and women discussed portfolios, exchanged papers and talked on mobile phones. A secretary at the front desk asked the new arrivals to kindly register their particulars, which they did, with Lucia handing over her business card. Once it was established that everyone was now present, 'Penelope' called all to order, directing them to the printed agenda.

'Ladies and gentlemen, before we begin the meeting to seek your authorisation to proceed with the activities of Auric Investments, I'd like to introduce two prospective partners, Dion Westford and Lucia Ximenes, just arrived from Dili. Please give them a warm welcome.'

They did. Dion and Lucia beamed, called out their thanks, waved to the group then sat in the back row on the chairs reserved with their names affixed.

"George' and 'Penelope' sat at the front, with the former chosen as chair. A dutiful secretary sat between them, poised to record the minutes on a laptop. 'George' began, using a data projector to outline maps of Timor-Leste and likely gold sites, statistics and details. Clearing his throat, he then went on to refer to Auric's possible 'reserve activities', should the meeting agree to them. There was much good-natured digging of the ribs and mild laughter.

'There is a motion before you proposing authority for Auric to engage in such reserve activities within Timor-Leste when and as they may present themselves. This is to offset any expenses should our search for the described gold be unsuccessful. May we have a proposer and seconder for that written motion?'

A forest of hands went up. 'George' continued, turning towards the eager minutes secretary.

'For the minutes, I declare Roger Delbridge as proposer and Sylvia Watson as seconder. Does either of you wish to speak to the motion?'

Roger Delbridge did so, outlining the advantage of the unstated 'reserve activities' that were likely to produce a considerable income stream. People smirked and gave each other knowing looks as Roger spoke, all noticed by Dion and Lucia. Sylvia in turn declared that she supported all the points Roger had made.

'Does anyone wish to speak against the motion?' Nobody did. The knowing looks continued.

'In that case, will all in favour please say aye.' The chorus of ayes was almost deafening.

'Those opposed?' Deathly silence.

'I declare the motion carried unanimously.' 'George' continued over the clapping and cheering that followed the decision.

'There is now only one other item of business. That is to confirm our previous meeting's decision for Auric Investments' partnership list to be finalised by the closing of business today so that we may begin activities in Timor-Leste immediately. Ladies and gentlemen, that means you have until five pm to ensure you've paid your stakeholder's fee of $500,000. You will recall this was in the minutes of our previous meeting.'

'Hear, hear!' went the general murmur, though two people raised their hands. The chairman allowed them to speak.

'Yes, Miss Atkins?'

'Mr Chairman, I did have some trouble paying my fee, even though the money is in my account. It's all clear now so I take it you can accept a transfer to Auric after this meeting?'

'Of course. There is enough time before the five pm cut-off. And Mr Deloso – you had the same problem? If so, the answer is the same.'

'Yes, Mr Chairman. Thank you for clarifying.'

Dion and Lucia had appeared agitated on hearing the cut-off time, but on hearing the chairman's reassurance, they relaxed. They'd be in time to join Auric, too.

'Thank you, ladies and gentlemen. That concludes the meeting. I invite those who still want to join and pay their fee to do so now. Otherwise, refreshments are served.'

Delvene Atkins, Tony Deloso and Dion came forward. A man whom Dion took to be the treasurer processed the payments, with each using their mobile phone to transfer the required fee to Auric's account in large parcels. Dion kept checking his watch. There was still time before the cut-off, but you never knew with bank transfers. It took a while but he was gratified when it all went through from his CBA account. The whole $500,000. He'd put it over that witch Roberta Koning at last and he was a proper partner, with the meeting's secretary confirming it with supporting paperwork. Ha, this was the answer – Auric's Darwin account had beaten that damned Roberta. He was free to move his funds now. Rodriguo Fuentes could get his cursed money and Dion's great scheme would be underway.

Easy Street was just around the corner.

Over refreshments there was much back-slapping and joviality as the informal part of the meeting eventually wound down. Dion and Lucia had booked a return flight to Dili later that afternoon and 'George' obligingly drove them back to the airport in the still-gleaming Lexus.

As it drew away from the kerb with a delighted Dion and Lucia ensconced in the back seat, a number of their new 'friends' gave a farewell wave. As soon as the Lexus was out of sight, Phyllis turned to the assembled troupe and beamed with delight.

'Performance over and bait well and truly taken. Troupers, you were magnificent!'

CHAPTER NINE

Kayla Westford was having a really bad day. Both her young daughters were sick with the flu, Sky especially. So Kayla had taken time off work, shifts she could scarcely afford to give up. It didn't go down well with Little Jewels; sympathetic as they generally were, a car accident had meant that one of their best teachers was laid up in hospital. Kayla would normally have covered for her.

How had life gone so wrong? Before getting married she'd been a happy-go-lucky young woman, enjoying all the normal things people do in Sydney. A cherished home in Bondi, the beach, friends and plenty of outdoor activities. She was seen as a bit of a surfie chick when she'd met the dashing Dion at her local beach, then again at Bronte and Tamarama. He stood out as a top surfer, very handsome and sure of himself. A young man definitely going places, it truly seemed.

He didn't appear overly impressed she was 'only' a preschool teacher – he was more besotted by those with finance qualifications and a private school education. But, still, she'd charmed him. It seemed curious to her at the time that he appeared interested in what her parents were worth, with their modest beachside home. She'd even asked him why.

'Men's business, Kayla. Don't worry your pretty little head over it.' She dropped the subject.

After doing some calculations on the land value, Dion had even discussed a development with her father, who, despite being the down-to-earth parent he was, was initially flattered by the attention. But on thinking it over, Dad had backed off, never saying why. Not showing any disappointment, Dion proposed marriage. Dazzled, she'd accepted, with her father happily shelling out on his eldest daughter's wedding. Her two younger sisters were keen bridesmaids.

Their first home was a flat on the edge of the same suburb. Dion worked his way up through a number of different banks, finally gravitating to Zenith, a prestigious merchant conglomerate. Then came the surprise move up the north coast to Sunrise Point, from where Dion worked remotely before suddenly resigning. It had all seemed a bit odd, but by now she was effectively sidelined from his life, with his many surfing trips overseas. Well, there was no point in crying over spilt milk, as it were. That was then, this was now. Now she had sick kids to attend to. Kayla cast her reflections aside.

'Coming, Sky. Try not to cry, Mummy will read you a story. How about *Spot's Adventures*?'

Kayla's mum had come up from Sydney to help out with the worst of the girls' illness but needed to return home. Prior to Dion leaving, Kayla had definitely been a happy, optimistic daughter, her mother felt. However, having him not just walk out but take all her money had been a massive blow. Casting around for a way to help, Helen had suggested counselling by Lew Stein of Sunrise Community Church. Kayla initially resisted. Dion had always laughed at any idea of Christian belief, committed to his idea of being a self-made man. Why believe in an imaginary being in the sky, he'd mock? Nevertheless, Helen insisted.

'Well, his attitude doesn't have to be yours, you know. Dear, you were sympathetic to the idea of church worship before you got married. Why not go and see Lew?' So she had. The pastor had been very kind, had prayed with her, arranged some practical support and urged her to have faith. Well, we'll see, she'd thought.

But now things were getting worse, not better. The strain of dealing with sick kids took its toll and the money pit kept getting deeper. She was in over her head and couldn't see a way out. Then came the phone call. She sighed. 'Yes?'

'Kayla, it's Gary Bishop. I've some news. Have you just checked your bank account?'

'No, Gary, it's too depressing. A sea of red.'

'Well, humour me. Log on to your computer and do a check.'

Puzzled, she did so. Then she almost fell off the chair in amazement.

'I can't believe it, $350,000! What happened?'

'I'll give you the whole story later. But we've managed to get your money back from Dion, not that he knows it. What he took plus some interest. A bit of compensation for all your heartache. Anyway, put it towards a house of your own once you sort things out.'

'You're not a PI, you're a genius!'

'Not really, I had some help from wonderful friends, one in particular. More on that later. I've now got to sort out Mr Westford and his new girlfriend – they're still causing plenty of mischief.'

'Bye, Mr Miracle Worker. Thanks SO much!'

'Don't mention it. See you, Kayla.'

First she made a celebratory phone call to her mum, then one to Lew Stein. The wonderful pastor must have a line to heaven after all.

Back in Dili, Dion and Lucia were on top of the world and ready to implement their ruthless scheme. Dion in particular couldn't believe his luck. He was a partner in Auric Investments with the possibility of a share of gold treasure. In any case, he'd be part of their 'reserve activities' once he got the details of George and Penelope's money laundering scheme. That would come soon enough, no doubt.

Not only that, but he could use Auric's Darwin account to free up his considerable assets still in Australia. He would use it to transfer his skimmed Zenith funds to his Dili bank, the BNCTL. No problem, he was a partner and had the paperwork to prove it! Best of all, he could pay that rip-off merchant, Rodriguo, his 'advance fee' of a million dollars and get going on his own plan. That was where dear Lucia would come in.

Did he love Lucia for what she was, or was he just using her? Time would tell. For now, he was entranced by her beauty and vivaciousness. Her position in that government office was useful, very useful. How lucky that he'd met her just after he'd moved his 'operation' from Bali to Dili. Sure, it wasn't great that the Bali drug lords had chased him out of town, but he was determined to make something work here in Dili.

Lucia had walked out of the surf at Manatuto when the waves were running wild. They'd each caught some great breakers. Man, she was a veritable vision of pulchritude. He'd seen her in the distance in the surf, her prowess matching his own. How he'd admired her Firewire surfboard, not that his own was in any way deficient. This chick had used it to great effect.

'Great surf, eh?' Not the best pickup line he'd ever used, but it was good enough. Lucia had been entranced by the handsome Australian. After some small talk, she'd accepted his invitation to a drink at the nearby beach bar and the relationship had gone from there. Long walks and romancing on the beach at sunset. It was a bit of a downer once she realised he was married, but he insisted the marriage was over, even though poor Kayla thought he was just on yet another surfing holiday.

Yes, once Dion became aware of Lucia's government position the plan had crystallised. She, too, was keen enough to make money and leave the relative poverty of East Timor to relocate with the man of her dreams.

If only the intelligent, dark-haired beauty, holding down a responsible government position, had realised it was all about him.

Dion Westford was a complete and utter narcissist.

CHAPTER TEN

Despite the landmark vote of independence from Indonesia in 1999, East Timor continued to experience turmoil. Indonesian-backed anti-independence militia groups instituted a violent backlash, eventually quelled by firm action from UN troops, in particular from Australia. It was during one especially violent conflict that the venal, much-hated General Arif Harbianto was killed in a vicious firefight.

In his research before leaving Australia, Gary had read about Arif Harbianto and realised it could be useful in his strategy to undo Westford. Harbianto, a native of Bandung in Java and well-connected to the country's ruling political party, had been a career officer in the Indonesian army. No stranger to the evil of 'korupsi', he'd used this method of bribery to influence those in power and advance his position. It turned out to be a spectacularly successful strategy.

Once he became aware that Indonesia was about to attack East Timor in 1975, Harbianto, lusting for personal gain, arranged through his contacts to join the invasion forces as a senior officer. Eventually rising to the rank of general, he'd been able to exploit the situation very nicely. Soon he was engaged in a scheme of extorting valuables from the vulnerable East Timorese population. To his great satisfaction, Harbianto accumulated a large booty of gold. The only thing he didn't factor in was Australian intervention and was shocked when he and his army were outgunned.

After his death, the gold treasure he'd accumulated suddenly disappeared, hence the mystery. Many people believed it was still buried or hidden within the country, rather than having been spirited back across the border to Indonesia, which was the most popular theory.

How likely was it for the keen partners of Auric Investments to turn it up? Dion mulled over this question as he busied himself with the Auric paperwork he'd brought back from the Darwin meeting. Once back in Dili at his still-reserved top floor room at the Esplanada, he and Lucia had gone through everything assiduously, scrutinising the maps that 'George Barham' had kindly provided, along with the proposed details of coming searches, which would be conducted by local contractors. 'George' had offered to stay in touch to keep the couple apprised of any likely developments and would return to Dili shortly.

Dion soon tired of the written material. He made a decision. A surf trip was needed, to celebrate. After all, Darwin had been a coup and he and Lucia could now move on to the real game, their own scheme. He phoned Lucia, who was hard at work back in her office catching up with a backlog of files.

'How about hitting the waves at Bacau this weekend, darl? Let's celebrate.'

'Sure! Pick me up from the office at five on Friday. I'll have my bag packed. You arrange the accommodation.'

By five-fifteen that Friday the couple were driving east from the capital in Dion's rented Peugeot, which he'd hired longterm from the moment he'd arrived back in Dili. They passed Manatuto, and soon approached their Bacau destination - the Shangri-La Inn, a stunning tourist hideaway. Once ensconced in a magnificent room overlooking the ocean, they made full use of their luxurious surroundings, delighted that their plans were working out so well. Once their romantic desires were sated, they turned to thoughts of tomorrow. They were of one mind.

Hit the surf!

Bacau, the second-largest city in East Timor, boasts several surf spots along its coast. Dion and Lucia's favourite was Praia dos Surfistas. It offered long, peeling left-handers, and was not for the faint-hearted. Sure, some intermediate surfers could cope with its demands, but it was better suited for more experienced surfing aficionados, such as them. They might also check out nearby Wain Huno, with its remote, secluded location. But Praia dos Surfistas was their preference.

Saturday morning and the weather was ideal. The surf was running high. Psyched up for a thrilling session, Dion and Lucia paddled their boards out past the first, then the second line of breakers, eagerly anticipating what was beyond. They were ready to crest the waves, and were not disappointed. Here came the surf!

Lucia got a floater, and rode up and over a section of the breaking wave, using the whitewater as a ramp. Dion countered with a bottom turn, carving a move at its foot to generate speed. He executed the turn superbly.

'Magnifico, Dion!' Lucia applauded him as he completed a cutback, a perfect follow-up manoeuvre where he redirected his DHD board back to the breaker, allowing him to maintain speed and continue along the wave's face.

He praised Lucia for her later 'snap', as she completed a quick, powerful turn at the top of a wave, expertly generating a wide spray of water.

After several hours of repeating their dazzling manoeuvres, their strength and fitness began to ebb. It was time to exit the bombora. They paddled slowly back to the beach and stretched out on the sand to recover, thinking of refreshment at the near-by bar to restore their energy.

Lying back, enjoying the sun as it warmed his fit, tanned and superbly-conditioned body, Dion gave a self-satisfied smirk. He had a gorgeous surfie chick of a girlfriend to cater to his every need, he'd got rid of his ordinary wife whose only ambition was for a conventional lifestyle, and- thanks to his undisputed business acumen- great wealth was beckoning.

Life was working out superbly.

Lucia Ximenes also felt that she was on the up-and-up. In her case, considering the deprivation and trauma of her youth, it was about time. At twenty-five, she considered herself lucky to be alive, having lived as a child through the horrific years of East Timor's frantic struggle for independence. Born in 1992, at the height of the Indonesian military repression, she'd grown up in a small village outside Liquica, to the west of Dili. She well remembered Indonesian troops storming into the village and ransacking the family home in a vain search for resistance fighters. In their frustration, and as a reprisal for earlier defiant acts by the villagers, several innocent men were executed, shot by a firing squad in front of the assembled villagers. It was a terrible atrocity the five-year-old Lucia would never forget.

Australian troops dispatched by the United Nations had been their saviours, and Lucia had loved anything to do with the Aussies ever since. Like so many others, she got caught up in the euphoria of the independence vote in 1999, only to endure the shock of the backlash from Indonesians who were furious at losing their 'new province.'

Full, official independence from Indonesia came in 2002, on May 20 – Lucia's tenth birthday. Everybody rejoiced with Xanana Gusmao, the country's first president. Life after these extraordinary historic events soon became something of an anticlimax for the young girl. She was fortunate, under the new regime, to complete her high school education in Liquica, and then win a scholarship to Dili's main business college, where she graduated in office administration.

The best outlook in the early 21st century for a young East Timorese woman was employment in the government service. It offered security. So Lucia joined the public service and began rotating through different departments until arriving at her present position of personal assistant. The future of any ambitious civil servant depended on a knowledge of English. Lucia applied herself assiduously to the after-hours course offered, quickly becoming proficient. Without doubt, she was doing well in a number of directions.

'Wow, that's impressive. I want to join them!' Lucia's first sight of Aussie surfers came at Jimbaran Beach on a holiday to Bali. She rented a board, and got some of the surfing tourists to show her the basics. With a natural talent, Lucia Ximenes was soon up and away, shooting the waves with the best of them. At the end of her holiday, she used the last of her savings to buy a decent surfboard of her own, taking it back to Dili to help the nascent surfing industry in Timor-Leste. She was there from the ground up, supporting and urging the movement along. Every weekend and holiday saw her at Dare Beach, Maubara or some other surfing hot-spot, perfecting her moves.

'Hi, I'm Dion. You looked real good out there today…' After a few initial comments about the surf, the tall Australian surfer she encountered that day used a healthy dose of flattery to chat her up. It worked. She thought he was pretty hot and, well, his blandishments succeeded. One way or another, they became an item. Dion made it clear he was going places, and that suited Lucia Ximenes just fine. She wanted a future.

'So, tell me about your work.' Was her new boyfriend really interested in her, or did he have an ulterior motive? Just the same, she liked the way Dion hung on her every word as she described her work, her colleagues and their positions, both her superiors and those at her level. She was impressed when he took notes and asked searching questions. She'd had a boyfriend or two before Dion, both East Timorese men. They'd never been seriously concerned with her achievements, possibly because hers outshone their own. However, Dion was as involved as anyone could be in her career.

'Hey, are all Aussie men like you, taking such interest in their girlfriends' profession?' His answer was a bit evasive. 'That depends. Sometimes yes, sometimes no. I'm the sort of guy who shows attention – I'll never ignore you.' Lucia had to be happy with that. He was indeed different.

Soon she was deeply in love, accepting his assurance that his marriage to... who? - oh, Kayla- was over. Lucia was unsure what this Kayla had done to upset Dion and he was vague when asked about it. Well, he'd have to get divorced before the two of them could marry, that was for sure. She wasn't interested in bigamy! Prepared to wait till he was a free man, Lucia probed to find out about his kids, Elise and Sky. She had no idea how she could ever be a step-mum to them, but Dion showed absolutely no interest in discussing the matter. The love-struck woman supposed the girls would simply stay with their mother and that would be that. In any case, it was a problem for another day.

Lucia's roller coaster love affair with the ambitious Dion was simply too exciting for her to worry about such details.

CHAPTER ELEVEN

Gary felt under the pump. Sure, he'd retrieved Kayla's stolen money from Dion and he was tempted to just mark the matter 'case closed'. But he knew in his heart the nefarious, faithless husband had another scheme on the boil. His police training told him that for certain. As an ethical professional, he couldn't let it rest, partly because every fibre of his being called out for justice. Dion needed to be stopped.

Using his laptop in the Mitchell Street rented office, Gary booked a flight for two days' time, the slight delay giving him the opportunity to organise a car for transport once he arrived. Again, he turned to the helpful Carmelita Soares for this, giving her a heads-up. Staying on in Darwin, the ever-obliging Phyllis had seen to the return of the hired fixtures and fittings, with the key to go back to the estate agent the next day. The Torrens Troupers hosted a celebratory farewell event at their hotel that evening before their own flight back to Adelaide, with an enthusiastic vote of thanks proposed by the grateful Gary. They responded with a thunderous cheer.

Pete, the designer of the popup Auric Investments website that had so impressed Dion and Lucia, received a standing ovation in his absence. No doubt the significant deposit into his bank account to pay for his professional expertise would have been gratifying. Gary proposed a toast to Phyllis for her generosity, having funded the whole exercise.

'Happy to help, laddie!' *Who said Scots were mean?* The magnificent Phyllis Cameron certainly wasn't. A philanthropist to the core, that she was.

Knowing he'd need a decent vehicle in East Timor, Gary decided to use a portion of the money he'd acquired from the nefarious Mr Westford to buy one. Carmelita quickly struck paydirt- a serviceable Toyota Rav 4, left behind by a departing staff member of the Australian Embassy. Gary transferred the purchase price to Carmelita's account and she texted him the vehicle's location in the Dili Airport carpark, the car key to be secreted under the bodywork.

Just before his flight, Gary sketched out his plan. A clue was in Lucia's business card: Personal Assistant to the Minister for Petroleum and Minerals. Based in the Rua 20 de Maio, the street name commemorating the date of the nation's declaration of independence in 2002. How about the deceptive Mr Westford? No business card, he had just put himself down as 'investor.' The PI reckoned he could bet his bottom dollar that Dion was targeting Lucia because of her position. He intended to make her a source of great return. For him.

The trouble-free Qantas flight from Darwin to Dili allowed plenty of time for Gary's mental preparation. He'd brought along multiple business cards advertising Auric Investments, maps of likely 'hot-spots' and supporting documentation. Phyllis remained contactable by phone as his 'business partner' should she be needed.

With landing, luggage collection and progress through customs causing no problems, Gary was soon out in the carpark looking for his Rav 4. Yep, there it was, gleaming white in the tropical sun. A Honda or Nissan would have done, too, but the Rav 4 would give no dramas. He retrieved the key and was soon driving the short distance into town, keen to check out Lucia's ministry. The GPS made it easy, but he'd acquired a map as well, just in case.

He drove up to the imposing building in the Rua 20 de Maio. OK, what next? He could hardly bowl in and ask the calculating Lucia to reveal all. No, it would require covert surveillance. Gary noted the cars parked outside in what he took to be the staff parking area. Alighting from his Toyota, he decided some refreshment might be in order. He purchased a flat white from a nearby street vendor, rewarding the man with a decent greenback tip.

'Obrigadu!' Gary responded with a friendly wave.

No sooner had he returned to his vehicle than who should emerge from the Ministry but Lucia Ximenes herself, getting into her own car, a Mitsubishi. She drove away but soon returned with some items she must have bought from a local shop, then went back into the building.

'OK, so that's her car, is it?' *Take every opportunity*, he thought. It was the PI's maxim.

One indispensable piece of PI equipment is a small tracker, and he had more than one in his box of tricks. When the coast was clear, Gary walked over to the parking area and surreptitiously placed a high-resolution tracker under the rear of the Mitsubishi, then walked a circuitous route back to his own Toyota. He checked – good, it was functioning.

It wouldn't be long until five pm, when office hours were over. All he could do was hope she'd leave work on time and not be caught up in after-hours meetings. Of course, she might simply just go home, or have a romantic evening with dear Dion, but he felt more was likely to transpire.

Fortunately, he was right. At five-fifteen Lucia emerged from the Ministry and who should appear at the steps to greet her with a kiss, but Dion Westford. They walked hand-in-hand to her Mitsubishi and departed. Gary followed at a discreet distance in his Rav 4, not unduly worried by Dili's peak hour traffic, which mostly consisted of pushbikes, motor scooters and tuk-tuks rather than cars, although, in the general chaos, there were plenty of those as well. All typical of a developing country.

They drove west to Dili's outskirts and pulled into a worksite with the sign 'Croesus Oil Exploration.' Lucia parked outside and they walked into a mobile office. Keeping his distance, Gary watched through a window. Dion was having an animated discussion with a man who looked like he could be an executive of the company. Then they came out, Dion's body language indicating some satisfaction, got back into Lucia's car and drove off. Gary tracked them all the way to the Esplanada Hotel.

'So he's back there, is he?' It was time for some direct action.

Returning to his old room at the Beach Garden, Gary made a phone call.

'Hello, Dion. George Barham from Auric. Is it convenient to talk?' With a smile, Gary wondered how romantic Dion was getting with Lucia at that moment.

'Oh, sure, George. What's up?'

'Well, as promised at our Darwin meeting, we're in hot pursuit of the missing gold. As you're now a partner, I'd like to update you with a progress update?'

'Oh, all right. Did you mean now?'

'If that suits, otherwise I can make another time. It's just that some leads will take me out of Dili and I'm free now.' Yeah, strike while the iron is hot.

'Right. I'm back in the same room at the Esplanada. Lucia's here, so why not come up?'

Minutes later, with his briefcase of material, 'George' was knocking on their door.

'Come in, George. Do you want a drink?' They were both downing martinis.

'Thanks, Dion. Just a mineral water will do.' Lucia obliged him.

'So, what's happened?' Dion was quietly gratified how industrious Auric seemed, he hadn't expected any developments so soon.

'Look, no actual results but we've got hot tips re locations.' He opened his briefcase and drew out some maps with coloured dots affixed, referring to the names of likely contacts.

'Alright, what next?' Dion seemed a bit puzzled. Was this worth interrupting his martini hour for? He opened his own briefcase, ready to file the Auric material for later perusal.

'I'm here following up, so you may expect to see me around town, but I'll keep out of your way unless there's something to report. Finally, here's a summary of the Harbianto gold history. You know, estimated amount, suspected location, key persons of interest. I should have given you this in Darwin.'

Really, is this George OCD or what? Dion wanted to get rid of him. He had bigger fish to fry than this. *What good is the gold history? If there's not a problem, why is he here? On second thoughts, he did have one issue to raise, so may as well.*

'George, there's been a problem using Auric's Darwin account to transfer my money from the CBA through to my Dili account. I though you said it would work OK as a conduit. Some pest of a woman at the CBA is stopping direct transfers. I need to make a big payment to a colleague.' *I bet you do*, thought George.

'Look, Dion, I'll phone my bank and see what the logjam is. I'll get onto it asap.'

'Thanks.' *You'd better,* thought Dion darkly.

'Well, that's it for now…' Getting up to leave, George clumsily knocked over his mineral water. It spilled down onto the carpet, wetting Dion's shoes. He turned the air blue with a series of profanities.

'Mate, I'm so sorry!' 'George' was not merely embarrassed, he was mortified. Dion was far from impressed. Those Jimmy Choos had cost a fortune. Still cursing, he fossicked for a handkerchief to dry them as Lucia raced to get a hand towel from the kitchen. Unnoticed, the heartily apologising 'George' was able to slip a small device into a gap he'd noticed inside Dion's briefcase. He continued to convey his regrets profusely, insisting on finding another hand towel from somewhere to complete the drying of the carpet – and the precious Jimmy Choos.

Finally, Lucia said that it had only been mineral water and worse things could happen. Yes, indeed. Once the hubbub was over and 'George' felt he'd probably overdone the apologies, he gathered his material, ensuring that Dion put his own copies away in his briefcase before closing it. Then, without further ado, he took his leave with a firm handshake of each. The door closed behind him.

'Stupid idiot!' Dion spat out, far from mollified. 'He'll have to do better than that or he'll never find any gold!'

A perceptive observation that was, ironically, spot-on.

CHAPTER TWELVE

Settled back in his car in the Esplanada's parking area, Gary's interest was piqued by the conversation the listening device was picking up. Dion had evidently poured more martinis to compensate them for the inconvenience of the accident caused by stupid, clumsy 'George'. As the alcohol relaxed him, his frame of mind was clearly improving.

Once he had consumed a couple more martinis to console him for his ruined Jimmy Choos, Dion calmed down enough to consider the situation in more detail. He had to agree with Lucia's suggestion that Auric would do them one favour, at least. The account George had allowed him access to could be instrumental in releasing the million dollars Rodriguo was demanding. So as soon as George sorted out this temporary glitch, their clever scheme would be underway. Then the siphoning would begin! It'd start tomorrow for sure. Oh, they'd soon be rolling in it!

Don't be too sure about that bit, my friends! Gary was sitting in his car in the hotel carpark, listening eagerly to every word and recording it all on his mobile.

It became clear to Gary that Dion had concocted an elaborate plot, a fiendishly clever one in fact. With several international oil companies conducting exploration in the Timor Sea between Timor-Leste and Australia- ConocoPhillips, Woodside

Petroleum, Santos Ltd and Petronas to name a few- oil revenue was starting to flow into East Timor's coffers. The income was desperately needed by the developing nation, but it was also an attractive target for those who wanted to help themselves.

With Rodriguo Fuentes on board with Dion's scheme- pending his payment of a million dollars fee upfront - Dion and Lucia could skim ten percent of the revenue. From their local account they'd transfer it to their offshore holding in the Cayman Islands, a Caribbean hideaway where they would be free of the fear of extradition. Once they terminated the scheme, after carefully calculating how long they could get away with it, there'd be an extra fee to Mr Fuentes. This was unavoidable- because he was the minister's head clerk, they needed his connivance to implement the scheme.

Just the same, it'd be a good little earner. But there was more.

Following East Timor's official independence in 2002, the new nation came to rely heavily on a great number of undersea oil and gas reserves. Desperate to access them, the new government signed the Timor Sea Treaty with Australia, outlining revenue-sharing arrangements that were heavily biased in Australia's favour.

With this arrangement being the best the new nation could achieve at the time, the Petroleum Fund was created to manage oil revenue and ensure sustainable development. It was this source of income that Dion and Lucia proposed to siphon off. By its very nature, it was a cruel and selfish scheme, one which would deny the country much-needed revenue. But what did Dion care about that? And was Lucia so dazzled by her new boyfriend that she was prepared to betray her beloved country? Either way, they appeared not to give two hoots about the repercussions. It was all about them.

Now the tiny Timor-Leste was in dispute with Australia over the maritime boundary between the two countries and was seeking a more equitable arrangement. Many people thought it was about time. If achieved, it would allow a greater flow of much-needed extra oil and gas revenue into the developing nation's treasury, and was something the more established and prosperous Australia could surely afford. Negotiations, however, were currently stalemated.

Gary was on tenterhooks as he continued listening in to Dion talk animatedly about East Timor's oil exploration leases. He was explaining to Lucia how, under the Timor Sea Treaty, a Joint Petroleum Development Area was established, divided into several blocks for oil and gas exploration. The main ones were the Bayu-Undan Field, the Kitan Field, the Timor-Leste Exclusive Area, the Greater Sunrise Field and the Laminaria-Corallina Field. A newcomer to the world of oil exploration, Croesus Oil, wanted to get ahead of the game and get a jump on the major players.

So this is how Croesus fits in. Gary was intrigued.

The conniving Dion Westford, ever the opportunist. With Croesus Oil seeking to steal a march on the larger company players, Dion had convinced the chief executive that, owing to his own Australian government connections, he could ensure the boundary dispute would be settled in East Timor's favour. And Croesus Oil would have a monopoly on the new concession, effectively locking the others out. It would be a bonanza for Croesus, with Chief Executive Carlos Goncalves becoming a multi-millionaire.

This arrangement was all for a large fee in advance to Dion Westford, of course. A very large fee, that would even further fatten his wallet.

Gary Bishop had heard enough. It was time to return to the Beach Garden, play all this back and take more notes to ensure he'd missed nothing.

Then it would be action time.

CHAPTER THIRTEEN

Carlos Goncalves knew a good wicket when he found one. Through a policy of glad-handing influential superiors, he'd gradually advanced up the ranks of Croesus Oil Exploration to the very top – Chief Executive Officer. He'd done well, blessed by good fortune. Born in Dili, he'd availed himself of a scholarship to study in Lisbon just before Portuguese rule of the colony collapsed. By adroit manoeuvring he'd stayed overseas during the period of the troubles, gaining excellent qualifications along with valuable experience, and only coming 'home' once independence was established, and East Timor was poised to profit from the oil industry. He'd then married a local woman.

True, Croesus wasn't exactly a world-beater in oil exploration and at times he'd considered jumping ship to take another position at Shell or perhaps ConocoPhillips. Still, Carlos had persevered with his present firm. The breakthrough came with the opportunity, through the new nation of East Timor, to drill in the oil-rich Timor Sea.

He keenly followed the progress – or lack thereof – of the negotiations between East Timor and Australia. East Timor was desperate to seek a better deal but Australia, perhaps harshly, seemed to be blocking this much-needed opportunity. Then came a ray of hope, a gift from providence for Croesus. An up-and-coming merchant banker with an essential entré to the Australian federal government promised to arrange favourable terms for his oil company – in essence, a monopoly on a new concession – for the payment of an advance fee to himself, albeit a huge one.

Watch out, it could be a scam! Carlos was cautious, not unreasonably. So he checked out his proposer. Dion Westford had a great track record with Zenith Bankers, a respected Sydney merchant bank with branches in other state capitals. The bank had significant connections with the Australian federal government and was responsible both for advocating and funding a variety of government projects. Dion was now here in Dili in a liaison position with the Ministry of Petroleum and Minerals, working closely, it appeared, with the minister himself. Well, he was certainly close to the minister's PA, Lucia Ximenes. Anyone could tell that!

'Why an upfront fee, Dion?' Carlos had quizzed him when the Australian quoted the amount of one million dollars.

'Carlos, you might say I need to grease the wheels!' Carlos definitely knew about bribery, so he was prepared to cook the books. The sum was simply a 'consultancy fee' accounting adjustment, with a further four million dollars to follow once Dion locked in the desired concession, guaranteeing Croesus' monopoly. Mentally calculating the zeros, Carlos assured Dion the 'fee' would be forthcoming; it would just take a little time.

Carlos became impatient. He was eager to scout part of the future concession at least, no matter how premature it might be. He wasn't a man to let the grass grow under his feet. Pressing a button he summoned his driver, José, who brought Carlos's official Mercedes up to the office door.

'Where to, sir?'

'A bit of a jaunt down to Betano. You won't be coming home tonight.'

The long-suffering José blessed the fact he was a widower and didn't have to answer to anyone at home.

'Of course, sir. As you wish.'

Within minutes, they were speeding south out of the confines of Dili. Soon the Mercedes bypassed the junction leading to Gleno, heading for Lequitura. Here CEO Goncalves, comfortably settled in the back seat, ordered José to stop at a roadside stall and get refreshment for the two of them. Next stop Same, before their destination of Betano.

'Before we start again, please radio ahead to have my helicopter fuelled and ready for take-off. No doubt you can amuse yourself somewhere for a few hours while I'm gone.'

'Very good, sir.'

Carlos had forgotten, however, to tell his long-suffering wife, Filomena, that he wouldn't be home that night. After the helicopter flight there was a girlfriend in Betano he wanted to call in on, where he expected he'd be comfortably catered for till morning. José could fend for himself somewhere. Carlos would chuck him a few greenbacks by way of travel allowance. That'd do.

Poor Filomena knew better than to complain or she'd get a backhander- at least. She'd had plenty, and worse. Then, feeling slightly magnanimous at the thought of the evening ahead, he relented and texted, 'Not home tonight.'

She'd better be happy with that.

Things were getting a bit tense in the office of the Ministry of Petroleum and Minerals and it was just as well the minister,

Francisco Martins, was away at a meeting. Rodriguo Fuentes, his head clerk, was sick of Dion Westwood's stalling.

'Dion, we agreed on a million dollar advance as a sign of your good faith. What's the holdup?'

'It's with my bank, don't you get it? I've already told you. There's a problem with the transfer through Darwin. I'm involved with another deal and I'm using that account. I've spoken to the Aussie guy I deal with and he's promised to fix it. You'll just have to wait.'

'Three more days or the deal's off. That's it!'

Dion swore. And again.

Then, suddenly aware that he might be cutting off his nose to spite his face, Rodriguo relented a bit.

'Look, I only need evidence you've got the dough in your account, that's all.'

'OK, here's my last bank statement.' Dion was starting to get desperate and was annoyed that the Auric account was still blocked, despite George's assurance. Rodriguo was certainly impressed with the large balance, so felt confident he could take the next step.

'Let's go over the procedure again', Rodriguo explained. 'Here's the computer program to do the skim. See how it's set at exactly ten percent? We'll start the very next day after the account is audited, which gives us a whole month to transfer the dough to our account before the auditors come back. Ten percent is the maximum we can take from the revenue stream before there's an automatic trigger to bring the auditors back, but there'll be plenty of gravy money for the three of us. Thirty whole days to pocket the proceeds, ensuring we have our air tickets booked to leave before the period expires. I want my special fee because I have to oversee the process – extra danger money, if you like. As the architect, I'll cop the hard jail time if we're caught.'

'Well, we won't be, Rodriguo!'

'Of course not.' Dion's mobile rang.

'Yes, Carlos. What's up?'

'Dion, I spent a wonderful afternoon yesterday in our helicopter, exploring the likely concession. I'm very excited!'

'Delighted to hear it, my friend. So you're right for my fee?' Damn this waiting. He'd try the direct approach, it was more hopeful than waiting for Auric to clear. Time was marching on.

'It'll be on the way soon. Bye now.'

'Bye.'

Rodriguo was puzzled. 'Was that Carlos Goncalves?'

'Yes. Any problem?'

'I can't stand the -' he stopped himself before using language he might regret.

'Why so?'

'He's married to my sister, Filomena. Beats her up when he feels like it. Next time, I'll go around and sort him out, even if he's a CEO. I tell you, if you're involved in a deal with him, all bets are off!'

To emphasise the point, he grabbed the coffee cup Dion had just emptied, smashed it on the floor and stalked out.

Suddenly, the fat was in the fire again.

CHAPTER FOURTEEN

Dion needed every ounce of his considerable ability as an 'influencer' to pacify the furious Rodriguo. He chased after him and caught up with him in his office.

'Mate, I had no idea!' At least that part was true. 'OK, I'll ditch him. You mean far too much to me. Can we please get back to where we were?' It took a full hour, with Dion plying Rodriguo with whisky someone had in a nearby cupboard, but Rodriguo was back on board. Dion smiled. He had no intention of keeping that promise, he just needed to be more circumspect.

Meanwhile Carlos, highly motivated following his helicopter jaunt over the wide blue expanse of the Timor Sea, deposited the million dollar fee into Dion's local bank – after swearing absolute discretion because of his irate brother-in-law. This amount was in turn immediately passed on to said brother-in-law. Rodriguo was finally appeased. Fortuitously, the monthly audit had been completed to the minister's satisfaction that very morning, so it was all-systems go for the big scam. All three – Dion, Carlos and Rodriguo – were able to check after an hour that the 'skim' was working, with ten percent of the nation's oil revenue flowing into their newly-established three-way account. Thirty whole days of lovely moolah. Visions of their future life in the Caymans lay before them: sun, surf and sand – and endless pina coladas and mojitos.

Dion rubbed his hands in delight. The clever merchant banker had won again.

Now aware of the nature of the scam, Gary sprang into action and immediately drove to Dili's main police station, the National Police of Timor-Leste Headquarters, or PNTL. He practically sprinted up to the enquiry desk.

'Bondia,' he greeted the enquiries officer. 'Sir, do you speak English?' The man shook his head but within minutes had found someone who did. The new officer listened attentively, but was dismissive.

'I'm sorry, sir. You're reporting an embezzlement that is about to begin? I'm afraid we have more urgent things to deal with, like civil unrest for a start. Surely embezzlement can wait until the scam you allege is underway, in which case we'll have more evidence. Were we to take action today, where would be the proof?' He had a point.

'We're talking about millions of dollars of government revenue.'

'Point taken. In that case please come back tomorrow. I hope Inspector Amaral will be free, but it depends on the civil arrest being quelled.' Frustrating as it was, Gary had to accept that.

The next day he had no more success, except that this time the same officer took down details and promised to pass them on to the inspector. Perhaps such crimes weren't a high priority in developing countries. Direct action was needed. He headed for Rua 20 de Maio and the Ministry of Petroleum and Minerals. Gary had his cover story worked out. Parking right out the front, he bounded up the steps and demanded to see Lucia Ximenes. Taken aback by his urgent tone, the receptionist ushered him straight into Lucia's office.

'Hello, George. What can I do for you?' Lucia couldn't hide her surprise.

'Lucia, I need to see the minister urgently. We've just had information that the gold'... he looked around slightly conspiratorially in case there was anyone else there – 'is within an approved minerals lease. It's right in the centre of the country. We need specific approval from the minister to enter.'

'Well, he's very busy right now. Can it wait for a while?' Somehow, with their new 'income stream' flowing, the prospect of profit from Auric seemed less urgent. She didn't trouble him about the still-blocked account.

At that moment Dion entered the room with two coffees from the staff café. He wasn't exactly delighted to see the visitor.

'George! What are you doing here?' He got the same story. This chase for gold was getting a bit tiresome. Would they ever find it? Dion was considering asking for his half a million stake back.

'I suggest you try again tomorrow, George. I'll check the minister's schedule, but I know he's got an important meeting with President Ruak at ten.' Taur Matan Ruak, a former resistance fighter, now had a largely ceremonial role, but in view of his respected reputation, it was still an important one.

'Thanks, Lucia. I'll come back then. Bye, Dion.'

'Bye.' Annoyed, Dion sipped his cappuccino, glad he'd made it double strength.

'What a turkey! I can't imagine how he got the job of leading such an important consortium. They loved him at that meeting in Darwin but he's dashing here and there and everywhere now. I don't get it! He needs checking out...'

'Hey, hon!' Lucia interrupted him. 'Look at these figures coming in. The returns are much better than we thought! I see Easy Street in the Caymans coming up!'

With this information Dion forgot his annoyance, got onto a spare computer and sought out the price of villas in the Caymans. Those right on the beachfront, of course. Then he scrolled down to the local surfing conditions. Ah, a villa! Perhaps they'd call it 'Pirates of the Caribbean!'

That'd be a nice touch.

Friday morning dawned. Today was do or die. Gary was determined, and had his revised plan ready. There was no chance of seeing the minister before the ten am meeting, and who knew how long that would go for, perhaps all day. Just as he got into his vehicle his mobile rang. It was Nick Vassallo, his fraud squad contact.

'Gary, your hunch was right. Our friend Dion has embezzled funds from multiple clients. We're onto it now with Zenith.'

'Thanks for the update, Nick. I'm onto his case here in Dili. Sorry – gotta go now. Bye.' Well, that news was hardly a surprise. His trip to the Ministry was beyond fast.

He parked his car nearby and waited. Just after nine-thirty the chauffeur brought up the minister's Holden Commodore. Fancy, an Australian car. To soften international relations, perhaps? A minute later, down the front steps walked Francisco Martins, splendidly attired in the latest Zegna suit. The distinguished official was every inch an important government servant. The chauffeur got out and held open the back door. Greeting the driver politely, the minister got in and buckled up for the ride to the presidential residence.

Just as the chauffeur entered the driver's seat ready to depart, Gary sprinted over and, with lightning speed, opened the front passenger's door and got in. Startled, fearing an assassination attempt, the chauffeur reached for the Glock automatic on his waistband.

'Please, I mean no harm!' burst out Gary. 'I'm a friend from Australia with urgent information for the minister. I need to speak to you NOW!' There was something about his manner that gave Minister Martins the confidence to put his hand on the chauffeur's shoulder.

'It's OK, Antonio. Let's hear him out.' The chauffeur relaxed.

'Thank you, Minister. I'm Gary Bishop, an Australian private investigator. I've become aware of a criminal scheme that is stealing millions of dollars of your oil revenue as we speak. Your PA, Lucia Ximenes, your head clerk Rodriguo Fuentes, and an Australian accomplice on site have set up an elaborate computer program to skim off revenue...'

As Gary spoke, Francisco Martins' eyes grew wider with the revelation of each extraordinary detail.

'Sir, you must stop it now!' The minister didn't need to be told twice.

'Antonio, wait here! Mr Bishop, please come with me!'

Minster Martins was a man of faith who started each day with a personal prayer time with the Lord, believing strongly that the Almighty would send him a message for his day's work. He always did. Today it was, 'be strong and expect the unexpected.' Gary Bishop's unauthorised arrival had certainly fulfilled that.

As chance would have it, at the very moment the two men were striding up the steps back into the building, Dion had been having further thoughts about George Barham, wondering if he would return today, as Lucia had suggested. What a klutz he was! Dion remembered the soaking of his precious Jimmy Choos with the mineral water. The guy was as clumsy as all get-out. And something didn't quite ring true. Inspired to do a check, Dion had a good look through his briefcase. He remembered George had given it one glance too many that day. So why?

It was then he noticed the tear, a gap that had been there before but was now slightly bigger. And what was that bulge at the bottom? Pushing his fingers down, Dion retrieved a small object. What the heck! It was a listening device – he'd seen them before. Why, the rotten -! What was his game? 'I'll fix him, and get my damn half a mil back!' he screamed.

'What's up, love?' His girlfriend was puzzled. Dion held aloft the device.

'Lucia, look what that George planted in my briefcase! What do you reckon his game is? He can't be fair dinkum!' It was an Australianism she hadn't heard but she got the meaning.

At that moment Francisco Martins and Gary Bishop burst into the office.

'Lucia, move away from your computer and you, too, Dion.' Martins instantly regretted his recent decision to employ Dion Westford as a 'special consultant'.

'Sir, what's this about?' As if they didn't know.

'I've buzzed for security. Based on information just received, we need to do a thorough check of all programs. You are both suspended from duty until this matter is resolved. That applies to Rodriguo Fuentes as well.'

Shocked as they were, they knew the game was up.

But Dion Westford wasn't done yet.

'Let's go!' He urged Lucia into the corridor just as Gary grappled with him, both falling to the floor. Dion was up first, ready to catch up with Lucia, who was sprinting to the entrance. Gary, keen to have another go, started back to his feet.

Dion was ready for anything and meant business. He drew a Smith and Wesson revolver he'd acquired for just such an emergency. He'd picked it up from a street dealer in Dili. Pointing it right at the shocked Gary he screamed, 'Cop this, George Barham – or whoever you are!' and pulled the trigger.

The weapon jammed. In frustration, mouthing profanities, Dion threw it at him and missed, then took off down the corridor.

'Mr Bishop, leave them to security! We'll arrest Rodriguo Fuentes, too. We're in your debt.' Gary hesitated for a few seconds then decided to follow his instinct.

'Sorry, Minister. This one is personal!' Racing off after the two in pursuit, he unlocked his car and jumped in, just as Lucia and Dion's vehicle left the carpark. No worries, the tracker was still underneath! He followed the comforting blip on his screen. There was no need to get too close, he could guess their next move. They'd want to escape to Indonesian West Timor, from which extradition was unlikely. In the meantime, while East Timor made a case, they could draw on whatever ill-gotten funds they had elsewhere to escape overseas.

Given it was a Friday, with the weekend ahead, Gary figured he knew how they'd do it. He'd seen their surfboards strapped to the roof racks, already anticipating a lovely surfing weekend at Hera, Wain Huno or maybe even Tutuala – as far east as you can go. Well, those places were all up the spout, that was for sure. Oh, they'd know the border posts to West Timor would all be closed to prevent their escape. But not a surfing exit. If they could get close enough to a beach right near the border... with their surfing prowess, it wouldn't be a problem.

Gary was thinking like them. Two options. Head west from Dili to Liquica, which Lucia knows well, being her home town. Then via Maliana and Atara, a direct link to the border. Shorter but more obvious. Lucia would know the back roads and they'd be able to skirt any towns where there'd be roadblocks.

The other was a more indirect route that would take them to a beach on the southwest coast, then to freedom. He would bet on the second choice. Either way, the tracker would confirm it.

The moving dot on the screen indicated they were heading south and, noticing Lucia had ignored the turnoff to Gleno, the shorter way, it looked like option two was correct. That was confirmed for Gary once Lucia got as far as Lequitura. As he predicted, she bypassed the town, using the backroads. Time for him to call for support. Fortunately, he'd had the foresight to key in Inspector Amaral's phone number while he was visiting PNTL. He dialled.

'Inspector Amaral? Gary Bishop here. You've no doubt been alerted to the two fugitives Ximenes and Westford by Minister Martins? I'm currently pursuing them in the direction of Soro, probably heading for Suai. Please alert your units.'

The surprised inspector hurried to do so. 'Obrigadu, senor!'

Gary was vindicated.

It was all very well to alert all units, but East Timor, as a developing country, was far from well-equipped to field numbers of officers to stop escapees. Nevertheless, they did what they could, setting up a roadblock at Soro. It was to no avail, as the wily pair, anticipating such a move, skirted around the town by bush tracks. The police tried again at Suai, where their forces were stretched even more thinly, but with the same result. The two eluded capture.

After Suai, it was back roads all the way. Gary's Toyota Rav 4 bounced along, and he was grateful he'd had the foresight to ask Carmelita to find a suitable vehicle. He hoped it would hold up as it hit one large pothole after another. *Not much chance of a decent resale price – I'll be lucky if I can get it back in one piece!*

Checking the map on the screen, it was clear the couple's destination was an unmarked stretch of beach right near the border. From there it would be a quick surf to freedom. Gary stopped and phoned the inspector again.

'Sir, it looks like they're heading for a spot to the west of Suai, beyond Batu Lappa Beach. No name I can find, it's the strip of sand just before the West Timor border. Can you get your units there? They've obviously got around your roadblocks. I'm still in pursuit.'

'Will do, Mr Bishop. Leave it with me!' Inspector Amaral was highly embarrassed at letting an Australian private investigator do his force's work for them. He decided to be creative. He placed a phone call.

'Mr Carlos Goncalves? Inspector Amaral, Dili Police. Sir, we urgently require your two helicopters that are based at Suai. We are in pursuit of two fugitives. Can you please have the helicopters fuelled and ready for a flight to the West Timor border immediately. Roster a pilot for each. My men will be there to collect them in half an hour. We'll settle the bill with you later.'

Carlos Goncalves knew better than to refuse a request from the government. He needed their co-operation to approve his oil exploration with Croesus Oil. He agreed right away, but his curiosity was piqued.

'Always happy to help, Inspector, but may I ask, who are these fugitives?'

'Sure, I might as well tell you. It'll soon be public knowledge. Lucia Ximenes from the Ministry of Petroleum and Minerals and her boyfriend, Dion Westford. A smooth-talking Australian confidence trickster, some sort of merchant banker. I won't trouble you with the details because no doubt you've never heard of him. That's it, OK?'

Carlos Goncalves nearly fell off his chair. Dammit, he could sure kiss his million dollar fee goodbye.

CHAPTER FIFTEEN

The two duty pilots were none too pleased. They'd been ordered to prepare their helicopters and await the arrival of police. It wasn't so much the rush to fuel up- although it was far too hurried for their liking- it was the threatening sky. An electrical storm was forecast to hit at any time, and their very location was at the epicentre. Conditions prevailing over the Timor Sea coast made the region vulnerable at any time, especially at this time of year.

However, Carlos Goncalves wasn't an employer to be trifled with, nor was a police inspector with men on a mission. They had no sooner completed the fuelling and done a flight check than two carloads of police screeched to a halt on the edge of the airstrip, slamming doors and rushing up to the helicopters.

'Men, are you ready?' yelled the senior police officer.

'Yes, sir. Please get aboard and buckle up.' With three police plus the pilot in each copter, it was a full complement. That done, the officer issued an identical order to each pilot.

'Southwest to the Indonesian border. See this stretch of sand? West of Batu Lappa!'

'Roger. Taking off now!' Each one inwardly gulped. The threatening storm clouds, huge cumulonimbus conglomerations, were more intense than ever. As professionals, it was their job to carefully check the weather report each morning, whether rostered to fly or not. Today's was especially grim. Warm air near the surface of the sea, holding a lot of moisture, had risen, cooling and condensing to form the ominous clouds. Add to that atmospheric instability, just the ingredient to intensify the coming thunderstorm. Moreover, there was a strong element of wind shear, and a change in wind speed and direction would only heighten and prolong the longevity of the atmospheric fury that was surely not too far away.

Would they make it? It was a tossup, yet they dared not refuse.

Looking grim, the police officers were just as apprehensive, but duty called. Inspector Amaral was a demanding taskmaster. It was better to obey, even if they died in the attempt. Their reputations as professionals depended on it.

Steadfast in their resolve to get to their destination and tackle the fugitives, every man on board tried to ignore the gathering storm, counting down the time until they were again on terra firma. All eight were quietly praying to whatever higher authority they acknowledged.

'Please get us there soon. And safely.'

The border was coming up on the RAV 4's GPS. Not far now. The tracker hidden under Lucia's Mitsubishi showed they were getting as close as they could. At this point of the border there was no official crossing point, and Gary supposed people might cross unofficially, although he had no idea where. Still, he knew how these two intended to make their escape- simply surf around the border from a point two or three kilometres away. In that case, they'd need to access the beach, so it wasn't that hard to guess where. Especially with the beeping from the tracker to guide him.

As to how he was going to apprehend them, that was another matter. Citizen's arrest? He had no authority, nor a weapon. Did Dion have another firearm? It was a miracle the revolver had misfired and Gary was still alive. It might come down to his knowledge of self-defence techniques. He was grateful for the basic training he'd taken with Queensland Police.

Look at those storm clouds! Gary had caught glimpses of the threatening sky through the tall trees as he bumped along the rough bush tracks, the surfaced road from Suai having long petered out. Curse his luck, a huge storm would be another factor. Suddenly the GPS stopped beeping. Gary saw the stationary Mitsubishi up ahead. They'd arrived.

He pulled up just out of sight, turning off the engine. The couple started to unhitch their surfboards. What to do now? Clearly, within minutes they'd be down to the beach and away, out to sea, the waves choppy and threatening, the storm clouds gathering.

Knowing he'd be out of earshot if he stayed in the Toyota, Gary's only option was to phone the inspector, hoping he'd get a signal for his mobile. Somehow, he did. Perhaps the Indonesians had a tower on their side? No matter, he got through.

'Inspector, the fugitives are right at the border, close to the beach. Yes, that border strip well west of Batu Lappa. I need backup!'

'Mr Bishop, I'm expecting you'll have help from above any minute. Hold on till then!'

What? Was the man on some sort of religious trip? Believe that if you want. Gary was a man of direct action. And he was ready to take it before the rain came down in sheets and the imminent tempest hit with all its fury. Already rain was falling in huge drops, and the light was quickly fading in the gathering gloom at an hour when the sun should have been blazing.

A convenient tree branch the only weapon he could find at hand, Gary snuck up on the couple, who by now had stripped to their swimmers, affixed backpacks with essentials such as money and passports, and had their boards under their arms. *Here goes nothing…*

'Hold it right there, you two! You're not leaving East Timor. You're under arrest!'

They looked up, the shock showing on their faces. 'Oh, yeah, you and what army!' Dion snarled nastily, pulling a knife from his backpack and wielding it viciously. 'A pity I didn't finish you off last time. You'll get it this time!' He lunged forward, but slipped on the now muddy terrain, sprawling on the ground with his knife hand outstretched.

Whack! Gary came down with a massive blow towards the knife, hoping to shatter Dion's hand. In his desperation he was partly off-cue, the knife rather than the hand taking the full force of the strike. Dion's knuckles were merely grazed, but he lost the weapon, which Gary grabbed and threw into the bush. Dion jumped up, impeded only by his backpack, and the two grappled. Lucia kept her distance, not knowing what to do.

'Lucia, grab your surfboard and make a run for the beach, like we discussed! I'm going to finish him off!' Gary was down now, having also slipped on the mud. Dion grabbed the branch and swung at Gary's head, mostly missing but grazing his head. It was enough to disorient him for a few seconds and he saw stars.

Dion, seeing Lucia now almost at the water's edge and thinking Gary was finished, grabbed his surfboard and raced to join her just as the storm, with brilliant flashes of lightning and great bursts of deafening thunder, burst with all its force. Gary thought he must be more dazed than he felt when he saw two helicopters manoeuvre through the rain clouds and land deftly on the only clear stretch of beach, the sound of their engines completely muffled by the raging elements. So this was the salvation from above! Six hyped-up police officers leapt out of the choppers.

'Stop and surrender! You're both under arrest!' yelled the commander. Lucia, being closer and knowing resistance was futile, complied. She dropped her backpack before being cuffed and detained, her face one of total dejection.

Not so Dion. He'd sprinted further down the beach carrying his surfboard as four of the police followed, but he had a lead he was determined to keep. One officer drew his automatic and fired two warning shots which only spurred Dion on. *Stupid cops – I'll beat them!* He plunged into the roiling waves, the storm's fury fully unleashed amidst the flashing of the lightning and peals of thunder.

An expert surfer, Dion used every ounce of his expertise to paddle out, knowing the cops weren't likely to be surfers, and in any case had no boards. All he had to do was get around the next point and go ashore in Indonesian West Timor and he'd be a free man. He had his essentials in his backpack and he could at least access his Australian bank account. The ill-gotten gains from his time at Zenith would be a start for a new life somewhere. A pity that rotten George or whoever he was had foiled his scam in Dili, but nobody would beat the clever Dion Westford!

As he surfed out of range of any further pistol shots from the police, he knew he'd eluded them. He turned back to see George coming down the beach to watch. Not finished off? Oh, he should have hit him again! No matter, he'd soon be round the point and free. He'd find another gorgeous surfer girl to delight him in Indonesia, or perhaps the Caymans. He couldn't resist a moment of personal adulation, of triumph over his recent opponents. And of his hopeless girlfriend, who had meekly surrendered. Just gave in. Weak as water! She could take her punishment!

Damn this rotten storm! Balancing upright on his surfboard, Dion focused on his coming freedom. At that moment, in between the lightning flashes, there was a brief pause in the frenzy, an unexpected quiet moment, and Dion seized it to shout his defiance to those on the beach. Raising his fist as he turned the surfboard around, he stood as upright as the surfing conditions allowed and bellowed with all his might. Oh, how he bellowed!

'Idiots! I've beaten you all! Nobody gets the better of Dion Westford! NOBODY! DO YOU HEAR THAT? NOBODY!!!'

In that instant the storm resumed its fury. A bolt of lightning arced down from the heavens, striking the tallest object it found out there in the Timor Sea- one Dion Westford. Around a million volts surged through his shocked form, his entire being suffused by the massive charge. His body remained upright, swaying too and fro for mere seconds before collapsing. Dion was probably dead before he sank into the surging maelstrom, weighed down by his too-heavy backpack.

Those on the beach ran for cover, the lesson of the criminal's demise not lost on them. Seek shelter while you can. *Like right now!*

Thanks to the unprecedented meteorological disturbance that occurred that night, Dion's body was never recovered, but his fate was not in doubt. His DHD surfboard was found days later, washed up further east along the coast at a small village some distance past Betano. Despite the board being in far less than pristine condition, it delighted the village children, who would use it to develop their surfing prowess for years to come.

It's the ill wind that blows nobody any good.

EPILOGUE

Once the storm's fury had passed, the police placed the handcuffed Lucia in one of the helicopters and both machines took off and headed straight to Suai Police Station. The officer displaced by the prisoner was delegated to drive Lucia's vehicle back to Suai for impounding. He ordered Gary to follow in his Toyota, which was now very much the worse for wear due to its enforced misuse. Scrapes from roadside bushes had done nothing to improve the duco. Ruefully, the Australian could only imagine what condition it'd end up in. He comforted himself with the thought it's a RAV 4 and could take some off-road conditions- just maybe not those potholed bush tracks through thick scrub. Trying to keep up with the trained police driver only worsened the wear and tear as Gary slid around in the muddy conditions.

Arriving at the Suai base was a relief; not so his full and detailed explanation to the English-speaking local police sergeant, who required a complete report. So it was definitely a consolation when the same man then produced an official letter addressed to Gary explaining the need to 'co-opt' the RAV 4 as evidence into the police operation. The government would pay handsomely- the price of a new vehicle, in fact.

Gary knew his next task was to call to Kayla and tell her of Dion's dramatic end. She took it bravely, but with terribly mixed feelings as she wondered how to break the news of their father's death to Elise and Sky. Lew Stein was a tower of strength beside her as she did so. The little girls were more resilient than she could have imagined.

Hospitality in Suai that night knew no bounds. Gary was billeted at the sergeant's home, and was the toast of his grateful family. The operation had certainly done no harm to the officer's reputation and subsequent career, quite the opposite.

'Mr Bishop, please try this offering from Cooper's Brewery!' It seemed the Australian beer had been flown in some time before from Darwin, ready for a special moment such as this. It was a superb celebration.

The next morning Gary refuelled his car at police expense. It was in better shape than he had thought. *Thanks, Mr Toyota, you sure know how to make them!* Then came the long drive back to Dili, where the police had instructed him to leave the vehicle in the airport car park before he left the country. However, Gary had another port of call first.

When he arrived back at the building he had last vacated in such haste, the Department of Petroleum and Minerals was still agog from the recent shocks. Minister Martins had recruited both a new secretary and head clerk to substitute for the two jailbirds. Lucia's replacement had heard of the courageous Gary Bishop and ushered him into Francisco Martins' office right away. He'd be a welcome visitor at any time.

'Mr Bishop, I've received a full report both from the Suai police sergeant and Inspector Amaral. Well done, indeed! I'm so glad you not only survived but played a large part in the arrest of those criminals. Imagine, they were right here in my department! Fortunately, yesterday I was able to contract a forensic accountant to access their computer program and repay the ill-gotten gains they'd transferred to their account. We were shocked to estimate the millions that would have flowed out of our coffers had their scheme been undetected for the full thirty days. Under police interrogation, Mr Fuentes has given us the full picture.'

'Minister, I can only imagine the amount would have been huge- something a country like Timor-Leste could ill afford.'

'Absolutely. We need every cent of revenue for our development. So, as a friend of our nation, you are in our undying debt.'

'Happy to have helped, Minister. I daresay I know what your important meeting with the president was about last Friday – the one I so rudely interrupted...'

'Well, you were a man on a mission. In your position I would have done the same. OK, so you've guessed my schedule. Does that have some significance?'

'Indeed it does. May I make you an offer? I have some expertise in the area you and the president have canvassed and I realise certain discussions are likely to soon reach a climax. Here's how I'm prepared to help if you want me to...'

Minister Martins listened intently. When Gary eventually left the office it was only after the warmest of embraces, each man having a tear in his eye. Francisco Martins offered a heartfelt prayer of gratitude. The man was an unexpected, undeserved gift from God.

Carlos Goncalves was a broken man. Dismissed by a previously compliant Croesus Oil Exploration board of directors because of the loss of his unauthorised million dollar fee to Dion Westford, he was lucky to be re-employed with a rival company in a menial role. This was despite the fee being later retrieved from Fuentes after his arrest. To add to Goncalves' woes, Filomena was no longer cowed by him, having been convinced by a female friend to take self-defence classes. The next time he tried giving her a backhander, she adroitly grabbed his wrist, twisting it until it almost broke before tripping him over.

'Try it again and you'll get worse!' He couldn't believe it. Women weren't supposed to fight back!

He staggered off with his sprained wrist to start another shift of drudgery for a few greenbacks in pay, one that would have him dog-tired after hours of manual labour. The dispirited Carlos, while obsessed with his own fall from grace, reflected on the fate Westford's two co-conspirators were facing – years of incarceration in Dili's Becora Central Prison. Curse them both, they deserved it!

How the mighty had fallen.

Beyond grateful to Gary for retrieving her life's savings, Kayla was determined to leave no stone unturned. She knew now how dishonest her faithless husband had been with his clients at Zenith Bank. After getting her urgent phone call, the bank put her in immediate touch with Felicity Le Mesurier, Zenith's chief auditor. Felicity was busy following up complaints from puzzled investors, querying the deficiencies in their accounts. The full picture was rapidly emerging. She'd already discussed it with Nick Vassallo, confirming all the rumours and suspicions. They were now well and truly alert to the scale of the fraud. On hearing the full saga of Dion's schemes and his sudden demise, she whistled.

'Wow, you poor thing. You've really gone through the wringer!'

'Yeah, but some of your clients have as well, I reckon. Once a cheat, always a cheat. Felicity, you'll need to get to the bottom of it for the sake of the bank's reputation. Now he's gone forever, chase the money trail.'

'Rest assured, Kayla, I have been doing exactly that. Once we've got official permission to access his personal Commonwealth Bank account we'll enforce restitution, using every available legal means to do so. Given your situation, however, we'll bend over backwards to ensure you and your daughters aren't left destitute. We'll separate his embezzlement from what you are entitled to. Are you managing OK?'

'Sure. Thanks to wonderful advice from my father and a gift from God of an astute PI I've got back the joint savings Dion stole. Elise, Sky and I will be alright.'

'Delighted to hear it. Well, on with the task.' Felicity sighed. 'Quite a hunt I'm on. Bye for now.'

'Bye, Felicity – and good luck.'

The chief auditor would have quite a job in front of her. Just as well she was happy to burn the midnight oil.

Gary's return to Tweed Heads was a brief one, giving him time only to check with his long-suffering PA, Jilly, on the state of play with other clients before driving to Sunrise Point for a much-promised homecoming dinner with Kayla and her young daughters. He was embarrassed when they'd decorated the dining room with a banner shouting: 'Welcome home, Gary.' He'd bought souvenirs from East Timor, little provincial costumes for the girls and a full-sized one for Kayla. They in turn had thoughtful gifts associated with his love of surfing. He'd have enough board wax and various paraphernalia to last the rest of his life.

He and Kayla relaxed with a celebratory champagne, specially chosen for the occasion, while the girls retired to their bedroom to change into their new costumes.

'I'm back to Dili in two days' time to finish up some unfinished business, then I expect to return here for good. Plenty of work's built up in Tweed. Poor Jilly can't handle it indefinitely.'

She took his hand. 'I'd love to help with the office if I can. You've been so kind. Please let me. I can take leave from Little Jewels. They're well-staffed now.'

'Kayla, I'd love you to. Yep, you're hired. An equal colleague.'

'Pro bono – I won't take a cent in pay, not after what you've done for us.'

'We'll see about that. But putting you on staff solves one dilemma.'

'Which is?

'I was going to ask to see you again. Which would break the rules of the PI Code of Ethics. But if I fire you as a client and appoint you a colleague, there's no problem.'

'Gary Bishop, I thought you'd never ask! Consider me fired!'

As they kissed, a fire of a different kind was lit.

Gary's trip back to Dili would be as brief as circumstances allowed. There was too much to do back home.

'Gentlemen, may I introduce a special negotiation consultant with an abiding interest in Timor-Leste, Mr Gary Bishop. For the record, Mr Bishop has just completed a mission here that greatly contributed to both our economic welfare and a poignant law and order issue. It's fair to say that he has our economic and social concerns at heart. Being also an Australian citizen with qualifications and expertise in negotiation matters, he will be able to see the issues before us from both sides.' President Ruak's welcome was effusive. Minister Martins, seated next to him, nodded in agreement, smiling wryly to himself.

It appeared the Australian negotiators in the Palacio Presidencial had been wrong-footed, but could do nothing about it. They'd expected a lay-down misère from Timor-Leste, but this upcoming argy-bargy would be a challenge. There was nothing to do but get on with it.

Despite the cogent arguments the Australians had anticipated would give them the lion's share of the disputed Timor Sea Maritime Boundary, with the corresponding opportunities to extract an oil bonanza from the depths, the combined forces of Xanana Gusmao, Taur Matan Ruak, Francisco Martins and Gary Bishop prevailed. While it was generally agreed there would be a 'mutual resolution' to the sea boundary, the final decision was a much-needed win for the new nation. This outcome was not achieved because they gained domination over Australia, but because it was a fair agreement, one that would allow them to achieve economic success at last. They were grateful for Gary Bishop's dedication and expertise with these vital negotiations.

It was a much-needed win. Finally signed in March 2018, the treaty established a permanent maritime boundary and addressed the distribution of revenue from the Greater Sunrise oil and gas fields.

Greater Sunrise. A new dawn for a new nation.

This time the homecoming was even more delirious. Gary was back for good, clutching a personally signed Certificate of Appreciation from the prime minister of Timor-Leste, along with many gifts. A delighted Kayla smothered him in welcome kisses and he responded in kind. Then it was time for a serious talk.

'Kayla, I know you're now no longer a client, but I feel I need to check how you've been provided for. You said something about your kind father. What did he do?'

'After initially being dazzled by Dion's acumen, Dad stopped being impressed with him, although went along with my choice of partner. The man was too smooth by half, he reckoned. He got that right, of course. Well, Dad insisted I take out term life insurance on Dion's life. Somehow he thought Dion had an exotic lifestyle that could impose some risks. Good one, Dad. So I took out a policy giving me a benefit of $200,000 which I've now claimed. Thanks to the East Timorese police witness statements and your own attesting to Dion's clear death, Global Life will pay out, not even requiring proof of his body. Nobody could survive a lightning bolt of that magnitude, let alone after falling into the storm-wracked sea and never resurfacing. He's gone.'

'No doubt about it. You're a free woman.' She smiled.

'Will I be free for long?'

Gary blushed. Then kissed her. 'We'll have to see!' Now he appeared a touch more serious. She noticed.

'Is something up?'

'Yes, in a sense. I've always seen myself as a self-made man and after Lesley died, I resented the idea of God. After all, despite her faith, God didn't save her. But, you know, things then just started happening by coincidence. First, a sudden rainstorm that stopped me heading out to sea to end it all when I was really on a downer. It had come out of nowhere. Then straight after that, the job offer by Adam. Add to the coincidences, people such as wonderful Phyllis and her troupers so ready to help once I got onto your case. Man, I'll do anything I can to repay a whole host of them.

'Finally, I've had remarkable adventures in East Timor and everything worked towards achieving justice for Dion's crimes. Somehow, I escaped serious harm- like when he went to shoot me and the gun jammed. I thought it must be a faulty firearm. But do you know the police ballistics people tested it and it fired off all six shots. It was a quality Smith and Wesson! So why was I spared?'

A sudden tear ran down Kayla's cheek. 'Somehow, miracles happen and we've each felt them. I thank God for mine!'

'You're right, it's all made me think. I might just discuss this with your friend Lew Stein. After all, I'm getting the feeling I'll be calling upon him to perform a special ceremony for us before long.'

'Gary Bishop, do you mean..?'

'Before I answer that, can I just say this. You may have noticed I've brought along my good old JS Industries board, and the surf's up. So for now, can I nip into your laundry to get changed into my togs while you hop into your room and do the same? I just looked out the window and the conditions are ideal. Check out those breakers! So let's head out with our boards and we can talk after we've put them to good use out there. That is, if I can still get down on one knee! I reckon your two lovely daughters need a father. And how we feel about each other- it's magic!'

'You're on. Sunrise Point Beach, here we come. I'll call Lizzie next door to watch the girls and we'll hit the waves. They're really running!'

'Kayla, I reckon they'll take us to new heights!'

RETRIBUTION

PROLOGUE

As he perched precariously atop the lookout's safety fence, Edward Goulston balanced his weight as best he could to get his desired photo. He raised his camera and aimed it at the spectacular scene far below. It took only a second for him to feel his footing disappear before he pitched forward. Dropping his precious camera, he hit the edge of the clifftop before plunging headlong into the void, screaming in terror as he fell.

Transfixed by the bloodcurdling scream, nobody was able to stop the strange-looking man from fleeing the area.

CHAPTER ONE

Tour leader Jean Wallace was really hoping for an easier time today. Her assembly of twenty-two eager tourists gathered around her, keen to board their bus as soon as it arrived. Their vigour certainly exceeded hers right now. Yesterday had been very busy, and she was feeling the weight of her responsibility.

The group had taken advantage of the favourable conditions to cruise Coles Bay on Tasmania's east coast, with the vessel anchoring at a secluded beach for lunch. A delightful and picturesque spot, it afforded the skilled photographers aboard many opportunities to snap away before the captain moved them on to explore the bay's scenic offshore islands. The boat rolled to and fro gently in the mild swell, but Jean couldn't relax. Her attention was focused on one of her charges, Edward Goulston, who was consuming a disproportionate amount of her energy.

'I loved the stunning sheer cliffs we saw yesterday, and those sea lions!' Edward commented to Jean as they waited for the bus. *Oh, Edward*, she thought, *you're giving me grey hairs*! The young man was a concern.

'Yes, they were great,' she replied, 'but did you have to take such chances to get their photos? Remember, no tricks today up at the Cape!' What was it with this bloke, Jean wondered. He was a mild-mannered public servant from Melbourne- unfailingly pleasant and polite- but he sure took risks trying to get the best photographs. He even brought along a collapsible stool to get a better vantage point. Oh well, he'd signed the usual waiver agreement, as had all the others. It was on his own head. Nevertheless, he flirted with danger and Jean felt a great duty of care for all her charges, which she took to heart. She'd have to keep an eagle eye on Edward.

Once the bus arrived from its nearby parking spot, it was 'all aboard'. The passengers were now used to the drill of finding their allocated seats, rotating each day to ensure equal opportunities for 'the best view'. Norm, the happy driver, greeted every traveller, who were practically old friends at this stage of the tour. Once they all were buckled up, Harry got them quickly underway, negotiating the winding road from Freycinet Lodge up to nearby Cape Tourville. Today's schedule was to spend part of the morning at the local national park, with plenty of time to walk around and explore the area before returning to their accommodation for lunch. The afternoon was scheduled as free time – a rare opportunity on this busy trip – giving committed hikers the chance to do some extra bush walking. The less mobile or enthusiastic could simply relax at the lodge and have a leisurely afternoon tea. Following a second night's stay, they would continue on with the tour in the direction of their final destination, Hobart.

Arriving at the cape's parking area, Jean instructed the group to walk up the path to the lookout, where she intended to give them a short talk on the history of the national park. The fittest set a good pace, striding ahead of the main group. As they walked, several others- private tourists who weren't on their tour- joined them in the throng progressing up the steep path.

'Jean, can you help me, please? I'm feeling a bit breathless.' Ruby, one of the more elderly on the tour, was struggling with the ascent. It wouldn't have been difficult for anyone with a modicum of fitness.

'Sure, Ruby.' Jean took the older woman's arm. As she slowed her pace, she continued to worry about Edward. What would he get up to today? Still, right now poor Ruby was her major concern, although with the extra support, she seemed much more comfortable. As they got close to the top, Jean was horrified to see Edward setting up his 'perch' and climbing up on top of the safety fence, scanning the coastline far below looking both north and south for the best and most scenic shot. Watching him closely was a stranger Jean hadn't noticed before.

'Edward! Be careful!' she yelled in Edward's direction. Impeded by her need to shepherd Ruby, she was unable to get any closer. She looked around and noticed a lovely couple from Canberra, who were on her tour. They also seemed concerned by Edward's antics and were trying to make their way through the crowd to reach him.

'Josh and Rachael, can you stop Edward – he's gone too far this time!'

'We're on it, Jean!' They were doing their best to get there, but were also struggling to get through the crowd headed for the lookout. They found a gap and ran towards Edward, also noticing the lurking stranger who seemed so interested in Edward's every move. Suddenly...

'Aar – Aaarrgh!'

It had taken less than second for the stranger to shove the unsuspecting Edward over the cliff, surely to his death.

'No! No! NO!' The immediate onlookers shrieked, horrified. They couldn't believe their eyes. Yet it had just happened. Why, why, why?

Of course, the catastrophe could have been avoided- Edward's carelessness for disregarding the safety warnings and Jean's clear instructions had put him in the face of imminent danger. And yet... that stranger, who lurked so close to Edward, hidden among the crowd of sightseers, watching his every move, had been an assassin waiting for the right moment.

It was an opportunity he took ruthlessly. Having quickly dispatched his target, the culprit made his immediate escape, sprinting down the path from the lookout to the car park, where he jumped into a waiting vehicle driven by an accomplice. They sped him from the scene, tyres screeching, before any of the shocked witnesses could react.

Josh and Rachael Kovacs heard Edward's horrified yell as he fell. Owing to the crowd of tourists blocking the walkway, it was too late to try and apprehend the offender, but they needed to check on the hapless victim – and urgently.

Galvanised into action, they frantically reached the lookout through the milling crowd, where they slid themselves over the safety fence and gingerly approached the clifftop. Peering over gave them some slight hope; a protruding stone ledge about five metres below the drop had arrested Edward's deathly fall. They could see Edward, barely conscious and clearly in a state of delirium, slowly inching towards the edge of the ledge, where the void below meant certain death.

'Rachael, quick! Call the State Emergency Service! I'll try to get down there and stabilise him.' Josh was onto it. Rachael, equally astute, was punching in the numbers already.

Praying silently for divine help, Josh found rough gaps in the cliff-face that allowed him to reach the stricken Edward, pulling him back from the edge and a final plunge to eternity. The victim was in a bad way; critically hurt, possibly internally. Josh took off his coat and placed it under Edward's head, holding his hand as a gesture of comfort. Above came a yell from Rachael.

'Josh, the Cliff Rescue unit is on its way- hold on!' Well, he would. 'They've alerted the ambos and I've called the cops!' That was some consolation at least.

During the longest half hour of his life, Josh continued to support the injured man, who was lapsing in and out of consciousness. In one of Edward's more lucid moments, Josh's curiosity overtook him.

'What happened, Ed? Why were you pushed?' A mumbled vague reply was the only answer.

'Sorry, what was that?'

'Sanchez…it was Sanchez.' *So who was this mysterious Sanchez?*

'Why, then?' No answer. The poor man was out to it. Probably a mercy. Then a yell came from up top.

'Cliff Rescue. Coming down!' Thank the Lord, Josh muttered. There must have been a group based somewhere locally.

Two men abseiled down with a stretcher, the short distance hardly an effort for them. Professionals - they'd done this before.

'Right, mate. We'll take him first, then come back for you. OK?'

'I got down here. I reckon I can get back up.'

'Yeah, probably. But one false step and it's curtains for you. Don't risk it!'

No argument with that.

After checking his vital signs- which were far from good – the rescuers carefully secured Edward onto the stretcher.

'Right, we'll get him down to Freycinet Airfield and do a medical assessment while we wait for the Flying Doctor. They'll take him to Royal Hobart, I reckon- that's the nearest major hospital. Anyway, that will be up to the doctor.'

Hobart was Tasmania's state capital, so that made sense. God bless the Royal Flying Doctor Service, with its fleet of air ambulances.

The men from Cliff Rescue headed back up the cliff with their unconscious patient and were soon out of sight. Minutes later, Josh heard the slamming of ambulance doors from above, and a vehicle departing at great speed, siren blaring. Then the abseilers returned with a harness for him, repeating the need to avoid any unnecessary risks. Before he knew it, he was back up top, to the clapping and cheering of his fellow travellers. Their adulation disguised his shaking, which was uncontrollable for about five minutes. Seeing his reaction, Rachael hugged her hero husband and planted a huge kiss on his lips, both out of love and for distraction. Once he had calmed, she knew what he'd say next; something she was sure she'd agree on.

'I think our holiday's over, Rach. We've got to get to the bottom of this mystery. When I asked him who pushed him over, Ed muttered the word 'Sanchez'. He's badly injured and probably won't survive. Why was that crim so desperate to kill the poor bloke? We owe it to him to find out.'

Rachael was of the same mind. Their holiday coach tour of the state had been great so far but now, with the cops on the way, duty called. So it would be farewell to their wonderful trip around the Apple Isle with Van Dee Tours (the name was a nod to Tasmania's original name, Van Dieman's Land). Hobart, Queenstown, Cradle Mountain, Stanley, Burnie, Launceston, St Helen's and the rest of the scenic east coast were behind them. The final leg southwards back to Hobart would have to be sacrificed, along with the stunning vistas of the Tasman Peninsula.

Given their background, they'd do nothing less.

CHAPTER TWO

'Right, everybody, gather around. Nobody is to leave until we've got all witness statements!' Sergeant Harvey McIlroy from Bicheno was on the ball, having rushed down with his senior constable, Brian Zoadski, from their picturesque home town some distance to the north. The nearest settlement, Coles Bay, had no police presence.

Jean Wallace dutifully marshalled the group, separating those who had actually seen the incident from those who were so distracted by the magnificent vista from the lookout that they had nothing to offer. Given their assertive action, Josh and Rachael provided the best information. When they were able, the couple took the police aside and asked to be involved in any later action, indicating why. His eyebrows, raised, Sergeant McIlroy agreed, then addressed those gathered once he'd collected all the statements supplied.

'Well, everybody, that's it for now, you're free to move off. We'll be in touch if we need any further details. Thanks for your co-operation. Mr and Mrs Kovacs, will you please wait behind for some follow-up?'

Once Jean had organised the group to walk down to the car park for the short bus journey back to Freycinet Lodge, the four of them were able to speak more freely. Josh began.

'Thanks for letting us get involved. This was clearly a murder attempt and I'm wondering if there's a clue back in Ed's room at the lodge. His belongings could prove interesting.'

'Agreed. Let's go – you come with us.' Once underway, Sergeant McIlroy negotiated the police car down the winding road back to the lodge at great speed, pulling up in the parking area shortly afterwards. It took just a minute to access a passkey from the concierge and gain access to Ed's cabin, where they quickly assembled his belongings. He'd brought along a work briefcase; clearly he was apparently unable to switch off while on holiday. Was he a workaholic, or simply highly committed?

The sergeant emptied the briefcase and placed the contents on the coffee table. First up was a photo and a dossier on one Diego Sanchez. From the information in the file, he was in his late seventies and had a wife, Esmerelda, who had died a couple of years ago, and two sons, Luis and Javier. Their last-known address was in East Kew, Melbourne. The two police officers and the Kovacs looked at each other knowingly. Rachael was the first to speak.

'A very revealing dossier. So Ed's been doing some private digging with a view to launching a prosecution of Sanchez, based on his nasty acts committed overseas. Well, that's certainly a motive for murder! Sergeant, you'll of course have the carriage of the criminal investigation to try and track down the actual culprits. However, as this case surely has wider implications that affect our own work, can Josh and I be apprised of any developments?'

'Of course. We can clarify the separation of our different roles and share information. You'll both have our full co-operation. Is there anything else you can tell us about Edward Goulston?'

'The only thing he told us in casual conversation earlier in the tour was that he was a clerk with the Department of Home Affairs, based in Melbourne. That's about all. Otherwise, his passion was for photography, especially nature scenes- he talked incessantly about that. Finally, he tried to hint he liked football and followed St Kilda, which was more or less a local team for him. I think that was just to find a conversation topic – I doubt his heart was in it. But photography – a definite yes.'

Senior Constable Zoadski chimed in. 'Good luck to him following the Saints, if he really did. We here in Tassie are keen to have our own team if it comes to that. How about the Tasmania Devils? I reckon that has a nice ring to it!'

As the four went through the rest of Ed's papers, they found plenty of material on his background. They tasked Brian Zoadski with using the police office photocopier to supply them all with sufficient copies for follow-up. With nothing further to be done at the lodge, the police took their leave. Their next urgent task was the hoped-for apprehension of the culprits- the would-be assassin and his getaway driver. Might that be Luis and Javier Sanchez, by any chance?

Josh and Rachael left to collect their luggage from their room and brief Jean Wallace on their imminent departure for Hobart. After passing on their fond farewells to the tour group, the pair booked the first available flight back to the mainland. But first they planned a quick visit to Hobart Hospital, assuming that was where Ed now was. Rachael did a quick phone check that confirmed he'd been admitted to the Intensive Care Unit in a critical condition. Could they get more information by a personal visit? It was worth a try.

Fortunately, Coles Bay Cabs were up to the challenge.

'Hobart Hospital, then the airport!'

CHAPTER THREE

Despite Sergeant McIlroy's efforts to apprehend the fugitives, and an urgent all-points bulletin for their arrest, the two Sanchez brothers eluded the net. They ditched their stolen Subaru RX sedan at Launceston Airport in favour of a Toyota Corolla they helped themselves to from the long-term car park. Having now laid a false trail and careful to observe all the road rules, they motored to Devonport, from where they took separate charter flights with Bass Air to Melbourne. By the time the stolen vehicles came to the notice of police, Luis and Javier Sanchez were in Victoria in their well-prepared underground lair, ready to flee overseas with false passports, obtained for $2,000 each through the dark web.

The scheming brothers celebrated with champagne. 'A copybook operation!' They clinked their glasses. 'Revenge is sweet!' The two brothers were peas in a pod, their outlook and attitude equally ruthless. In their late thirties, with Luis Sanchez two years older than his sibling, they had never married. Any girlfriends they had eventually tired of being mistreated, exploited or ignored. Self-centred to the core, the Sanchez brothers were not exactly husband material. It was all about them. Well, who cared about others? They were just there to be used, women especially. Even murder was all in a day's work- and in this case, it was job done.

There was just one more task to complete before a new life abroad awaited.

From the back seat of the Coles Bay cab, Rachael Kovacs reflected on the dramatic turn her life had taken during the last few years. She had grown up in the delightful English county of Shropshire, and at just eighteen married the mercurial Rhys Morgan, only to be tragically widowed a year later when he was killed in a horrific motorbike crash. Even a Harley-Davidson has its limits when you lay it down around the sharp bend of a wet road.

Through the kindness of others and a deep spiritual understanding, Rachael rebuilt her life. She qualified at university and joined Britain's anti-espionage agency, MI6, with the dream of helping safeguard the nation's security. While based in Ankara, Turkey, in 2019, she had met the efficient and charming Aussie, Joshua Kovacs, who was working with the Australian Secret Intelligence Service to destroy a joint criminal operation that threatened her country. Britain honoured both of them for the stunning outcome, which put paid to the scheme of a Silk Road country's ruthless oligarch. A whirlwind romance swiftly followed.

'Rachael, please do me the honour of becoming my wife.' It was Christmas 2019, and Josh's proposal produced the inevitable 'yes', followed by her loving parents' blessing once they met Josh at the Prentiss family home. Cultured and educated, a wild colonial boy he was not. Their only reservation was that she might be lost to England forever. Well, with a wedding not planned until the following September, there was time to consider the options.

Or so it seemed. Unfortunately, a pandemic and the scourge of Covid-19 intervened early in 2020. With looming lockdowns and the imminent cancellation of international air travel, it was decision time. Josh and Rachael had a last-minute wedding in March at the Prentiss family church just before all ceremonies were postponed, with a honeymoon in Australia to follow. Scrambling for a flight, the loved-up couple took the very last plane before all international travel there was closed down. It was too close for comfort.

'Welcome to Australia, Rachael!' Having heard all about Josh's 'English rose,' the Kovacs clan in Sydney was eager to meet her, and she certainly didn't disappoint. The couple managed a honeymoon at Palm Beach under difficult circumstances, with lockdowns happening everywhere. Then it was back to work. Rachael recalled her MI6 Field Director's interview in London just before the wedding.

'Mrs Morgan, it is only your meritorious service in the Silk Road oligarch affair and your honouring by Her Majesty that has produced a decision in your favour, allowing you to work in Australia. That and our deep understanding with the Commonwealth of Australia on security matters under the Five Eyes agreement. As you know regulations dictate that on marriage to a foreigner, you would normally have to resign from MI6.'

Rachael nodded as the Director continued.

'However, as Joshua Kovacs is equally distinguished in security matters with ASIS and has himself rendered great service to Britain, we are making an exception. At your request, you will be transferred to the British High Commission in Canberra to work on matters of mutual security as directed. I trust that arrangement suits your needs?'

'Perfectly, sir. Thank you.'

'Good. You are free to go. And best wishes for your wedding – and to beating this damn virus. Stay healthy, and pray for a vaccine!'

'Thank you, sir. I'll definitely do that, and I thank you for your decision.'

'Don't mention it. Good luck!'

'Same to you, sir!'

Their prayers had been answered. Josh was transferred to the ASIS Canberra headquarters and would stay abreast of security matters remotely, with all travel restricted. Rachael's work at the High Commission for MI6 was performed in the same way. With so many of their colleagues falling victim to Covid, they kept the lowest possible profile, as worried about infection as they were about the security projects that came their way. Their Canberra flat was a safe and welcome refuge.

'It's time to spread our wings a bit, what do you reckon?' In 2022, with vaccines widely available and the pandemic lessening as a factor, Josh suggested a trip to Tasmania. 'In a way, it's a bit like England, so I'm sure you'll love it. You've seen some of the mainland, so why not try a coach trip around our island state? Check out this brochure from Van Dee Tours.' Josh read from it aloud. 'Tasmania was first confirmed by the Dutchman Abel Tasman in 1642… Exploration wasn't all just down to your Captain Cook, though he did pay it a visit and nobody realised it was an island until…'

As keen on history as her husband, Rachael soon got the whole story, and readily agreed to the trip. Which had been totally relaxing and enjoyable until somebody attempted to murder Ed Goulston right under their noses. Working in international security, there was always something to upset the applecart. But why did it have to be during their holiday?

Rachael sighed as she thought about their plans from here on. But there was nothing she could do until she and Josh were alone in Hobart. Then there would be time enough for their own 'security conference.' Putting their heads together, they were bound to find the way forward.

Or so she hoped.

Fred, the taxi driver, looked at Josh and Rachael in the rear-view mirror. He was more than happy to have the long run down to Hobart from Coles Bay; it was far better than the usual short trips around town. And he was sure he'd pick up return passengers at the airport to bring him back.

'Are you the one who rescued that bloke who took a fall off the cape? Bit heroic, wasn't it?' News spread fast in a small community.

'Well, we were on the spot and just did what anyone would do.' Josh was grateful Fred didn't press the subject, and was now more interested in tuning his radio to a favourite station. They didn't want to parry awkward questions about the murder attempt. Josh was feeling uncomfortable and had not been his usual self since the clifftop episode. Memories of past challenges still disturbed him, and Rachael had made the odd comment. What was it with those shakes? Still, he dismissed any negative thoughts and concentrated on the task in hand.

The Tasman Highway took them down the scenic east coast through Swansea, Triabunna and Orford, before turning inland to Buckland on the last leg southwest to the state capital. The trip was some small compensation for missing the Van Dee coach tour, which would soon visit the same locations.

Crossing the Derwent River on the final approach to Hobart, Fred broke away from his devotion to the music on the radio.

'Be there in a moment, the city centre is coming up fast. I know where I can park for a while. Been here before plenty of times, you know.' They nodded approvingly.

As good as his word, he pulled up in Royal Hobart Hospital's short-stay area and the couple alighted.

'We'll be as quick as we can.'

'Take whatever time you need. It's all on the clock.' How grateful they were for their government-supplied taxi vouchers. Otherwise it would be one expensive trip.

Quickly directed to the ICU, they were met by head nurse Amelia Merton.

'Ah, Mr and Mrs Kovacs. I'm sorry to tell you that Ed Goulston's condition is exceptionally grave. We're doing everything possible and he's now in theatre. He suffered massive internal injuries. However, in a brief moment of consciousness he muttered a few words. I wrote them down once I got Mrs Kovacs' phone call.'

'Fantastic, what are they?' Amelia Merton showed them the paper.

'Tell Josh – diary at home. Do you know his address? Ed's wallet came with him to the hospital and we're keeping it safe until he or a family member can claim it. Accident and emergency protocol, of course. Normally we wouldn't disclose his personal information but under the circumstances...'

'Thank you, Nurse, that's helpful but we obtained his details separately. We'll certainly follow that up. We guess there's nothing more we can do?'

'Just pray and stay in touch. You can phone any time.'

With a glance at each other, the couple silently agreed. They'd certainly pray for Ed's recovery, unlikely as it seemed.

'You've been wonderful, we're so grateful. Bye for now.'

'Goodbye, Mr and Mrs Kovacs. And thanks for what you've done so far.'

Minutes later they were back in the cab with Fred and on their way to Hobart Airport. Their next move was obvious. They had Ed's address, so it would be a flight to Tullamarine Airport then a quick trip to number 10 Heritage Street, Caulfield. They also had a contact phone number and names for Ed's parents. *They'd better be at home.* The moment the couple left the cab at the airport and had a moment's privacy, it was time to check.

Rachael dialled the number.

CHAPTER FOUR

The Kovacs needn't have worried about finding the Goulstons at home. An anxious Mrs Goulston had answered the phone immediately, hoping it was news from Hobart Hospital. She and her husband were waiting for the signal from the ICU that Edward was conscious, so they could make the quick dash down there to rejoice over his recovery- as slim as that chance seemed. Or, sadly, if he failed to revive, to say their final farewell. She welcomed the call from Rachael and confirmed they would be home. So after arriving in Melbourne on their Virgin flight, Josh and Rachael used yet another cab voucher for a speedy trip to the home in Caulfield.

It was an unassuming but neat bungalow in one of the suburb's quieter locations, not far from both the racecourse and the station. They let the taxi driver go rather than wait. Who knew how long their visit would take? Rachael rang the doorbell.

'Yes? You must be the Kovacs? My wife told me you phoned.' A man in his sixties answered, his face smiling as he spoke, the furrows of worry lines now easing. He had received a phone call from Sergeant McIlroy in Tasmania telling of Josh's intervention, and was keen to show his gratitude. 'Come in, please come in and meet my wife. After what you did to help poor Ed, you'll always be welcome here!' He effusively introduced himself as Levi and his wife, Sarah. Edward was their only child.

'Please, you will have tea with us?' Both Josh and Rachael willingly agreed. It had been a long day and was still far from over. They began by expressing their sympathy to Levi and Sarah over Edward's critical injury. The Goulstons urged them not to feel guilty, especially in view of Josh's heroics, for which they continued to thank him profusely.

Over some much-needed refreshment, the visitors learned more about the Goulstons. A devoted Jewish family, their original name had been Goldstein. Levi's father Elias, originally from Poland, had been a Holocaust survivor who had come to Melbourne after World War Two as a refugee. He settled in Caulfield, considered the heart of the city's Jewish population. The family always worshipped at the local Hebrew Congregation, a focal point for the whole community.

'Father taught us to try to give back, to go the extra mile to help people and that's what we've always done as a family. Edward in particular spent his whole life helping others, so what's now happened to him is a catastrophe. Do you have any idea who did it?'

Rachael answered circumspectly.

'There are definite clues, which we're following up. We hope you can help us by showing us his diary. He mentioned it at the hospital while he was briefly conscious. The Tasmanian police have agreed that we can make our own enquiries.'

'Of course. Let's go to his room.' They followed Levi, who chatted about his son. Thirty-year-old Ed, to his parents' frustration, had shown little interest in marrying, preferring to concentrate on one worthy cause after another. He had a number of posters representing them on his bedroom walls. Victims of wars and civil unrest, starving children, homeless people, sufferers of domestic violence. On it went.

'How did he manage to do his government job?'

'Sometimes with difficulty, but he'd use his recreation leave on whatever 'project' he was absorbed in each time. Also his money – he had few savings and what he had he spent on his only other passion, photography. We had to talk him into taking time off to go on that coach tour of Tasmania. We're devastated it may have cost him his life. We are ready to rush down to his bedside once we get news he's conscious. The ICU staff asked us to wait a bit.'

'You've got to admire his commitment. The ICU are certainly doing their best. We're all praying he pulls through OK. Can we please see his diary?'

Sarah was prompt to answer.

'I know he kept it in his bedside table drawer. I didn't ever dare check it, but know that's where it is.' Just then the phone rang. Levi took the call. It was Victoria police looking for evidence; they had been tipped off by Sergeant McIlroy in Bicheno. They had an urgent request to check Ed's room and go through his effects. Scribbling a note on a piece of paper, Josh held it up to Levi: 'Stall them- we need an hour.' Levi nodded, making an appointment for an hour's time, then hung up.

'We need to photograph his diary before the cops take it,' said Josh. Sarah quickly retrieved the voluminous record and handed it over. Josh and Rachael leafed through it eagerly. Every entry related to the murder attempt caused them to either raise their eyebrows or whistle in surprise. A full picture of Ed Goulston was dramatically emerging. Josh and Rachael clicked away busily on their mobile phones.

Ed had been a very busy man indeed.

CHAPTER FIVE

The diary had been a complete revelation. On the flight from Tullamarine back to Canberra, Rachael and Josh couldn't tear themselves away from their mobile phones, on which they had recorded the entire diary over the last several months, both the mundane and meaningful entries. They'd each taken a record, both for security backup and their separate analysis of events. Just seconds after their taxi had accelerated away from the Goulston's home at number 10 Heritage Street, officers from Victoria police arrived to gather their own evidence on the murder attempt, principally Edward's diary. Levi and Sarah's farewell embrace of the couple and earnest pleas to stay in touch were something neither Josh nor Rachael would ever forget.

Their preoccupation with the diary was noticed by an elderly gentleman on the other side of the plane's aisle. 'That's the trouble with young people,' he remarked to his wife. 'You'd think that lovely couple would get their noses out of their mobiles and talk to each other. No communication these days..!'

With their noses well and truly in their mobiles, the Kovacs continued scrolling...

Three months earlier.

It was a day like any other. Edward Goulston caught his usual train at Caulfield station to the city centre, mentally going through the routine files at work he needed to review, and mulling over the recommendations he had to make. The Department of Home Affairs' Melbourne State Office was located in Bourke Street, Docklands and his regular commute took him from Caulfield to Flinders Street Station. From there, he would exit and head towards the tram stop on Swanston Street, boarding tram route 70 towards Waterfront City. He would then disembark at the Docklands Park tram stop to walk the remaining short distance to his office.

Today, however, his train had only gone two stops to Armadale when his attention was taken by the elderly woman who boarded the train and plonked herself down in the seat next to him. She was crying.

'I'm sorry, but you seem upset,' Edward spoke to her gently. 'Can I help you at all?'

'Oh, I'm having a bad day. Today is the anniversary of the murder of my son. It is the day they killed my poor Roberto, just for his politics. He was my only son. And now I've come face to face with his killer – that monster! – right here in Melbourne!'

Shocked, Ed introduced himself and gently pressed the poor woman for details. As the train rattled onwards, she told him, the facts coming out, jumbled but heartfelt, as they passed Toorak, Hawksburn, South Yarra, Richmond and finally onto Flinders Street, where she too needed to get off; she had a part-time cleaning job in the city. Gone was Ed's preoccupation with work. He urged the woman to join him at a nearby café and unburden herself further. She agreed, willingly.

Over coffee came more details. The woman introduced herself as Paula Torres. Aged in her mid-seventies, she was originally from Santiago, Chile. In her late teens she had married Miguel, and they had an only son, Roberto. Tragically, they'd lost a daughter in infancy during a whooping cough epidemic.

Later, the family were caught up in the maelstrom that descended on that country when the right-wing military dictator Augusto Pinochet came to power following a coup in 1973. Pinochet formed the Directorate of National Intelligence (DINA) and went on to perpetrate egregious human rights abuses against perceived political opponents, dissenters and civilians.

'Mr Goulston, you can't believe it. Mass arbitrary detentions, torture and ill-treatment, forced disappearances, assassinations, censorship and even international terrorism. My poor Roberto ran the student newspaper at the University of Santiago, it was called *Libertad-* you know, *Liberty.*'

Ed nodded as Paula continued.

'Roberto was a keen student of political science, so he knew his life was in danger when he continued to publish articles calling for democracy and an end to the arbitrary arrests. One day in 1986, on his way home, witnesses saw four men jump out of a van and accost him. Roberto was bundled inside and never seen again. For the next four years my husband Miguel and I tried to find him, constantly enquiring with police, but they always fobbed us off. It was only after that wicked regime fell in 1990 and the records became available that we were able to learn the truth, along with other grieving parents of the many 'disappeared' young activists.'

'So what happened?' Ed had become totally caught up in Paula's story.

'Poor Roberto – he was only twenty – had been arrested at the DINA headquarters the day he was kidnapped and thrown into the dreaded Interrogation Unit. He was handcuffed, beaten and then injected with sodium pentothal, the so-called 'truth serum', to extract information. All of this was under the direction of an absolute monster, a man called Diego Sanchez.'

'Tell me more about Sanchez.'

'Well, I found out he's a clever biochemist. Oh, yes, he's really qualified, please believe me. That man – if you can call him one- was easily able to use his knowledge of drugs and horrible chemicals to get what info he needed from prisoners.'

'That's awful!' Ed was horrified. His knowledge of the time was small. 'Drugging those innocent victims.'

'Yes, that's exactly what he did. His rank was colonel and he headed the unit I mentioned. Later in the 1980s they promoted him to general, once Pinochet realised how effective the monster was. I can assure you many hundreds of poor souls suffered the same fate as Roberto. There could have been thousands – all because Sanchez hated their politics. It's in the records.'

'I'm appalled. I know this is painful, but what was your son's fate?'

'Months later, when he'd given up any useful information, the DINA had no more need of him. Sanchez signed his death warrant. I still have a photocopy of it! He gave Roberto yet another drug injection to sedate him, had him bundled into a military cargo plane with at least a dozen other prisoners who were due to suffer the same fate. It took off from the nearby air force base outside Santiago and, when they were flying over the Pacific Ocean, they put all the prisoners into weighted sacks and threw them overboard, like rubbish. Then the plane returned to base, possibly for another 'jettison run'. The date of my dear Roberto's death is on the photocopy of the form. At least I have that! Those DINA monsters kept good records.'

'I'm so sorry, Paula. But how did you happen to identify Sanchez here in Melbourne?'

'Well, getting the official news about Roberto was a real shock, I can tell you. Dear Miguel had somehow always clung to the hope that our son would be found alive, perhaps in jail. On the same day his death was confirmed, Miguel collapsed and died from a heart attack. Being now alone, I made the decision to migrate far from Chile and was eventually successful in coming here to Melbourne.'

'Did Sanchez do the same?'

'Yes, as it turned out. Knowing that there was an arrest warrant out for him because of his many atrocities, he evidently fled the country after faking his own death. Apparently, his own family also migrated.'

'So how exactly did you catch up with him?'

'Purely by chance, I had no idea he was in Melbourne. As I told you, I'm a cleaner and normally work after hours alone. One day there was a storm that caused some water damage to ChemLabs International here in the central business district, and I was called in to clean up. Just as I finished and was preparing to go home, in walked that cursed Diego Sanchez! I knew it was him; I had a photo of him taken in Chile. Every day since I have been praying to the good Lord for justice, and then in he walked! I'd recognise him anywhere, even though he's now in his seventies, like me. He worked as a consultant, and had an appointment to discuss some technical matters with one of the firm's executives, I assume.'

'I can understand your shock. So what did you do, Paula?'

'I pretended to take special care to clean up some more then waited till he left and followed him home on the bus – he took public transport to save expensive city parking fees. Typical! He lived in a well-appointed home in East Kew. I confronted him about Roberto but the monster just laughed in my face. I remember his mocking words, "You're raving, you damned obsessed woman. Get lost!" Then he treated me to some unprintable Spanish curses. He yelled at me, telling me I could never prove anything. He was Declan Saunders now, so I should forget all about Chile, or he would fix me the way he fixed Roberto.

He told me he had a lot of scores to settle, and could easily add me to the list.'

'Oh, Paula, that's absolutely terrible. I hope you went to the police?'

'I did, but they had no evidence. The man was, apparently, Declan Saunders, a respected biochemist doing contract work for chemical companies like ChemLabs, and living a blameless life. The police weren't willing to pursue it, so I was left high and dry. But today, on the anniversary of his death, I just couldn't cope any more. I know it's well over thirty years ago, but I want justice before it's too late. Can you help?'

'I'll do my best, Paula. Now, what is the address of that home in East Kew?'

The diary reading had to stop here as Josh and Rachael landed back in Canberra.

CHAPTER SIX

Happily ensconced back in their flat, the Kovacs continued their study of the diary information, transferring everything to their home computer. Josh was determined to squash any negative thoughts arising from the clifftop escapade, but because of their shortened holiday, they each had a number of days of recreation leave left and they used the time carefully, unable to tear themselves away from the screen. Edward had recorded as fully as possible the significant events, and Josh and Rachael filled in the gaps with their likely interpretations.

Three months earlier...continued

Ridgemont Avenue in East Kew was located just off the High Street, not far from neighbouring Balwyn. Number 39 was as appealing a cottage as you'd find in that pleasant suburb. Edward used a ruse to gather information from the next door neighbour, an elderly woman pruning the roses in her front garden.

'Hello, I'm checking out some local properties on behalf of Domus Real Estate in Balwyn.' Edward offered the woman a generic card he'd managed to 'souvenir' from a casual visit to that business. 'Would you or your neighbours be interested in selling? We're particularly taken by your homes and there'd be buyers waiting. The market's pretty hot at the moment.'

'Not me, love. And I doubt my neighbour – or in fact, the actual owner- would want to sell now, with things as they are.'

The woman looked like one of those neighbours who would know everything that went on in her street. Ed had struck gold.

'The occupant, Declan, is a widower with two adult sons. For some reason they both still live at home. Declan's wife Esmé died of cancer about two years ago, sadly. He's some sort of bio-chemist and does contract work from a home office. That was really useful for him during the height of this cursed virus, with all the lockdowns. He has very interesting visitors, that's all I can say. Various clients, I guess, come and go. Otherwise, he has meetings in the city.'

'What did you mean about the real owner of the house not wanting to sell?'

'Well, Declan recently sold his home to some investor on the proviso that he and his sons could continue to live there as preferred tenants until they gave notice. If you're with Domus, wouldn't you have heard that news through the real estate grapevine?'

Embarrassed, Edward was on the back foot. 'Oh, I've just joined the firm. It would be in the back notifications, I'll have to check. Thanks for the heads-up.'

'You're welcome, love. Have a good day.'

'You, too. Bye now.'

Declan Saunders- in reality, Diego Sanchez- peered through the curtains in his upstairs home office, watching that nosy old woman next door talking to a stranger. It seemed a bit curious. They were looking over at Declan's home. OK, who was that guy? You didn't get to be a top interrogator with the DINA by ignoring little details or anything out of place. Alarm bells rang. So what could they be talking about? It was a pity he wasn't a good lipreader. Declan wasn't a man who took chances, especially not at this critical time, just ahead of his coming plot, soon to be put into operation. Grabbing his mobile phone, he took a few photos of the stranger, as surreptitiously as he could through a gap in his curtains.

As soon as the stranger left, it was time to satisfy his curiosity and hopefully put his fears to rest. Declan left the house and sauntered over to Mrs Nosy and discreetly asked about the visitor. As always, she was happy to chat and told him the man was from Domus Real Estate and had enquired about the Saunders and their family situation. So was the investor putting the home up for sale? That'd really throw a spanner in the works; he and his sons wanted to stay put for a while yet. Thanking his neighbour, Declan walked back home and immediately put a call through to the real estate firm. They knew nothing about the visit!

By now alarm bells weren't merely ringing, they were clanging fit to raise the dead. So who in heck was that guy? Why was he pumping Mrs Nosy for info on him? Only one thing to do. After quickly locking the house, he jumped into his Audi in the garage, pressed the remote to open the door, drove out and was soon away.

Good, there was this mystery guy waiting at a bus stop for his return trip to wherever he came from. Probably the CBD. Declan stopped the Audi, found a convenient park and quickly assessed that his target was about to take bus route 200 towards Bulleen. A bus pulled up right away. Declan grabbed a spare copy of The Age from his front seat, locked the car and moved to mingle with the waiting commuters, as far away from the guy as possible.

At the end of the queue, he had the newspaper ready to shield his face should there be a glance in his direction as he boarded. He needn't have worried, as the man was in a window seat, looking outside and apparently lost in thought. Good. Maybe he didn't know what Declan looked like, anyway. But you could never be too sure.

Some sixth sense told Edward that he was being shadowed. When the bus got to the Hoddle Street and Bridge Street stop, Edward got off, then walked the short distance to the tram stop on Bridge Road. His intuition still made him think that someone was behind him, But with the city crowds nothing seemed obvious, so he couldn't be sure. On reaching Flinders Street station, feeling more than a little shaken he stopped at his usual takeaway coffee vendor for a much-needed lift before entering his workplace at Number 808 Bourke Street, Docklands. He was already far too late and his manager would no doubt scold him for unapproved use of flex time. It had been a challenging start to the day.

Discreetly shadowing his quarry, Declan kept his distance and as soon as the man disappeared into the building he approached the coffee vendor. Did he know his last customer, that young man of thirty or so? The answer was gratifying.

'Yes, sir. That's Mr Edward Goulston of the government building just there, you know, the Department of Home Affairs. He buys coffee here all the time. He seems to work very hard at what he does. I think he deals with migration matters and other stuff. Why do you ask?'

Shocked at the implication that he was under surveillance for some reason known to the authorities, Declan replied, 'Oh, I'm likely to have some business dealings with him. Thanks for that. May I have a large cappuccino, please.' The human rights abuser also needed whatever stimulation he could find. Immigration? Hadn't he covered his tracks well enough, especially at this critical time?

The situation was indeed ominous.

CHAPTER SEVEN

'What do you reckon, darl?' Josh felt the need to consult with Rachael and use her MI6 expertise on the conundrum they faced. They could use their recreation leave during the next few days to get on top of the mysterious murder attempt on Edward. However, the more they analysed his diary, the more the situation had wider implications for their work, and it would have to become an urgent project once they returned to duty. He could see it spiralling into a threat not only against Australia and Britain, but worldwide. Hence of vital interest to both their agencies.

'OK, let's consider our course of action.' Rachael grabbed a writing pad.

Joshua Kovacs was no newcomer to espionage intrigue, but he valued his wife's expertise. Originally from Concord in Sydney's inner west and growing up in a tight-knit and supportive family, his university results guaranteed him entry to the Department of Foreign Affairs and Trade's program to train candidates for overseas diplomatic service. On his first appointment to the Australian High Commission in Pakistan, the High Commissioner, eager to fill an unexpected vacancy, requested Josh to work temporarily as the post's Australian Secret Intelligence Service's officer. Thrown into an urgent security operation, Josh had distinguished himself by saving Pakistan's prime minister, Imran Khan, from an assassination attempt.

Josh's desperate rugby tackle saved Khan from a hail of bullets. As a result, he'd brought down an entire criminal network. Then there was Turkey...

'God brought us together in Turkey, for sure, Joshie.' Her husband nodded in clear agreement. After Pakistan he'd elected to stay full time with ASIS and take on further training before being posted to Ankara. Meeting up- by chance as it seemed- he and Rachael had become enmeshed in a joint challenge to bring down a ruthless Silk Road oligarch that started in Turkey but ended in Britain. The real blessing of that do-or-die involvement was a romance with Rachael that had begun as MI6 and ASIS wrapped up their mission.

Now they faced another intriguing situation together.

They might still be on holidays but it was down to work.

Diego Sanchez, aka Declan Saunders, hadn't been this worried since that day in September 1973 when his greatest hero, General Augusto Pinochet, the Commander-in-Chief of the Chilean military, came to power after a dramatic coup. As a twenty-nine-year-old colonel in the Chilean Army, Sanchez had a vested interest in the outcome and had been instrumental in laying the plans for the coming coup, brought to its head by Pinochet. But he needn't have worried about the coup's success.

To be sure, there had been a series of political and social upheavals that destabilised the country. Chile's political climate was deeply polarised, with escalating tensions between the socialist government of Salvador Allende and the conservative opposition forces, including business elites and many in the military. Economic instability, exacerbated by Allende's policies, had led to inflation, shortages and a general sense of crisis.

How I loved September 11, 1973! Sanchez reflected. *That glorious day of the coup!* It had been swift and decisive, with Allende dead, his government toppled and Pinochet in power as the head of a military junta. The army Commander-in-Chief dissolved the Congress, suspended political parties and imposed martial law.

He knew how good I was, and exactly what I wanted! Pinochet had appointed Sanchez with a position on the committee for Operation Condor, and Sanchez revelled in it. The notorious Operation Condor was a campaign of state-sponsored terrorism and political oppression targeting left-wing dissidents across Latin America. Pinochet's rule had all the hallmarks of authoritarianism, censorship and human rights abuses.

Later appointed as head of the dreaded DINA's Interrogation Unit, Colonel Sanchez was in his element. Rich and arrogant, he expected nothing less, having devoted himself to his twin careers of biochemistry and the army. This meant he had married Esmerelda later in life, but they were still able to produce two sons, Luis and Javier. The family, one of Chile's elite, lived in Las Condes, one of the most exclusive and upscale neighbourhoods in Santiago's eastern part, with tree-lined streets, luxurious homes and fine establishments. The suburb positively reeked prestige. Having inherited a fortune from his parents, who were members of Chile's business cream, Diego Sanchez was set for life. His background and family influence had ensured stunning promotions in his army career.

Esmerelda was from a similar background, although her husband often joked that 'she only came from Vitacura', as though it were a slum. Far from it. Adjacent to Las Condes, Vitacura was another affluent suburb favoured by the wealthy, with spacious estates, gated communities and upscale residential developments. It was also renowned for its elegant architecture and proximity to the Mapocho River. Esmerelda was cut from the same cloth as her arrogant husband.

As a qualified biochemist, Colonel Sanchez used his considerable skill to great effect as head of the Interrogation Unit. Victims slated for interrogation were routinely beaten, then injected with chemicals to loosen their tongue. Many died under this technique, although all were eventually dispatched one way or another. The DINA certainly got what it wanted.

Damn those interfering western countries! With his authority gradually undermined by constant human rights pressure from abroad, and despite his promotion to the rank of general, Diego Sanchez realised the writing was on the wall in the late 1980s. Frustrated, he burned with rage against those countries he imagined had wronged him or his hero-god, Augusto.

I'll fix them! A scheme came to mind. He had no chance to put it into practice just yet, but he was prepared to play the long game if that was what it took. *They'll pay – dearly.*

The family made preparations to flee Chile before Sanchez's likely arrest for human rights abuse. Just as Pinochet stepped down in 1990, Sanchez began his plan, starting by laying a false trail. Liquidating his assets, he faked his death, sending the family ahead of him to Australia as 'priority migrants.' He had to lie low for a long period until, fluent in English, he was later able to join them in Melbourne, reborn as Declan Saunders. The best forgers in Chile, for a large price, were able to present him with a perfect set of new papers.

To all intents and purposes, Diego Sanchez no longer existed and Declan Saunders, a distinguished and capable Melbourne biochemist, was available as a consultant to that industry. Exactly what he wanted.

Now it was time to lay plans for his campaign of revenge.

CHAPTER EIGHT

'Let's list the issues and see where we stand,' advised Rachael. 'Remember, we each need to make a strong case at work on Monday.' Upon their return to duty, the couple would make a proposal to both MI6 and ASIS for a joint operation, based on the assumption that the information they had discovered had wider – and international – implications for several allied countries.

Josh agreed. 'If Ed recovers, albeit against the odds, McIlroy and the Tasmanian police will interview him for follow-up. That's one factor. Victoria and Tasmania police are doing their best to apprehend the Sanchez sons, if they haven't already slipped the net and gone overseas. Then they'll look into Diego Sanchez for murder, quite apart from his human rights abuses. So the cops will do what they have to – another factor.'

Rachael was quick to add, 'If the crims are all abroad – quite likely given their degree of planning – then there's the need for both an Interpol Red Notice and alert for that country's authorities, if we can find where they've gone. So we'll have to liaise with the Australian Federal Police. Importantly, to keep faith with Ed we need to mount an International Court of Justice case against Sanchez – or 'Saunders' – once he's caught. We've got the procedure in our training manuals, so all we have to do is follow it. Joshie, anything else you can see?' Josh had printed off all the diary contents and was leafing through it.

'Paula Torres may have some extra info. I think I'll phone her. Who knows, Ed may not have recorded everything. Fortunately, he noted her phone number. In any case, she needs to hear the bad news about Ed, although I expect the Melbourne cops have been in touch once they've gone through Ed's diary.'

'Great idea. Give her a call.'

A sniffly Paula, dealing with a cold, answered and patiently listened to Josh's opening statement. Yes, Victoria police had been in touch to tell her about poor Ed and she was shocked. No doubt at all that monster Sanchez was behind it. Where was justice? Grateful to hear of Josh and Rachael's involvement, she offered to help if she could once she was over this cursed respiratory infection.

'Thank you for what you did for Ed, Mr Kovacs. And I've just remembered- when the police phoned me, they asked me to make a statement at the nearest police station to where I live, in Armadale. That's the one at Malvern in Tooronga Road. I'll go there tomorrow if I can.'

'That's good. Is there anything else you can tell me, maybe about ChemLabs International? What I mean is, has anything else developed since you last had contact with Ed?' Josh had had a sudden thought.

'Oh, yes. I've since realised Sanchez has set up his own laboratory in the office basement. I reckon he's bribed one of the executives to let him do it, based on their body language that day I saw him in the office. I've been specifically told not to clean it. It's always locked when Sanchez isn't on the premises.'

'Very interesting! Can you tell me more?'

'Well, I may only be a cleaning lady, but I had a responsible administration job in Chile. I'm more observant than most people give me credit for. Sanchez thinks only he has a key to the lab but guess what? The executive I mentioned is pretty cunning too, and has his own spare key, along with spares for other sensitive ChemLabs locations- which I reckon Sanchez doesn't know about. All of them are labelled. They're kept in a safe and I'm pretty sure I know the combination to open it. It's amazing what pieces of paper you see thrown into bins if you've got time to nose around after hours.'

'That's fantastic! Any chance you could access the safe?'

'Sure. I think I'm well enough to clean tonight if I dose myself up a bit. After hours, I'll have the place to myself. How about I get into the lab and take some photos? I can then email them to you.'

'Paula, your blood's worth bottling! Please do exactly that. Bye for now.'

Puzzled by the expression- she assumed it was a compliment- Paula said she'd be in touch, farewelled Josh and hung up. Paula Torres, secret agent? She liked the sound of that.

For the first time in a week, her cold symptoms strangely eased.

Each primed by a strong cup of coffee, Josh and Rachael knew they had to put the best possible case forward at work on Monday for official action. The historic human rights violations in Chile were the bedrock of the matter. So it was back to the training manuals again, with a similar process followed both by MI6 and ASIS.

Step One: Gather Evidence. This could include witness testimonies – Paula Torres would certainly provide this. The document she obtained after the fall of the dreaded Pinochet regime definitely met this criterion, with research likely to turn up more. The Sanchez family's immigration history and fraudulent documents were additional evidence.

Step Two: Consult Legal Experts. Their agencies had these "on tap" to provide a briefing on the process of reporting to the ICJ. Step Three: Contact Relevant Authorities: The UK Foreign Office and the Australian Department of Foreign Affairs and Trade were a start, with other authorities likely involved later. The couple read on, taking notes and sketching action as they listed the later steps- Preparing the Complaint and submitting it to the ICJ, Follow-up and Co-operation, Legal Proceedings and finally, Verdict and Judgement. Yawning, Rachael needed a break.

'It's pretty involved, hon, a complex and lengthy process with success far from guaranteed!' Rachael could see the enormity of the task ahead.

'Agreed, but we're determined to give it a go, aren't we?'

'Sure are. What's that old saying? "The journey of a thousand leagues starts with the first step?"'

Josh had to agree. But as he rose to sum up their work on the computer, his hands were shaking. Excitement?

Maybe, but he couldn't be sure.

CHAPTER NINE

As cunning as the proverbial outhouse rat, Diego Sanchez knew exactly how to get information on his quarry. That damned Edward Goulston was a threat at this critical point in his plans; his research in Australia was almost ready to wind up before he set in motion the all-important second stage abroad. He cursed his bad luck in encountering that hysterical woman who'd accosted him at his own home. How had she got onto him? No matter, she was of no importance. But somehow since then, the immigration authorities had got wind of him. That was another issue.

Bribery and inducements were always a useful tactic. He had returned to the coffee vendor outside the Docklands office and had a conspiratorial talk to the man once they were alone, purchasing the largest takeaway cappuccino available to smooth the way.

'Look, can I ask you something? I- er... need a little help with an immigration matter, it's a worthy cause to help a friend. I know a customer of yours is a helpful bloke and I'd like to get to know him. Edward Goulston, you told me his name last time. He seems a nice bloke.' The lying words tripped off his tongue. 'Do you reckon you could connect with him on social media and maybe forward the link to me as your friend? I'd really appreciate it, and my mate is willing to help you out with some dough to repay the favour. What do you think?'

The vendor was a refugee from Afghanistan, and had always had to live by his wits. He saw Australia as the land of opportunity, but certainly knew all about the immigration difficulties people faced and sympathised, even if the story seemed a bit thin. Still, anything to get some rent money.

'Sure, happy to help.' He watched in amazement as Sanchez peeled off $500 from a wad of notes and handed it to him, along with his contact details, before he disappeared into the crowd.

Aziz the happy barista poured himself a huge drink in celebration. They were right. Australia was a veritable land of opportunity.

The plot worked nicely. Aziz was the essence of charm and Edward welcomed him as a Facebook friend, anything to help the nicest coffee vendor he'd encountered adjust into the Australian way of life. It seemed harmless enough, even when Aziz recommended his Australian friend 'Dave' to join the group. 'Dave' occasionally chimed in with the blandest of comments about certain information, but otherwise kept a very low profile. It was all good fun.

Edward shared news about his worthy causes and his love of photography, even showing photos of himself perched in the most precarious of positions to get the best nature shots. Otherwise, he was anything but a daredevil. Still, any useful information was duly noted by 'Dave'. Then he hit gold.

'Off to Tassie with Van Dee Tours in April!' was Edward's sudden news, a break from the worthy causes and photo stuff. It was a coach tour around Tasmania. 'Dave' followed up eagerly – not to Ed via Facebook, but with an email to Van Dee in Hobart.

'Hello, I've just learned about your April coach tour around Tasmania. It seems ideal for me and I'd like to join it. Can you please email me a brochure and a detailed itinerary?' The office manager was quick to follow up on the request and minutes later 'Dave' had laid his plans. Oh, yes, the rugged cliffs of that wonderful island state would present an ideal opportunity, especially for a keen photographer who'd risk his neck for the right shot. Rubbing his hands in glee, he called his sons together for a brief conference.

'Luis and Javier, there's something I want you to do…'

Then it was whisky and soda all round for a premature celebration as they joked about the unofficial Sanchez family motto.

The family that slays together stays together.

CHAPTER TEN

Paula Torres had a sudden coughing fit as she quietly let herself into the secret worksite at ChemLabs, and was grateful there was nobody else present. Apparently her cold wasn't quite better after all. Once in, she looked around in amazement at the array of bottles and equipment neatly arranged on the benches. It looked as though it was all ready to be boxed for removal and guessed the place might shortly be wiped clean. Maybe she was just in time.

Careful to move only those bottles and industrial-grade plastic containers whose labels needed to be revealed, Paula took a series of photos, then checked they were accurate. Good, she hadn't missed any. She took further shots from every angle so as to answer any questions the Kovacs might later ask her. All this was balm to her soul; she enjoyed taking actual action to redress the injustice of Roberto's murder, and her dear husband's tragic death from the stress of it all. That monster, Sanchez – how she wanted justice!

Once her covert operation was complete and the photos taken, Paula verified all was as it had been when she entered, relocked the lab and replaced the key in the right spot in the safe, which she in turn checked was closed and secured. Her routine cleaning duty throughout ChemLabs afterwards was an anticlimax, so much so that she realised later she'd overlooked a couple of usual jobs.

'Oh well, if anyone complains, I'll put it down to not being over my cold.' Then, proud of her growing command of English idioms, one came to her and made her smile.

Tonight I had bigger fish to fry!

No argument with that.

The Kovacs were ecstatic when Paula's emailed photos came through that same night. They stayed up late to record them, jotting down every substance listed. The key ones were CBB, which was somewhat mysterious, then Nutrient Broth – whatever that was- along with a range of amino acids, vitamins and minerals, trypsin, ammonium sulfate, some chromatography resins and glycine and albumin. Rachael send a wonderful 'thankyou' message to Paula as she and Josh scratched their heads as to what game Sanchez was playing. Whatever it was, it was clearly ominous.

'Let's sleep on it and work out our strategy tomorrow.' Given the hour, it was good advice. Tomorrow was Saturday and Monday meant a return to the office.

Next morning, Josh had an idea. 'I'll phone Rick Woodley, our chemical expert, he's got a master's degree in forensic science. I know it's the weekend but hopefully I can catch him.' Rick was out but Josh left a message. Then another. About midday, Rick phoned back.

'Hey Josh, you back from holidays yet?'

'Nope, but something has come up. It's urgent. Can you help?' He filled Rick in on Paula's spy mission and what she'd found, then repeated his urgent request.

'Sure, fire away.' Josh read out the list. Rick's exclamation of dismay at the other end was clear.

'Josh, this certainly is urgent. I know what CBB is. It's Clostridium botulinum bacteria, highly dangerous. The lab man must have got the spores he needed to start the process on the black market and grown the bacteria in sealed fermentation containers. You mentioned your friend Paula found some. Is that right?

'Yep.'

'All those other chemicals and substances are clearly to develop a highly refined version of Botulinum toxin as a weapon. The biochemist must be a criminal bent on releasing a nerve agent as a terror weapon. In the wrong hands, he could kill a whole city full of innocent people…'

'Thanks, Rick. I'll get back to you later. Bye!'

Seconds later, Josh put a call through to the Australian Federal Police's Melbourne headquarters.

'Joshua Kovacs of ASIS. Make an urgent raid on ChemLabs in the CBD. Hurry! There's a basement lab full of dangerous nerve agent chemicals. Show extreme caution. Go now!' He gave the special codeword.

He and Rachael prayed the AFP would make it in time.

About ninety minutes later the bad news came through. The AFP had broken into the secret lab but were too late. The lab was as clean as a whistle. With no evidence against them, ChemLabs would probably lodge a complaint about 'overzealous police' and demand compensation for the broken door, plus anything else a lawyer might dream up. Later, a report came through of a van parked outside in the street about six am and two men in their thirties loading sealed boxes of materials from the building into it, while an older man remained as the driver. About six-thirty it drove off. Nobody thought this unusual – it was ChemLabs, after all.

Thoroughly disappointed, Josh stayed in touch with the AFP, only to receive further bad news. A privately hired cargo plane had departed Tullamarine Airport at ten am, bound for Vancouver, Canada, with three people on board that met the same descriptions. The older man had lodged paperwork claiming approval to export certain harmless chemicals to be used in agricultural products.

Equally frustrated, the AFP arrived at the East Kew house, much to the concern of the elderly neighbour Ed had encountered, who by now was thoroughly aware that something exciting had been going on next door. The police found the home completely vacant, not a stick of furniture had been left behind. A later check with the managing real estate firm confirmed the Saunders- as they were now known to the police – had officially vacated the previous day, having given the requisite period of notice, with their rent paid up to the cent. They'd been ideal tenants.

The Kovacs kicked themselves for their 'holiday attitude.' Had they been officially on the job, they'd have organised a raid first and asked questions later. Why didn't they listen to their own suspicions? Only one question remained- what was behind the cargo plane's destination of Vancouver?

Josh had one final task before compiling a report and a dispirited return to work on Monday, following these early failures. Two phone calls to Canada; the first to Senior Constable Veronica Puglisi of the AFP, working at the Australian High Commission in O'Connor Street, Ottawa, and the second was to Zeke Leroy, also based in the Canadian capital. He held an equivalent position to Josh, that of an officer with the Canadian Security Intelligence Service.

They'd both likely have some urgent work to do.

CHAPTER ELEVEN

As their Beechworth King Air 350 cargo plane sped high above the Pacific Ocean, the three Sanchez men treated themselves to copious amounts of champagne. No whisky this time- nothing but the best vintage Bollinger. Diego Sanchez in particular was glad to have put the shores of Australia behind him; not just because he and his sons had avoided any possible retribution from the authorities, but also because he had nothing but contempt for the country that had unknowingly sheltered him from the clutches of justice for years.

Australia was too democratic by half, with its alternating Labor and Coalition governments sharing power over decades. A coup to bring in an extreme right-wing dictatorship? Now that'd shake the place up. How he would have loved to resurrect the now long-departed DINA and drop more dissidents to their deaths in the roiling waves, just like those he could see cresting far below.

As he tossed down yet another glass of Bolly and called for a fresh bottle, Sanchez comforted himself with the satisfaction of having had at least one Australian dissident dispatched to a quick death, albeit onto rocks if not into the depths of the Tasman Sea. *Farewell, Edward Goulston!* As the champagne took effect, he couldn't repress a wry smile. He looked forward to many more people like the interfering Goulston reaching a similar grisly end.

'Please fasten your seat belts, we'll shortly be landing in Fiji!' The pilot's voice came over the audio. They complied, knowing there was a compulsory refuelling stop in the Pacific island nation. So Sanchez had to cease his gloating for a while. After landing in Suva, he elected to supervise the refuelling process, which took place without incident. Even though he had taken the precaution to have extra fuel tanks added to the aircraft to increase its flying range to well over its usual 1800 nautical miles, this was an essential stopover.

After stopping at the airport for the shortest time possible, the Beechworth King Air was soon back in the air heading for the next touchdown – Howland Island, a speck of land just north of the equator. The final stop was Hawaii, before the plane landed in Canada. It was this last part of the journey that would really require the extra fuel.

During the flight northeast to Honolulu, Sanchez's thoughts turned from gloating to revenge as he reflected on the scandalous treatment dished out to his dear Augusto, with whom he compared the Roman emperor, Augustus. In Sanchez's mind, Pinochet had the same aura of greatness. How dare they treat him the way they did! Pinochet had been in London for medical treatment in 1998 when the authorities arrested him on a Spanish extradition request for human rights violations. He was held under house arrest in the UK for over a year before being released on health grounds. Over a year!

Enraged, he snatched a map of Britain and tore it to pieces. *Damn the British! I'll get them!* He mentally added that country to his hit list. Thank heavens the British had allowed Pinochet to return to Chile, where he was guaranteed immunity from prosecution only because he was a Senator for Life. Unlike Sanchez himself, sadly. As a mere army officer he – the talented, dedicated General Diego Sanchez – had no such immunity, either in Chile or abroad. No matter, he was going to level the score in his own way. Oh, yes, all the 'Five Eyes' nations will be in the firing line- Australia, New Zealand, Canada, the USA and Great Britain. Sanchez knew all about those countries' mutual arrangement for sharing intelligence information to combat outside espionage and terrorism. He'd tackle all five eventually, but Canada, Australia and Britain were priorities – they'd get his 'first wave.' The others would get theirs later.

Several hours later Hawaii was in sight. The pilot issued the same safety instructions, followed by a careful landing. The Beechworth aircraft taxied to a stop for refuelling, with extra time needed to top up the auxiliary tanks, and the relief pilot ready to take over. Sanchez had all his paperwork ready in the event of an inspection by US Customs but there were no complications.

'Please fasten seatbelts. We're about to take off for our final leg to Vancouver, Canada.' Both pilots were grateful for the Beechworth King Air's superb performance, known for its reliability and capability to fly such long distances. However, the three Sanchez men were starting to weary of the trip and looked forward to their destination. It was still hours away, but despite the inconvenience of a long-haul, they were sure it would all be worth it.

Canada – and the world – were in for a huge surprise.

On Monday morning Josh and Rachael returned to their separate workplaces, neither feeling properly rested. They quickly dealt with interested holiday queries from their colleagues before acquainting their superiors with the Ed Goulston affair. The Field Operations Directors of both ASIS and MI6 agreed there was a strong, even urgent call for involvement, and, within an hour in each case, confirmed their joint mission.

Josh asked about his colleague at the Australian High Commission in Ottawa, Madeline Arnold. Could they work together? He received a sad reply.

'Sorry Josh, no luck with Madeline. She's come down with Covid and is quite ill. We suspect she'll be unavailable for some time, so it's down to you. With Rachael as an equal partner, of course.' Josh nodded. He knew she'd be more than enough.

The agencies hurriedly set up a phone conference between the Kovacs, Veronica Puglisi and Zeke Leroy. All four agreed to resist the initial urge to just arrest the three Sanchez in Vancouver. Rachael was adamant.

'Sure, we'd get them on some charges but they're clearly part of a wider conspiracy. We want to get everyone in the net. Let's just keep them under close surveillance.' All were of the same mind. Josh finished the call on an optimistic note. 'Veronica and Zeke, we'll be on our way to Vancouver tomorrow. Can you please arrange a loan car to be available for us at the airport under the usual 'Five Eyes' arrangement? If you could email the details when you've made them. Bye for now!'

Zeke phoned back an hour later.

'Hey, Josh and Rachael. Forget Vancouver. We've just had word the Sanchez plane had another leg on their flight, not officially disclosed. They've landed in Calgary, where they unloaded the cargo and trucked it south to their final destination.'

'Where's that, Zeke?'

'The Meridian Eco-Lodge, in the boondocks south of Calgary and off Macleod Trail. Interesting, because it's open to the public. We'll keep it under close surveillance.'

'Got that, we're on our way. See you.' Josh quickly googled the location.

Looking at each other, the couple's thoughts were in sync. Josh spoke first.

'Well, darl, fancy a little stay at an eco-lodge?'

'Why not? Our holidays usually turn out to be very memorable, don't they?'

Touché.

It had been a very long trip but the three Sanchez were fired up for this final leg, the van trip south to Meridian. With money no object, they'd bought exactly what they needed for the transportation- a Ram ProMaster, ideal for the job. Funds were readily available from the Sanchez family's many assets, which had been squirrelled away abroad after the fall of the Pinochet regime. With the chartered cargo plane account settled and Canadian Customs no problem- thanks to the 'agricultural products' listed on the manifest concealing anything noxious- they were soon on their way from Calgary International Airport.

The city's network of trails – actually freeways – provided an ideal way to exit Calgary and within the hour they had arrived at Meridian, the name derived from a local landmark. A warm welcome awaited Diego, Luis and Javier Sanchez, as they were now to be known. They had jettisoned the Australian surname of convenience, Saunders.

'Greetings, Comandante!' Those saluting Diego were showing the height of respect. Some, like Sanchez himself, were extreme right-wing officers from Chile, similarly eluding justice. Others were a disparate group of extremists and anarchists drawn from several nations, all with a common purpose, the one Sanchez had outlined to them when they were recruited. Just one last task remained before they could relax from the long trip.

'Greetings to you, soldiers. Right, form a squad and unload the Ram. The real cargo goes to the laboratory. Dispose of the agricultural material in the appropriate place. Go!' They did.

Then it was time for a celebratory meal. The men enjoyed a sumptuous repast of grilled salmon, quinoa pilaf and steamed seasonal vegetables, washed down with the Comandante's personal selection of wines. Held in a private hall away from the public section, the dinner was a time for relaxation, and a raucous celebration of what they'd achieved thus far. For Diego, Luis and Javier only one thing would ever surpass it. Their mission's success.

Well, that wouldn't be long coming.

CHAPTER TWELVE

Yawning as they finally exited Calgary International Airport following their long Air Canada flight from Australia, Josh recalled an earlier visit to Alberta during his student days. Rachael had experienced eastern Canada through a brief work assignment some years ago but had never visited this delightful western region, one of the three prairie provinces: Alberta, Saskatchewan and Manitoba.

'OK, where's our vehicle?' Rachael had all the information on her phone, and they headed for Brenda's Florist, just outside and straight across from the airport building. Entering the small shop, Josh asked for Ron, the manager. Their security identification cards were all Ron needed to find the electronic keys to a late model Chevrolet Cruze sedan. He gave the couple a knowing glance, along with directions to the vehicle's location. They both signed for it, with the thoughtful Ron handing over a posy of flowers to the delighted Rachael.

'Welcome to Canada, Rachael. I wish you every success for your mission, both of you!'

'Thank you, Ron. That's most appreciated!'

They easily located the Chevy and were quickly away and out onto Deerfoot Trail, heading south. Josh drove: thanks to earlier assignments in Turkey and elsewhere in Europe, each was quick to adjust to driving on the right-hand side of the road.

It was the work of only a few minutes to make the necessary mental switch.

The GPS made driving easy but their intelligence training had taught them to memorise all landmarks and major roads. With Calgary's Foothills Industrial Area on their left hand side, they soon crossed the Bow River, recrossing it twice before Deerfoot Trail merged with Macleod Trail, well south of the city limits. By now they were well and truly 'out in the boondocks.' It was time to rehearse their undercover mission and remember their alias.

'Joshie, it's good the lodge has members of the public staying. We'd better keep our eyes peeled at all times. It's great we can get backup from Zeke in particular, with Veronica in reserve. They both seem on the ball.'

'Yep. Then there's our personal emergency backup- the Glocks- if our lives are in danger.'

'Too true!'

Bypassing Okotoks they soon saw High River come up. The GPS alerted them to take the 540 minor road to their right. Shortly after, the sign they were looking for appeared on the left: Meridian Eco-Lodge. Driving down the long driveway, their hearts beat a little faster as the office came into view. Josh steered the Chevy into one of the two empty car spaces.

Just before going inside, Rachael squeezed Josh's hand. 'Show time! Ready?'

'Yep. You, too?'

'You bet. Let's sort 'em out.' The office door opened automatically.

'May I help you?' The receptionist was efficient but friendly.

'Sure. Joshua and Rachael Kingston booking in. Here are our details.'

Another interesting holiday was coming up.

Before the couple left Canberra, ASIS and MI6 had jointly briefed the Kovacs under the principle of OPSEC, or Operational Security. For this mission they were to assume cover identities with the plausible backstory of being Australian journalists researching the operations of eco-lodges, analysing their healthy lifestyle, menus and basic philosophy, all for the magazine *Better Living*. ASIS came up with some 'samples', which they brought with them should they be needed. Clearly displayed in the editorial list were the names, Joshua and Rachael Kingston, Writers-at-Large.

'What do you reckon Rach? We make pretty good journalists!' They admired the impressive articles on healthy lifestyle, written under their bylines, which appeared throughout the sample magazines. ASIS was nothing if not resourceful. The magazines were entirely convincing, along with the associated website, manned 24/7 by an ASIS officer back in Canberra.

Settled in their cabin, Rachael perused the menu. Breakfast the next day offered a choice of fresh fruit salad, wholegrain pancakes or waffles with a dollop of Greek yoghurt, and eggs. This alternated with homemade granola, vegetable omelette and a smoothie bowl. Lunch was minimalist, mainly fresh vegetable crudités, Greek yoghurt parfait and an offering of fruit smoothies.

'Hey, hon. Dinner's not too bad. Take a look.' It was Rachael's turn to be impressed. 'Look at this: grilled salmon or trout, vegetarian stir-fry, roasted chicken breast, pasta primavera...'. They'd certainly eat well.

Comforting as that was, they still had to negotiate their way through the daily program to get to the real purpose of their mission. Firstly, as new arrivals, they'd face orientation by the guest manager before dinner. Tomorrow, the schedule would begin with an early wake-up call followed by a Tai Chi session, breakfast, and physical activities such as swimming, gym work or horse riding. After this came relaxation time, lunch, and nature walks. A map of the lodge and grounds showed a restricted area for staff and farm workers only. How easy would it be to get access? Maybe their 'journalist credentials' would do the trick.

It was time to work on a plan.

Inside the restricted area, in a locked building signposted as 'Veterinary Research. Strictly Staff Only', Diego Sanchez called the 'hit squad' to order. 'Squad, pay attention. We're almost ready for our targeted operation. The chemicals are prepared both in capsule and aerosol form. I've looked down the list and see you're all due for the antitoxin just before departure. Correct?'

'Yessir!' they answered in unison.

'Good. Now, here are the precise orders that I'll issue to your group commanders. Lieutenants Luis and Javier, please collect them. You'll have time for a final practice and to workshop any remaining issues.' His sons, dutiful as ever, did their imperious father's bidding.

'Please synchronise watches, read the instructions, do the practice and be ready on the day at zero hour, having done a last check of your equipment.'

The Comandante ensured all was in readiness then allowed an evil smirk to cross his face.

Canada was in for a little surprise.

CHAPTER THIRTEEN

'Good evening, ladies and gentlemen. I'm Maria Romero, the guest manager. Please introduce yourselves and then I'll take you through the daily program here at Meridian.'

The 'Kingstons' did so, along with just one other couple who had arrived at the same time, Elaine and Bernie Jarrett with their son Matthew, from Winkler in Manitoba. There were welcoming handshakes all around. Maria was a warm and friendly woman, her English pleasantly accented. She emphasised there was a 'research area' of the lodge property that was strictly out-of-bounds, otherwise, guests were free to use the facilities. Each individual activity had a trained facilitator. All guests were encouraged to set their goals for a healthy lifestyle and participate fully in what was available at Meridian.

'Any questions?' Rachael was quick to signal she had one.

'As we mentioned, we're journalists researching the healthy living options you outlined. We appreciate that you have a research area, but is it possible to find out something about it, even of a general nature?' A momentary frown crossed Maria's brow before she countered with a forced smile.

'Well, we have a generic brochure that is available on request. Will that do?' Rachael hoped she hadn't overplayed her hand.

'Yes, it'll be fine. We just want to be able to write a well-rounded story for our magazine. Readers will be impressed that Meridian is continuing to do independent research.'

Maria brightened a little. 'That's alright, I'll see you get a copy.'

'Thanks, Maria.' Just then a surly man burst in and interrupted. Both the Kovacs stiffened. He looked familiar.

'Maria, where's José? There's something urgent he needs to check!' Maria frowned at this unprofessional interruption as the man glanced around, uncaring. The penny dropped for both Josh and Rachael. This was a man they were expecting to see.

'He's in our quarters, you can find him there.' The man swore in Spanish as he rushed angrily out of the room, but not before glancing at the two Australian guests. Where had he seen them before? Oh well, he'd worry about them later. José was enough of a problem for now.

With the unpleasant interruption over, the orientation concluded with some friendly chit-chat about the meals and activities, then they all moved into the dining area to mingle with other guests for alcohol-free pre-dinner drinks – it was a health retreat after all – and a delightful meal. A choice between roasted chicken breast and pasta primavera for the main course, and for dessert, a magnificent selection of fresh fruit topped with delicious Greek yoghurt.

Josh smiled at Rachael, 'Hard gig, but someone's got to do it!'

Luis and Javier Sanchez were both in a foul mood, their plans upset by a problem that should have been avoided. Two of the aerosol canisters were faulty and had started to release some of their deadly contents. Not much, but it had meant a delay of a full twenty-four hours and a rechecking of the target's schedule- he could now have a commitment that would put him beyond their reach. Also, it meant vaccinating three men against the toxin, which was more than a mere inconvenience. Damn that careless Sergeant Romero! The next day Luis hauled him over the coals after summoning him to the restricted area to point out the faulty equipment.

'Idiot! I told you to check all the canisters carefully. How did those faulty ones slip through?' He followed with some choice epithets as the hapless José Romero stood there, frustration building, before being dismissed. 'Get out of my sight!' All José could do was scurry back to his quarters in shame.

Seeing his scowling countenance, his wife Maria made the mistake of asking what had happened, then probing whether he had in fact checked the canisters. She got a stinging backhander for her trouble before José stormed off to drown his sorrows in whatever alcohol he could find. Fortunately, there was plenty of it in the 'research area.'

With a black eye quickly forming, Maria Romero's mind was made up. How had she ever married this brute? This had happened before and she'd had enough. One beating was one too many, let alone the number she'd endured over the years. She just had to get away, but how? She really liked the look of those Australian journalists, maybe they'd help. Sure, she'd only just met them, but she felt there was something about them she could trust. She couldn't explain it, it was a gut feeling. In any case, she was beside herself and desperate. The tears just wouldn't stop.

The 'Kingstons' had just returned from a late afternoon horse riding session. They had thoroughly enjoyed it, but they did note how many horses were on the property, many more than the number of guests. When Rachael asked the supervisor why, he told them some of the horses were used for veterinary research, such as equine diseases. Josh gave Rachael a knowing look. Later, in private, he filled her in.

'That confirms it I reckon. They've developed botulinum toxin and the horses are used for producing botulinum antitoxin.'

'How?'

'The antitoxin is derived from the blood of horses that have been immunised against the nerve agent. When these low-life crims are hitting a target, they could also be at risk. So they'll immunise themselves first. They would no doubt carefully calculate how soon before the attack they need to have it. That's why they have all these horses – they're not really animal lovers!'

'Got you. So when and where is the hit? Lord knows!'

An answer came in the form of a weeping Maria Romero, suddenly appearing.

'Maria! Are you OK?' The poor woman clearly wasn't.

'No… no. I'm in trouble… can you please help me?' Of course they would. Rachael gave her a huge hug.

'Come in and tell us what's happened.'

For the first time in many years, Maria felt she had a chance to unburden herself, to free herself of years of abuse, to get away from a tough, uncaring spouse who didn't care about for her needs. She felt she could trust this lovely couple somehow, even though they were still strangers, it seemed right to do so. The dam wall of her emotions was breaking and she started to reveal all the horrible secrets she'd suppressed for far too long. She was determined to be free of it all.

Out spilled the story. A sad history of being slapped or beaten by a brute of a husband who had gradually become more and more dependent on alcohol. She was married to an extreme right-wing fanatic whose own father was an army officer under Pinochet, like Diego Sanchez. In 1990 the Romeros fled to Canada, where they eventually connected with Sanchez, who was recruiting like-minded fanatics from different countries, both when he was on the run and later while living in Australia. Under his remote directions, the group had set up the location at Meridian. Despite her personal reluctance, Maria had done much of the preparatory work, urged on by her husband. The Sanchez scheme was all part of the grand plan – an especially evil one.

Maria paused briefly. Josh and Rachael were looking expectantly at her, knowing there was more. Damn it, she thought, they deserve the full story. They're journalists after all. She continued with a sigh.

She told them that using Sanchez's knowledge of biochemistry, his henchmen had produced a refined and deadly nerve agent, along with a hit list of targets to be used for extortion and blackmail. Unless various governments 'paid up' there would be mass casualties.

'Do you know any more, Maria? Like, who is on the list? And who will be the first?'

'Someone important, but José hasn't told me who or where. He got chewed out by Luis Sanchez because he didn't check some faulty canisters. I think they're fixed now, so it will be soon.'

'Maria, this is very important. We can't let this go ahead. Can we ask you to go back to him briefly one more time and try and find out? We know it's a big ask, but once we have that information we'll help you escape and get to a women's refuge in Calgary.' Josh was adamant. 'In the meantime we'll phone an emergency helpline and find the closest.'

Scared as she was, Maria nodded, grateful that she'd now have a way out. Rachael's kindly arms around her were great consolation. Once she was calmer, they let her go, urging her to come straight back if there was a problem – and to definitely get back to them with that vital knowledge as soon as she found out any details.

Still teary, Maria walked back to her staff quarters.

Once in her cabin, which was some distance from the guests' accommodation, Maria found José in an easy chair, almost asleep from the effects of the whisky he'd treated himself to. At least in this state he was no further danger to his fearful wife. Plucking up all her courage and showing tenderness that she in no way felt, it was time to 'pump him.'

'José, are you OK?' she asked solicitously. He nodded.

'Can I help you get ready for that job?'

'Yesh, you better,' he slurred, unfit for anything but staggering off to lie down and nurse a coming hangover.

'Is it far away? Like, how far do you have to drive?'

'Too far. All the way to Edmonton.' He added some Spanish curses. The drunk was unable to drive to the main road, let alone the provincial capital.

'Where in Edmonton? Where are you going?'

'That damned rotten Government House. We're going to hit that guy – who's that guy in charge?'

'Do you mean the lieutenant governor?'

'Yessh. He's the one. And get his staff. Kill 'em all!'

'Why, José?'

'To get dough out of the Canadian government, otherwise we'll do other hits, you know, unless they pay- what's the word..?'

'You mean blackmail or extortion?'

'Yair, one of 'em's the right word. You choose!'

'When will you do it?'

'The men are leaving in half an hour – then they'll hit 'em later tonight, he's got a few staff living there.' Shocked, Maria had heard enough.

'Dear José. You seem tired. Why not lie down for a while so you're ready for the job. Let me help you.' With her husband too drunk to argue, she helped him to the bedroom, where he collapsed face down on the bed. Soon he was snoring away and would hopefully sleep for hours.

Taking the opportunity, Maria tossed some necessary effects into a holdall and went straight around to Josh and Rachael's cabin, where she passed on the urgent news. It was the work of just a few minutes to check details on the criminals' target, leave messages for Veronica and Zeke, and throw their belongings back into suitcases and into the boot of the Chevy. Maria was impressed with their efficiency.

'Wow, you both are pretty good for lifestyle journalists! Sorry to put this one on you!'

'No worries, Maria! Let's get going. Off to the refuge for you!' Nervously but secretively checking their Glock automatics, there would be no refuge for them.

Action awaited.

Racing along Macleod Trail back up to Calgary, the 'Kingstons' were curious about something.

'Maria, why did that criminal group base themselves in Meridian Eco-Lodge, somewhere open to the public?'

'The Comandante said he wanted to hide in plain sight. He owns the lodge, of course, bought with money he got out of Chile, like my husband's family. He thought it was less suspicious than a group based away from everyone. The 'research area' let them develop their chemical weapons, recruit fellow criminals and do whatever planning they needed. The horses were a good cover, too.' Rachael and Josh nodded. It made sense.

'Well, relax now and we'll get you to a safe place- Sanctuary Grove in the centre of Calgary.' Rachael had got through to a women's helpline and had phoned ahead to confirm there was a place for Maria.

It was more direct to stay on Macleod Trail rather than going back to Deerfoot, so just past Calgary's Talisman Sports Centre, Josh turned left onto 17 Avenue and, minutes later, pulled up right outside Sanctuary Grove.

'Thanks so much, you two. I'm so sorry to disrupt your holiday. I'm sure you'll pass that knowledge on to the police.' Josh and Rachael gave each other a knowing glance.

'Don't mention it, Maria. Yes, we'll certainly tell the police. Believe us, you've been very helpful. Now, please let me take you inside to check you'll be OK.' Rachael was insistent. Maria agreed, with a fond farewell wave to Josh as she exited the Chevrolet Cruze.

Soon after, Rachael was back at the car. 'OK, move over, Joshie. My turn to drive. You can't have all the fun!' He did. Traversing the city centre, she crossed Bow River then took a right at 16 Avenue to connect to Deerfoot Trail. Resolutely heading northwards, the Chevy was soon out of the Calgary city limits and on the main highway to Edmonton.

Government House was coming up.

CHAPTER FOURTEEN

For His Honour, the Honourable Percival Watkins-Emmett, Lieutenant Governor of the Province of Alberta, it had been a long day, so he was glad of the opportunity to wind down with a glass of his favourite port before having an early night. His wife, Her Honour Beatrice, was down in Alberta's far southeast in Medicine Hat, addressing a delegation of women about equal-opportunity issues. She wouldn't be returning until sometime the next day.

Oh, these bills from the provincial parliament requiring his assent, they seemed endless. Percival had chaired a series of meetings with constituents about a variety of constitutional matters. Somehow, he was seen as a sympathetic ear – more so than certain parliamentary members, to whom such concerns should have been directed. From now on, he was determined to take a harder line to reduce his workload. He yawned. This job was far from the sinecure he'd imagined when retiring from the army. Percival was looking forward to the end of his five year term in the job.

The Watkins-Emmett family had migrated from the 'old country' early in the twentieth century and done well in western Canada. As part of a large family, his parents had been ranchers and then his siblings had either concentrated on following in their footsteps in British Columbia or undertaking minerals exploration in Alberta. Rather against the trend, young Percival had entered the army, gained rapid promotion and served with distinction in various trouble spots, either under his national banner or that of the United Nations. Retiring early, he had anticipated a late career on the family ranch he'd just inherited a share in, but a recommendation by the prime minister for a Companion of the Order of Canada, his country's highest honour, was exactly the inducement he needed to take the position of lieutenant governor. Dear Beatrice, not overly enamoured of a ranching life, was especially delighted.

In his dressing-gown- and deciding another port and the rare opportunity of an hour's television before bed was just the ticket for the night- the Honourable Percival was determined nothing would spoil his hard-won moment of leisure.

If only it had turned out that way.

Once the hit squad departed, Diego Sanchez turned to Walter Nemisov, who was, as always, sitting over his computer, which was set up in an especially private area of the lodge's research facility. A mysterious man whose origin was somewhat obscure, Nemisov seemed to have no great skills other than being an expert in computer encryption and sending messages that defied tracing. The dark web was his friend and he was ready for action when given the signal. Having no particular allegiances, in this situation he was simply a hired hand. Diego Sanchez paid handsomely and the computer geek was fiercely loyal to the mighty dollar.

'Walter, it's essential the message is untraceable. Definitely.'

'Absolutely one hundred percent. They'll never find the origin. I'm an expert in the Tor network. You know, for secret computer messages.'

'Good. I'll double your fee once we get the payoff.'

'Thanks, Comandante. I'll guarantee success.'

Moving away, Sanchez took one last look at the script and allowed himself to gloat. He'd take this democracy for everything he could get. The conspirator relished the plot of his coming military-style operation. Just imagine- the Canadian federal government being extorted to transfer half a billion dollars to his offshore secret account by the specified date. Otherwise the next hit wouldn't simply be a lieutenant governor and his staff, but a major stadium with thousands of fans in it. They'd all die! He rubbed his hands in evil delight. So, Canada- proud of your democracy and human rights record? Taking action against so-called abusers abroad? Ha! We'll see about that!

Revenge would be sweet!

Racing up the highway to Edmonton in the Ram ProMaster, the hit squad leader Luis Sanchez reminded his men of the action procedure once they reached Government House at 12845, 102 Avenue North West.

First, eliminate any security personnel on the premises. They were armed with suppressed automatics for that very purpose. Next, stand prepared to turn off the electricity supply- but preserve it intact- at the first sign of trouble. Every man had an effective headlamp so light for the squad wouldn't be a problem. After that, gain entry quickly. They had just the right implements to do that, and had rehearsed in a mock-up of the Government House premises.

Following this, the target would be the staff, resisting or otherwise. Spray them with aerosol cans, then find the lieutenant governor and give him a similar treatment. Give them a large-enough dose to be fatal; the highly refined version of the toxin would do the trick. Leave nobody alive. Then the clincher:

turn off the power but leave pellets in the air conditioning system, left in the on-mode, to be activated once the first responders- hopefully, large numbers of police- rush in to investigate. Turning the power back on would be their undoing.

With the maximum dose applied, they'll choke to death quickly, causing huge casualties. That'll prime the government for extortion! Fiendishly simple, but very effective.

'And the long-term plan, Lieutenant?' One of the henchmen was curious. Javier was happy to respond.

'The Comandante has contacts to syndicate our method to patriots like us in other democratic countries. Australia and Britain are next on the hit list. For a price – a big one – the syndicates will get a supply of all the chemicals once we have more in production. Thanks to our 'research facility', that will all be possible. Now driver, how far to go?' Due to an excellent run on Highway 2, they had made good time.

'With the exit to Wetaskiwin behind us, we're about to see Leduc off to our right. After that, we'll soon hit the Edmonton city limits.'

Hit? *Not as good as the one we're about to make.*

CHAPTER FIFTEEN

Burning rubber as they raced towards their destination, Rachael urged Josh to contact Zeke Leroy and Veronica Puglisi in Ottawa immediately. Sounding frustrated, he told her he'd been trying but couldn't get through, nor had they replied to the earlier messages.

'I dunno, are we in a series of black spots? Don't worry, I'll keep at it. No need to nag.' A moment later, there was success- of sorts. 'Sorry I can't take your call right now, please leave a brief message…' What the heck, he thought, we need urgent backup! Only later did he find out that Veronica had a rare evening off, and had taken the opportunity for a girls' night out. The Rocky Mountain Funkadelics were touring eastern Canada so she and two girlfriends blasted their eardrums for several hours at their Ottawa rock concert. Even when she got home, her ears were ringing so much she didn't hear her phone go. Multiple times.

Zeke was on an undercover operation in Montreal with his phone off. Only later did he get Josh's desperate message. So much for backup.

'OK, so onto plan B. The Edmonton cops.' The duty officer answered promptly.

'Sir, you say you're with Australian security?'

'Yes, that's just what I said.' His frustration was growing. Rachael cast him a doubtful look.

'What is this month's codeword?'

'Eaglehawk.'

'I'm sorry, sir. That's incorrect. I can't process your request unless I have the correct word.'

'Well damn-well check again. I know it's the right word!'

After an interval, the duty officer returned to the phone with an apology. 'I'm sorry for my error, sir. You're right. Things are very stressful here right now. I made the mistake of opening the manual at the wrong page. 'Tarsands' was last month's codeword. 'Eaglehawk' is correct.'

Josh wasted no time before passing on the urgent message for all available units to secure Government House and protect the lieutenant governor. Once again, the reply was far from reassuring.

'Mr Kovacs, I appreciate the urgency but we have no units available right now.'

'What do you mean?'

'You may not have heard. There's been a huge warehouse fire in East Edmonton. Arson, we believe, because it took hold after some explosions. It's an abandoned building right in the middle of a built-up residential area. A number of new condominiums are at risk and all available police officers are evacuating residents. We'll get some units to protect His Honour and Government House as soon as possible, but I may not be able to contact the commander right away.'

'Well, keep onto it. They're planning to kill the governor. Phone his secretary to alert him, will you?' Josh would try, too.

Sadly, the run of 'outs' continued. That night at Government House, while Percival was enjoying his television program, his private secretary, Carol Pobje, had taken advantage of the rare spot of leisure time to phone her aged mother, checking on her state of health. The good lady ran through her various complaints at length and Carol responded with soothing advice, ensuring a long, drawn-out conversation.

Precious time elapsed and frustration grew as the phone kept giving a constant engaged signal. Josh tried Percival's cell phone. Switched off. After all, it was a gripping television show, rarely able to be enjoyed without interruption. Rachael knew how her irate husband might react and took the upper hand.

'Hon, it's down to us! Reckon we can manage it?'

'Sure, Rach. We'll have to. But give me some inspiration!' He was at the end of his tether. A thought from the Bible came to mind though she couldn't remember the exact words.

'How about, "I can do everything when God gives me strength?" That's the meaning, anyway.'

'Sounds good. Let's hope it applies to stopping criminals bent on murder!'

They would soon find out.

The Sanchez brothers and their henchmen were altogether more confident of success than were the Kovacs. What a great plan! Their two fellow criminals had phoned to boast of the 'roaring success' of the arson attack at the old warehouse. Fire, threat, panic. Hundreds of residents were urged to evacuate their homes, which were built too close to the warehouse for comfort. Hordes of firefighters were doing their best to extinguish the massive blaze while police struggled to control the growing crowd. It was pandemonium.

Elated at their achievement, the two arsonists wasted no time in driving south, back to the lodge and their agreed bonus from the Comandante. Once the 'special operation' against

Government House succeeded, there would be rewards all round before the next phase of the plan unfolded. Magnificent!

Whoever said 'crime doesn't pay' hadn't met Diego Sanchez.

Finally, passing Edmonton International Airport on their left, the desperate couple were in the provincial capital. Crossing the North Saskatchewan River and entering Edmonton West, they could expect to reach their destination in North West soon, according to the comforting message on their GPS.

Then came a welcome breakthrough. Carol Pobje had finished her phone call. Josh rang and she picked up. Relieved, he practically spat out the urgent situation. This time the codeword 'Eaglehawk' worked. The panicked private secretary raced up the stairs to the lieutenant governor and burst in, rudely interrupting his TV program just as the plot was coming to a climax.

'What the devil! What are you doing, woman? Explain yourself!' She did, trembling. Percival gulped, stubbed out his stogie and took a swig of his port. The emergency triggered an instant flashback...

It was in the former Yugoslavia... the Balkans erupting in war in the 1990s... a UN peacekeeping mission with the Canadian forces... his unit pinned down by hostile fire... he was personally targeted by an enemy hit squad. Percival had made a quick decision to extricate his men from peril and received an award for valour. Now, history seemed to be repeating itself. Could he pull it off again? Quickly, he assessed the situation.

Thank God his wife was away and out of danger in Medicine Hat. He had his secretary, three catering staff who were of no military use, and a replacement security guard, Sebastian Bartos, who was fairly elderly but could handle a firearm. Why did his efficient young protector, Al Curtis, have to be struck down with Covid right now? Damn rotten luck. Well, he was assured the two Australian security officers, racing to his aid, would do their utmost to turn the tide. He loved the Aussies. In military terms, as good as any backup you'd find.

But how many were in the hit squad? He'd have to expect five or six. Puffing up the stairs, Sebastian Bartos burst into the room as the Honourable Percival raised himself to his full height, ready to take charge of the property's defence.

'No need to say anything, Sebastian, I know exactly what you're thinking!'

Out of breath, the elderly guard nodded as the lieutenant governor continued.

'Action stations!'

CHAPTER SIXTEEN

Rachael pulled up with a screech at the entrance to Government House, then both she and Josh leapt out of the vehicle right under the eye of Sebastian Bartos, who was covering them with his automatic firearm until they identified themselves. 'Eaglehawk! Australian security and MI6!' Well, there was no mistaking the distinctive British and Australian accents, the latter so loved by many Canadians. Josh quickly took charge.

'Lieutenant Governor?' He emerged straight away. 'Josh and Rachael Kovacs, Australian Secret Intelligence Service and British MI6. We have no time to lose! Are these all the personnel present tonight?'

'Yes, Mr Kovacs. My secretary and security guard, plus three catering staff. Fortunately, my wife Beatrice is away.'

'Right, I'll have to hide our car. I considered a vehicle evacuation, assuming yours is ready, but the hit squad is only minutes behind. They could easily catch us on the road out. Also, we need to defend your property. Is there somewhere I can conceal our Chevy?'

'Sure, give Sebastian the key and he'll do that.' The guard nodded. Rachael then took over.

'OK, turn off all the lights inside. We need to leave the house, but there's no need to lock it. Lieutenant Governor, where is the best hideout? Sebastian, can you pull out the light fuse, hide the car, then follow us to our hideout spot. We'll regroup there and work out our tactics.' Sebastian sprang into action, went straight to the fuse box then moved the vehicle to an empty shed before following the others. Percy seemed quietly confident, leading the way to the best hideout in the bushes before speaking again.

'Mr and Mrs Kovacs, can I add my bit?' Rachael and Josh nodded. 'I don't doubt you're both armed and prepared.' They were. 'Well, we're somewhat more prepared ourselves than you may imagine. Every three months the lieutenant governor has to sign off on the Provincial Defence Charter. This goes back to nineteenth century colonial times when the province had to be prepared for hostile attack or possible insurrection. The constitution requires the lieutenant governor to inspect a sample of the weapons and equipment available to police, riot squads and any other organisations who may have to deal with civil disorder. This requirement, that the weapons and equipment are available, have been sighted and verified.'

'We'll have to update our training manuals!' Rachael was quite impressed.

'Yes, well, in short, this time the police brought a sample of stun grenades and tear gas for me to sign off on. They're due to be collected in a week before being replaced by riot shields and helmets, I believe. I'll have to check the schedule.'

'You mean we have these weapons for our use tonight?'

'Absolutely, right this way.' He led them a short distance through the bushes to a concealed bunker. 'Only I have the key. Fortunately, I grabbed it from my desk drawer once I heard of this emergency. And please include me in your 'platoon.' As an old army man I can still throw a grenade!'

Within minutes the Kovacs, the lieutenant governor and Sebastian had prepared themselves with a good supply of grenades and tear gas, and checked their firearms. Doing their best to get the unarmed staff comfortable and as far away from danger as possible, the four then crept back to the edge of the bushes to await the would-be assassins' arrival.

They didn't have to wait long. A large vehicle was now quietly but quickly moving down the driveway with its lights off.

CHAPTER SEVENTEEN

Parking the Ram ProMaster over to one side, the five conspirators, holding their weapons and canisters ready, crept up to the main door of the house. How strange- it all was in darkness, something they hadn't anticipated. Gingerly trying the door, they found it unlocked and they entered in single file. Watching them, the four defenders maintained their positions. Through the large windows, they could see the criminals' headlamps lighting the way, before they evidently found the light switches and, judging by their muffled cursing, flicked them on. Nothing. There was nobody home! More cursing. Looking frustrated, they checked all the rooms.

No longer needing to stay silent, their expletives filled the air, swearing in Spanish and a variety of other languages. Luis Sanchez called them to order.

'Come on, damn the lot of you – focus! Where the heck are they? Maybe hiding outside. Did they know we were coming? Come on, get outside and look around. Remove your suppressors and shoot them on sight if you find them! Go!'

Out they rushed. This proved a brief opportunity for the watching defenders. While the five attackers were gathered on the front steps, ready to spotlight the bushes, Percy- conscious of being the first law officer of the province- yelled his command. He knew he would have to write a thorough report later.

'Lieutenant Governor here! You lot are in breach of the law. Put down your weapons and surrender!'

Luis Sanchez, astounded, unleashed another string of Spanish curses, then fired three shots in Percy's direction. All three missed. Percy gave his hand signal.

'Now!' At Josh's command, four stun grenades flew through the air. Two were wildly off target –Percy and Sebastian were a little out of practice – but Josh and Rachael's were close enough. A cacophonous noise split the night, the flashes dazzling and disorienting. The criminals staggered around, coughing and spluttering. Luis Sanchez screamed an order.

'Shoot 'em! Get 'em, now!' Three of the five shot randomly, the other two were still disoriented. A volley of shots rang out. Sebastian Bartos fell. Hit in the leg, but he wasn't out of the fight yet. Ignoring his wound, he returned fire from the ground, killing one of the assailants. With the other two now recovered, that meant four still left to attack.

Furious, the Sanchez brothers yelled in unison. 'Surround the bushes and get 'em all! Go on!' Rachael aimed her Glock and fired, with devastating effect. One attacker was shot and down; his mate thought better of it and decided to flee. Curse them! No one told them the would-be victims were armed. And what was with those stun grenades! *Demonios! Diablos!* He was out of here, into the van and away...

Beyond furious, Javier Sanchez could see the whole plot dissolving before his very eyes. These Canucks were supposed to be soft targets. He turned to see his henchman about to flee. 'Coward!' He shot him twice. The man fell, and though badly hit, managed to reach the van and climb in as Sanchez fired two more shots into the vehicle. With the key left in the ignition, he was able to start the Ram ProMaster and, bleeding profusely from his wounds, move it from its parked position, frantically trying to find the driveway exit.

Seeing Josh, the desperate Javier shot at him, striking him in the shoulder. The brave ASIS officer staggered back, returning fire but missing. Rachael did likewise, though her shots also went wide. However, Percy, the old army man, was ready. He had no firearm but was awaiting his chance with a tear gas container. In desperation he tried a lob. It landed right in front of Javier, the choking gas stopping the would-be assassin dead in his tracks. The Chilean dropped his weapon, clutching his throat as the enveloping gas had a far deadlier effect than intended.

'Aargh! Aargh!'

Unbeknown to him, he had a rare genetic mutation that meant he was fatally allergic to tear gas. Writhing on the ground, gasping and choking, he was seconds from breathing his last. A minute later, there was no sign of life in Javier Sanchez.

All might have seemed lost, but Luis Sanchez wasn't going to give up. Furious, and filled with hate towards his would-be victims, he somehow managed to avoid their defensive shots, despite losing his own firearm in the process. With rat-like cunning and circling around his two unwounded opponents, he clutched the remaining weapon he still held – a canister of deadly, highly refined nerve gas.

He'd had the antitoxin, so it was harmless to him. Not so his opponents! And that damn woman- now he remembered. Back in Tasmania, where he'd pushed that cursed interferer over the clifftop- she and her husband were there! Then again at the lodge. And now here! They must be cops! How did they track him down? Boiling with rage, he had only one goal- get her!

'Rachael, watch out!' Josh, despite the pain of his wound, was still in the fight, catching sight of the attacker in the last second. Rachael turned and pulled the trigger of her Glock.

Nothing- she'd just used her last round. No time to reload, so she closed with him, blocking Josh's desperate bid to shoot the Chilean. Her karate chop, slightly off target, at least parried his determined bid to activate the canister right in her face. But in the struggle she slipped and fell, and was now helpless to ward him off.

'Sanchez!' Josh screamed, distracting the killer and causing him to involuntarily look up for a split second before he could turn to use the fatal gas. That was all the time Josh needed. He loosed off a volley of shots from his still-working Glock, the rounds hitting Luis Sanchez full in the chest. Shocked, the desperado staggered back, dropping his deadly canister harmlessly in the dirt as he thumped into a tree before slumping, lifeless, to the ground.

At that exact moment, three police vehicles raced down the driveway, sirens blaring and lights blazing. They were just in time to block the injured henchman in the van before he could escape, then arrest the remaining criminal lying bleeding on the grass.

With all the attackers disposed of, Rachael rushed to comfort the wounded Josh, with the Honourable Percy doing likewise to poor Sebastian Bartos. The four unarmed staff now emerged from their concealment, rendering first aid to the two casualties, who would survive to tell the tale. Percy allowed himself a historical reflection.

'Well, we've won! Well done, all of you. Like the Battle of Waterloo, it was a near-run thing. Here are the Edmonton police, racing in like Field Marshal von Blücher and his Prussians! A pity they cut it so fine!'

A tearful Rachael couldn't stop kissing and cuddling Josh, taking care to avoid his shot shoulder. She had to agree.

It was definitely far too close for comfort.

CHAPTER EIGHTEEN

Ambulances conveyed the wounded to Edmonton Hospital, while the two criminals were kept under police guard. One of the two would be lucky to survive. Sebastian Bartos needed an operation on his leg but was expected to eventually achieve a full recovery. The bullet that hit Josh's right shoulder passed cleanly though; his injury would heal completely, with no expected ill effect. His only remaining symptom were his periodic shakes. It certainly could have been far worse.

The lesser injured criminal knew the game was well and truly up and was prepared to confess all in the hope of a lighter sentence- not a light one, mind you. The police made that clear. He outlined the details of the devilish plot of murder, mayhem and extortion, both in Canada and abroad. The nerve gas would do its deadly work. That was simply a taste of further horrors to come.

The interrogation was persistent. The long-term aim of the operation was very clear: blackmail firstly the Canadian government, then others to pay a huge sum as an extortion demand, with the threat of larger targets with huge casualties. Botulinum toxin was ideal for large-scale assassination attempts; an indoor aerosol release in an enclosed space was a fiendish but perfect method. The Maple Leaf Stadium in Toronto was one such location on the hit list.

Luxuriating in his quarters at the Meridian Eco-Lodge, Diego Sanchez was holding an initial celebration with Nemisov and the two arsonists who had returned from the provincial capital. Having heard the glowing report of the successful conflagration of the abandoned warehouse that had effectively distracted the police, firefighters and other authorities from the larger target, Diego Sanchez was gleefully anticipating further glory. But when a series of flashing blue lights caught his attention, Diego choked on his prematurely-poured glass of Bollinger.

Edmonton had been quick to alert their Calgary counterparts, and a conga line of official vehicles screeched to a stop right outside Diego's quarters. Shocked, he heard the words, 'Police, open up!' before a police mini battering-ram forced his door open. Damn the cops, he wasn't going down without a fight. Instinctively, he drew his weapon, but was unsure which officer to target. He loosed off two rounds in the incoming force's general direction. A sergeant's well-placed shot to his right wrist convinced him further resistance was futile. Recoiling from the pain of the impact, Sanchez dropped his firearm. He surrendered, was arrested, cuffed by his uninjured left wrist and taken away, along with his three equally-shocked accomplices. The cops then rounded up other gang members still on the property, including the drunken Sergeant Romero.

Sanchez and his cohort didn't even get to finish their first glass of champagne. It would be many years, if ever, before they'd be able to taste it again.

EPILOGUE

Relaxing on their business-class flight home to Canberra via Sydney, Josh and Rachael Kovacs enjoyed the best of fare on their journey. Main meals offered choices around grilled salmon, beef tenderloin and chicken marsala, enough to tempt anyone. The obliging Air Canada crew, aware of Josh's temporary disability with his right shoulder and upper arm extensively bandaged, ensured his delicious meals were suitable for eating with a splayd- no trouble at all.

In any case, his attentive wife considered it her pleasant duty to help him, although desserts such as decadent chocolate mousse cake or tiramisu presented no problem. That, and any other tasks, were a pleasure for her to assist with, eternally grateful for a husband whose courageous action had undoubtedly saved her life.

The Canadian authorities had filled them in on all the details. Whatever information the surviving conspirators either hadn't known or divulged, Diego Sanchez, devastated beyond belief at the loss of his sons, was happy to cough up.

'My dear Luis, my wonderful Javier – dead. I'll never see them again!' His interrogators appreciated the irony. Working for the tyrant Pinochet, Sanchez had deprived so many parents of their own sons and daughters. Now he had lost his own. But those young Chilean people, so cruelly taken, were innocent. Not so his would-be murdering sons.

As all the details of the failed attack came to light, Diego couldn't help but gasp at the further irony. As the general in charge of the DINA, he had loved to authorise the use of tear gas against demonstrators, laughing at the sufferings of those who choked and writhed in the streets, before he let loose his goon squad with truncheons to assault the victims as they lay there. Now his dear Javier was dead from the very same substance. A genetic fault – who knew?

One thing he did know was the fate that awaited. Multiple charges by Canada for attempted murder, terrorism, extortion and other offences. After certain conviction and a long sentence would come extradition to Australia for his part in the attack on Edward Goulston, along with various indictments relating to the development of nerve gas. And no doubt, referral to the International Criminal Court in The Hague for crimes against humanity. Yes, all those thousands killed by the DINA...

A devastated Diego Sanchez wept at the prospect. All was lost.

He'd definitely die in jail.

Back in Canberra, Josh was on light duties for some weeks. He and Rachael underwent a complete debrief, shared equally between ASIS and MI6. The mission was of equal importance to both agencies. In a vain hope to eventually see a chink of light at the end of his long tunnel of imprisonment, Diego Sanchez had been very forthcoming and explicit concerning his goals.

The syndication of the nerve gas formula and precise instructions on its manufacture were designed to guarantee mass casualties. Later, Sanchez intended to develop even more heinous methods, such as Sarin gas or Ricin, based on previous DINA research in an infamous program another biochemist developed.

However, for now botulinum would more than do the job. The plot anticipated thousands – even hundreds of thousands – of casualties. He'd planned a supply of antitoxin with accompanying instructions to ensure that assassins wouldn't die by the same method as their multiple victims. Oh, yes, the preparation had been very careful indeed. Finally, the obsessed and vengeful Chilean had outlined careful procedures to extort hundreds of millions of dollars from fearful governments, who would be blackmailed into buying 'immunity' for their population.

The Kovacs nodded as their superiors trotted out the details. Rachael outlined her own thinking, entirely in line with what Josh had also supposed.

'We assume it was to be syndicated to neo-Nazi groups and the like? And anarchists?'

'Exactly that. They anticipated passing on the supply of nerve gas, data and full instructions to any extremist group with an avowed intention of overthrowing their government. Canada, Britain, Australia, New Zealand and the USA were to be the first targets. Then they'd try others. It really was a worldwide threat.'

'Thank the Lord we were able stop them – we mean that literally!'

'The free world is in your debt. We greatly appreciate your joint achievement. Is there anything else?'

'Yes, there are a couple of loose ends we'd like to tie up. People in Melbourne we need to see.'

Both agencies were in complete agreement.

'Take whatever leave you need. A month or more if you like. Joshua and Rachael, you're free to go. And thanks again!'

'Thank you, too. It was a pleasure to serve.' As he got up, Josh grimaced in pain for a second.

Well, not exactly *all* a pleasure.

The side flat, part of a larger house in Armadale, was neat but unprepossessing. Paula Torres answered the door almost as soon as they knocked; she had noticed the couple wending their way up the narrow front garden path.

'Wonderful to see you both, please join me! And come through to the lounge room.' One corner of the room was a veritable shrine to her lost family, their photographs proudly but sadly displayed for any visitor to see, along with little keepsakes on a nearby table.

There was the daughter lost to whooping cough in infancy, probably too young in those days for a vaccine – or maybe it was unavailable to those of a modest income in Chile. Her beloved Roberto, so cruelly murdered by the monster, Diego Sanchez, on Pinochet's orders and dropped from a great height into the Eastern Pacific, forever to lie in the ocean depths. And then Miguel, her much loved husband, dead from a sudden cardiac seizure; a broken heart caused by the emotion of losing both his children. But now Paula's face had cheered.

'You have achieved justice? And Joshua, was it at the cost of your shoulder? You poor man!'

'Oh, just a bit of collateral damage – I'll heal.' He groaned involuntarily and let Rachael answer Paula's question.

'Yes, we have got justice and Josh's wounded shoulder was an unfortunate part of it. Anyway, we firstly want to thank you for your 'detective work' in exposing that secret laboratory. It gave us all the background evidence we needed to take action. You were great!'

'My dear friends, I was happy to help – anything to put that man where he belongs. But please tell me all about it.'

They related whatever details they were free to disclose. The massive shootout in Edmonton could no longer be kept completely under wraps. Their own identities were kept secret for security reasons; the credit given to the Edmonton police. The couple swore Paula to secrecy about any involvement on their part. Officially, it didn't happen.

'Diego Sanchez arrested, due to spend the rest of his life in jail- and his sons dead. For years I prayed to the good Lord for justice, but never for vengeance. It looks like He has answered!'

'He certainly has, and we give thanks for that.'

'Well, please let me offer you tea and cakes for a small celebration. But can you tell me what happened to your shoulder, Josh?'

'Let's call it a small workplace accident. I got caught in the crossfire and didn't duck fast enough!' He winked at Paula.

'That calls for a double serving of sponge cake. It'll help the healing!'

For the first time in years, Paula Torres was a happy woman.

Her internal war was over.

Two hours later, after many 'final' embraces with the eternally grateful Paula, the Kovacs made their way to the Goulston home in Caulfield. Levi Goulston answered, his face much brighter than the last time.

'Please, Mr and Mrs Kovacs, come in. I'm so sorry, I wanted to contact you but things have been pretty busy here.'

'That's all right, we've been overseas on business ourselves. So you have news?'

'Sure, please follow me.' He led them along the corridor to a room and knocked on the door.

'Come in.' There, sitting on an easy chair was Edward Goulston, two walking sticks close by.

Josh and Rachael's eyes grew wider by the second. Amazing!

'Welcome back to life, Edward!'

Levi Goulston spoke. 'Yes, he came home by special charter two days ago. They eventually got him patched him up in Royal Hobart. It'll be a few more weeks before he's properly up and about again, but each day he's a little better. Tomorrow he'll be back at work from a home computer, till he can make it into the office. Well, we all got used to that during our many Covid lockdowns, didn't we?'

They sure did.

Josh and Rachael gently shook Edward's hand, with the homecoming patient expressing his gratitude for the clifftop rescue, tears in his eyes. He insisted on coming out to the lounge room, with a round of food and drink to celebrate, all willingly prepared by Sarah. On behalf of the other two Goulstons, she considerately enquired about Josh's 'bung shoulder.' Josh could now laugh off his wound with a brief explanation, but he knew he could hardly fit in another slice of cake.

Rachael was realistic, giving him a nudge and a quiet word. 'Darl, the diet starts tomorrow!' No doubt it would have to.

Much later, back in their rental Kia with his wife at the wheel, Josh had a thought. 'Hey, Rachael, how about we head back to Tullamarine and hop on a flight down to Tassie. We've got plenty of extra leave. Let's pick up on our interrupted holiday and go to the places we missed out on last time. We can hire a car there- and you drive, of course. We can see the stunning Tasman Peninsula, Bruny Island, Hobart with all its great attractions...have you heard of Mawson's replica huts? You should see them! Yeah, we could take a spin up to Kunanyi – Mount Wellington. It's a view to die for!'

Rachael smiled. Had her husband turned into a travel agent? Yep, she was up for it. There was only a single proviso- apart from the counselling she was going to suggest for his shakes. That might be the start of post-traumatic stress, and was a discussion with him she'd just have to have.

'Sure, Joshie. On one condition.'

'What's that?'

'This time, no cliffhanging! OK?'

He winced, his shoulder suddenly sore at the very thought. Head over a cliff again? No way.

'Darl, you've got a deal. Let's go!'

ACKNOWLEDGEMENTS

Following the 2024 release of my first published novel, 'Code 1990', I firstly confirm my gratitude to various family members, friends and readers who asked me questions along the lines of,'What's next?' Well, the answer is obviously now 'Beyond The Horizon.' I thank them for their individual forms of encouragement, for which there is no better substitute. I trust this publication won't disappoint.

Secondly, I acknowledge much general internet research to confirm geographical locations, dates and historical events that appear in the three stories. I made every effort to get these correct and very much hope I did so.

Thirdly, I am grateful to my sister, Lissa for her prompt reading of all three stories and for her practical comments. Next, Léonie as with my previous books, generously gave me the computer time I needed and was on hand to sort out technical difficulties as they arose. I thank all our adult children for their interest and encouragement, mentioning Jen, Annie and Chris for giving me useful feedback on the stories and providing helpful suggestions. In particular Chris passed on essential details of the scientific aspects of 'Retribution' to ensure correctness in the plot. Thanks indeed to all of you.

My dedicated editor, Ingrid Waltham carefully scrutinised all aspects of 'Beyond The Horizon' and rightly deserves my thanks both for her editing and her incisive comments. As well, Ollie and his team at 100Covers worked diligently to complete the task of formatting the book and cover as soon as possible.

Finally, I acknowledge good friend, Carmen Allen, herself a talented children's author, who provided much-needed help to finalise the production of this volume of three novellas.

ABOUT THE AUTHOR

Apart from times overseas, Ray Keipert lived in various Sydney suburbs prior to retiring north with his wife, Léonie in 2013. After joining his local University of the Third Age writers' group, Ray was motivated to write short stories and poems, contributing to the group's book publication project. A number of his short stories have received awards in Australia-wide literary competitions, including first, second and third place in various years.

In 2020 Ray published an edition of twenty fictional short stories, 'Life's Winners…and a Few Losers', followed by the 2021 production of five longer stories in 'Five in the Quiver.' Some of these were sequels to events and characters in his first book. In 2023, he published 'A Hand of Aces', two novellas in the one volume. To this tally he added his first published novel, 'Code 1990' in 2024.

Inspired by the lure of creative writing, Ray continues to plan and prepare further books. You are welcome to contact him via his website, **raykeipertauthor.com**

www.ingramcontent.com/pod-product-compliance
Lightning Source LLC
Chambersburg PA
CBHW050602190726

48283CB00007B/2249